MW00583209

The Edge

of

Courage

Elaine Levine

Published by Elaine Levine
Copyright © 2012 by Elaine Levine
Cover art by Hot Damn Designs
All rights reserved.
ISBN: 0985420502
ISBN-13: 978-0985420505

ACKNOWLEDGMENTS

Many thanks to my fabulous beta readers who field-tested this story: Barbara M., Ryan, Michelle, Joanne, Carol, and Barbara R. Thank you for your eagle eyes and endless patience!

A special thank you goes out to J.A. Konrath, Marie Force, and all the fearless indie authors who so freely shared their experiences and expertise as they blazed the way ahead of me.

Most of all, I'd like to thank my readers. Your emails mean the world to me—thank you for your support. You're why I write.

Other Books by Elaine Levine:

~ Men of Defiance Series ~

Rachel and the Hired Gun
Audrey and the Maverick
Leah and the Bounty Hunter
Logan's Outlaw

Chapter 1

He couldn't breathe, couldn't hear, couldn't stand, but his goddamned eyes could still see. Everything.

Women hurried in random directions, their faces filled with terror, their mouths open and straining with silent screams. Most of them were still in their house clothes, exposed in their panic to the eyes of men. Children were clinging to their mothers. Others cried where they stood. Or worse, lay silent and bleeding in the dirt.

He pushed himself up to his elbows and looked behind him.

Dust fell like snow. Not dust. Ash. Debris rained down on him. A boot. A brick. An arm. A scream pushed its way from his gut, cut through his heart, and erupted from his mouth.

Silent, like all the others.

Rocco landed on his stomach, his hands clasped to his ears. He pulled a deep breath, felt the air scrape his raw throat, then screamed again.

And woke himself up.

People surrounded him. Faces he didn't know. A room he couldn't remember. Where the hell was he? Men pulled at him. The jagged noise of their shouts slammed into his head like knives. They yanked him up to a sitting position, dragged him into the light, shaking him and gesturing.

"No. Don't. Don't touch me!" he shouted to everyone around him, in this reality and the one he'd just left. "Don't touch! Get the fuck off me!" They looked at him with odd expressions.

Christ, what language was he speaking? He looked at his clothes, seeking a clue from what he wore where he might be. He had jeans and a T-shirt on. Not a *shalwar kameez*. He was not in Afghanistan, then. He should have spoken in English or Spanish.

"What's he saying?" one of the men asked the others.

"Who the hell knows? He's still hallucinating. Shit, can't a man get a little sleep?"

"It ain't English. You heard him."

"It's Pashto. I served over there. I know that language. Look at him. He ain't American. He's a Pashtun, a goddamned haji."

More men gathered around, frowning, reaching toward him. He pushed himself back with the heels of his bare feet, shoving and tearing at the people around him as he did a crab-walk shuffle to the nearest wall. He couldn't breathe, couldn't get free. And the blood. The blood was everywhere. Tears spilled down his cheeks. He let loose a roar and shoved again at everyone around him, punching them, warning them.

But it was too late.

The burned flesh was already drying, sticking to

him, to them, to everything. He leaned to his side, bucking against the dry heaves squeezing his ribs. He sucked in a harsh breath, smelled the smoke of the burning village, and heaved again.

Rocco leaned against the wall as he wiped the spit off his mouth with the back of his hand. The cinderblock was cold through his sweat-dampened T-shirt. Keeping his eyes closed, he drew small breaths through his mouth. He didn't dare smell the air, fearing it would stink of smoke and ash and burning flesh. This world and the other kept flashing in and out, back and forth, like a TV that flipped between two channels. He squeezed his head between his fisted hands, trying to make it settle on a single reality.

Let it have been a dream. Just a dream. Nausea writhed in his stomach like a living thing. God, he couldn't take seeing Kadisha's home collapse again, tracking the cloud of dust that had risen from what had been her house. It wasn't real, this. It was a dream.

He cautiously opened his eyes. Someone had switched on the fluorescent panels, flooding the room with sterile, white light. He looked around, blinking, unable to reconcile where he found himself with where he'd just been—where his soul still was.

"Everything all right?" Reverend Daniels asked. He leaned toward Rocco, but didn't touch him.

"Hell no, it's not all right, Rev," one of the men said. "You heard him screaming. All of Cheyenne heard it. Ain't none of us can get any sleep with him here."

Rocco looked at the man who spoke. In deference

to the minister, his fellow vagrants had moved a few steps away. But they stood in a tight circle, staring at him as if he'd sprouted feet out his ears. The bus from DC had dropped him here three days ago. Faithful Heart Homeless Shelter. A holy fucking Mecca to all drifters, hungry and lost men, women and children.

"You ain't lettin' him stay, are you, Reverend?"

"He does this every night. He could hurt someone."

Rocco's gaze slashed toward the new speaker. He *could* hurt someone. It would be so easy. He bent his ankle, feeling for the strap of his knife's sheath. It was gone. All of his weapons were gone. No matter. An arm around the forehead, a quick twist. The end would be the same.

Sweet, goddamn silence.

"I'm sorry, son. I'm afraid they're right." The minister set his hand on Rocco's shoulder. Rocco jerked free, sending a quick look from his arm to the preacher to see if the blackened flesh had moved.

It didn't. Of course it didn't. It wasn't real. He held his arms up and looked at them, seeing only his bare skin, damp with sweat. He felt like vomiting again, but knew nothing would come up. He'd not eaten since he'd been here. He'd taken only water as his body rid itself of the meds the shrinks had pushed on him at Walter Reed. That shit fucked with his head. He needed to get clean, to start thinking straight.

"Get your things, son, and come see me. I've got some coffee on in my office," the minister offered.

Having nothing else better to do, Rocco moved to his cot. Someone had set it back upright. He shoved his feet into his still-new combat boots, struck by the oddity that after ten years' service, he didn't have a pair of boots that was broken in. Forcing himself to stay focused, stay present, he grabbed his jacket and green duffel bag, then followed the older man.

Reverend Daniels poured two cups of coffee. He was stirring sugar and powdered creamer into one. "How do you like yours?"

Rocco ignored the question. Answering it would involve too many decisions about preferences he didn't have. And way too many words. He shrugged. He'd drink it however it was served him. It wasn't as if food tasted like anything anyway. He took the proffered mug and sat in one of the chairs in front of the minister's desk.

"You got a place to go, son?"

"Yeah." That's why he was staying in this shithole.

"You serve overseas?"

"Yeah."

"Come back recently?"

Rocco sighed and leaned forward, scrubbing a hand over his face. The inquisition made him nervous. All he needed was for the helpful minister to put a call in to Walter Reed. They'd send a couple of muscles out with a straitjacket for him. Hell, they could come right over from F. E. Warren. He set the mug on the desk and stood.

"Thanks, Reverend, for the coffee, the place to

crash." Rocco slung his duffel over his shoulder and made his way outside. It was a few hours to morning. The chilly spring air cooled his fiery skin. Shoving a hand in his pocket, he dug out the key to the old Ford truck he'd picked up. He tossed his duffel in the truck bed and climbed inside. The vinyl seat was cold, the steering wheel like ice. He leaned his forehead on the hard, cracked surface.

Pressure had been building in his head since he woke, expanding his skull, throbbing against his eyes. He grew still, pretending his brain hadn't become an IED about to detonate.

Maybe it didn't matter. None of it. Maybe a person could will himself to die. Just stop breathing.

Just. Stop.

But if he died, who would save his son?

He dragged a breath into his lungs. And another. And then they came in rapid, ragged gasps.

God, he was fucked.

Chapter 2

The cell phone's shrill ring was loud in the morning's still air. Rocco let it go unanswered. He tucked his hands deeper under his arms then rolled to his back, his legs still folded uncomfortably in the short length of his truck's bench seat.

The phone rang again. How the hell was he even getting reception out here in the empty prairie outside Cheyenne? When he left the shelter, he'd driven to the ranch where he'd lived as a kid, only to find it was a ghost of its former self. No cattle dotted the wide range. The main house was abandoned and badly in need of maintenance. The outbuildings were gray and buckling from years of Wyoming's savage weather.

He'd managed to track down the aging foreman, who'd retired to a nearby trailer park. They'd had a beer and laughed about the old days. The old guy had kept Rocco's shotgun all these years. It laid against him now, its cold barrel biting into his side.

He was parked in a turnoff on a dirt road near the highway, out of sight of all but the occasional train.

This was as far as he'd gotten two days ago. He'd have to move along soon. Somewhere. He sat up and clicked to accept the call. He'd only texted his new phone number to two people and now regretted even that.

"Yeah," he said into the cold little panel.

"Rocco? Where the hell are you?" came a familiar voice on the other end. Kit Bolanger. One of his two handlers. He and Ty Bladen were the only Americans he'd had contact with in the seven years he'd been deep undercover in Afghanistan. All three of them had joined the service from Wyoming—Kit and Blade from the same small town. It was because of them he'd survived his secret Red Team assignment.

Jesus, he wished Kit would leave him alone. "Somewhere in Wyoming, I guess."

"You guess? I've been trying to get you for days. You check your messages?"

"Sure. Like, hourly."

"Hell. You been sleeping in that truck?"

Rocco looked at the barren, sunlit hills of short grass. "No." He couldn't sleep much of anywhere. "You calling to see if I've been brushing my teeth?"

"You were supposed to check in."

"I did. I gave you my number."

"And then haven't taken a single, goddamned call."

Rocco closed his eyes. "I'm not Red Teaming anymore. I don't need a handler."

"I'll tell you when you don't need a handler."

"Blow me."

Kit ignored that directive. "Blade's coming home."

Rocco sat up. "What?"

"Sniper got lucky. Blade took a round in his thigh."

"When?"

"While you were at Walter Reed."

Rocco felt gut-punched. For a minute, he couldn't draw enough air to speak. "Why didn't you tell me?"

"You were dealing with enough crap. Not like you could do anything."

"Except fucking talk to him."

"He wasn't taking calls. He was apeshit there for a while, almost as bad as you."

"How long will he be home?"

Rocco could hear the breath Kit pulled. "He's done. He's out."

Christ. "Did he lose his leg?"

"No. No, he's just done."

Rocco sighed and leaned his head back against the seat's headrest. He felt sick for Blade, worried for Kit fighting the fight without one of them. They had been tight for so long. He felt as if the Earth had shifted and now he didn't know where to stand, didn't know where his feet would hit solid ground.

He shoved his truck door open and got out, then tossed his hat on the bench seat. The wind was cool, but the sun instantly heated his back.

A train chose that moment to travel through. The conductor blew the horn a few times. The raspy, long whistle bounced around in the emptiness that ached inside Rocco. The tracks rumbled and rattled as the cars passed by. He bent his arm over the truck door and leaned his forehead on it as the train went on and on.

When the noise grew distant, he held the phone to his ear and listened to Kit breathe.

"You okay, man?" Kit asked.

"Yeah."

"Look, I need a favor."

"What?"

"I need you to go up to Wolf Creek Bend. Mandy has a parcel of land up there. Inherited it from her grandparents. She's starting an equestrian center and has an opening for a ranch hand. She can't seem to keep that job filled."

Rocco sighed. "I don't need a pity job. Jesus, Kit. Leave me the fuck alone."

"Right. 'cause you and that truck, you're tight, man. S'all you need."

"Kit—"

"Look, her land backs to Blade's. I'm going to bring him home in a couple of weeks, but I'm not sure how long I can stay. If you're there, you could check in on him now and then after I leave. And Mandy seriously needs the help. Something funky's going on up there. I don't think she's safe."

Rocco rubbed his eyes. Mandy was Kit's half sister. She'd been in junior high school and Kit had been a senior in high school before they ever knew they were related. Before both of their lives had gone to hell. Somehow, through letters and occasional visits, they'd become close over the years. If Kit said she needed help, then she did.

"What do you mean 'funky'?"

"Just weird shit. She can't keep staff. There've been some unexplained accidents on the construction site. The cops don't think it's anything unusual, but it don't sit right with me."

"You looked into the construction company?"

"They checked out." There was a pause filled with unsaid things. "I can't leave for a while yet. I'm getting out, as well. I'm going to work for a private company. Blade, too."

"You guys going merc?"

"Tremaine Industries isn't a firm of mercenaries. Owen Tremaine's hiring former Red Teamers. He wants the three of us. I'll talk to you about it when I get out there. Until then, I'd feel a lot better if you went up to Mandy's to see what's going on."

What the hell. What did he have to lose? He'd have work, a place to sleep. A chance to find normal again. A chance to heal. The sooner he got better, the sooner he could go back for his son.

"Fine. I'll head out today."

"Thanks, bro. I owe you."

Rocco had a flash of the afternoon Kit and Blade pulled him out of the pit he'd been stashed in after the explosion. He'd spent seven years in the Hindu Kush, four of them observing the infamous warlord, Ghalib Halim. No one else had come looking for him. No one thought he'd survived the blast—except for his two buds. Hell, he'd been Red Teaming so deep and so long, no one else even knew he existed. They'd given him a canteen, an MRE, and an M16 that day, then the three of them had taken the cave where Halim was holed up, executing a kill order that had been years in the making.

"No, Kit, you don't owe me. We're a long way from even."

"Rocco?"

"What?"

"Try to keep it together, feel me? I want an update in a few days."

"Roger that." Rocco dropped the connection.

* * *

Wind slipped past the low ranch house and curled around Rocco's legs, carrying a feminine whisper of ragged words. The late May morning bit like a winter day. He shoved the door shut on his old Ford pickup, letting its creak announce him. A slow look around the decrepit property showed him a barn in an advanced state of collapse, two large, overgrown pastures, a small, older farmhouse screaming for a new roof and a paint job, a steel building, and a larger ranch house that looked about a century newer than the little farmhouse.

Rocco shoved his thrift-store cowboy hat on his head and made his way to the steel building where he could hear a woman's frustrated mumbles. She had a weed whacker gutted on a counter and was leaning over it with a screwdriver. She still hadn't heard him.

"So—do you get off torturing small engines or did

that one just make you mad?" he asked, standing at the entrance to the big, cluttered workshop. The woman jumped about a foot, then sent him a glare over her shoulder. She looked away and swiped the back of her hand across both eyes. Then, drawing a deep breath, she came over to him as she shoved her hands into the back pockets of her jeans.

Light fell across her face. Rocco was unprepared for the effect she had on him. Her skin was pale, smooth like cream, freckles sprinkled lightly across her nose. Her cheeks were rosy with the day's crisp air. Straight gold-red hair the color of copper wire hung in loose streams over her shoulders. Her eyes were large and very green, like emerald cabochons. Her dark lashes were spiky with moisture. Had she been crying?

Rocco ignored that likelihood, focusing instead on the fact that good old Kit had given him a poor description of his half sister all these years. She wasn't anything like a redheaded, freckle-faced monster. As she looked at him, those green gemstones narrowed.

"Can I help you?" she asked in a voice so melodious he shivered.

"Kit sent me. Said you had a job opening."

Mandy took one look at the man standing before her and silently cursed her brother. She'd told Kit she needed a handyman—barely a couple of hours ago—and he sends her *him*.

The man was silhouetted against the stormy sky, which deepened the shadows in the hard angles of his face. He had dark-brown hair that curled a little at the edges of his hat brim. His beard, filling in from several days of not shaving, did little to gentle his jaw or obscure the shallow cleft in his chin. His lips were rounded and sensuous, though the lines bracketing his mouth gave him an edgy look. His nose was straight and narrow, flared slightly at the nostrils. His eyes were black. His gaze, obscured somewhat beneath the wide brim of his cowboy hat, was cold. Ancient. Impossible to read.

Her senses went on high alert. If Kit hadn't vouched for him, she would send him packing. She should anyway. He was every inch a warrior. She studied his eyes, trying to get a feel for what type of worker he would be, but she couldn't see past his stony expression. Wolf Valley Therapeutic Riding Center was to be a place of sunshine and healing, not the dark shadow world of a haunted soldier.

"Oh, no. No. No, Kit." She shook her head

The man leaned against the side of the shed and let his grin out, flashing white teeth against his olive complexion. "You're a fan of his too, huh?"

"I thought he was going to send a friend over."

"I am a friend."

"No. You're a Green Beret."

The man's face hardened. "I'm out of the service. I wasn't Special Forces."

Mandy frowned. "With all that's going on around here, I don't need you to take a job you're not going to keep. It's hard enough to get anyone to stay as it is, but putting an adrenalin-junky in a low-level handyman's position won't fly. Thank you for coming all the way out here. I'm sorry to have wasted your time."

"Well now, sweetheart," the man drawled, "you didn't hire me, so you can't fire me."

Mandy squared her shoulders as she met his steely gaze. Adding him to the mix of everything else that was happening was like holding a flame to a Molotov cocktail. A plain bad idea.

"I want you to leave."

"Negative."

"Mr—" What had Kit said his name was? "Whoever you are—"

"Rocco Silas."

"You're trespassing. How about I call the cops?"

Rocco quirked a brow at her. "How about you do that?" he agreed. Kit's sister glared at him. He sent her another grin just to see the flush rise on her skin again. Sun broke through the stormy clouds, streaming through the air to brighten a circle about her, igniting the highlights in her hair until it was the color of wheat washed in a red sunset. It fascinated him. It was as changeable and dramatic as the woman herself. Yanking her flaming mane around one side of her neck, she reached into her pocket and withdrew her cell. She hit one number, then lifted the phone to her ear.

If she was calling the cops, he didn't like the fact that she had them on speed dial—or rather, that she had a need to have them on speed dial.

"Your Neanderthal's here. Call him off, Kit."

Rocco took advantage of her preoccupation with

the phone call to give her a thorough look-over. Her jaw was a tempting line that ended in a narrow chin. Her neck was slim. Her shoulders looked thin and feminine in her jean jacket. Beneath it, she wore a top that emphasized a nice rack and a sleek ribcage. Her shirt was longer than her jacket, flaring out over her hips. Her legs were long and slim, her jeans tight enough to accentuate the toned muscles of her thighs. He stared at her legs, realizing she stirred something in him that had long been dormant.

Christ, this was not going to be an easy assignment. He had not expected to be attracted to Kit's sister. It was a distraction he could do without right now.

He cut her arguments short as he pulled the phone from her and held it up to his ear. "We're cool, Kit. I got this." He shut off the phone and handed it back to her. "Tell me where I can put my gear."

Mandy glared at him, sorely tempted to tell him exactly where he could put his things. *Just for the summer, Em. Please? I need to know you're safe. And there's no one I trust more than Rocco,*" Kit had asked so nicely before he'd been cutoff.

Silence settled between her and Rocco, broken only by the wind that whined as it curled around the toolshed's entrance. It caught her hair again, tossing it in front of her face, toward her brother's friend. She didn't look away from him as she drew it over one shoulder, didn't miss the way he tracked the path her hair made across her skin.

She glared at him, disliking the heat his gaze spread

through her. "I need a man who can pull his weight around here."

The humor drained from his face. "This ain't my first choice of gigs, either, sweetheart. Why don't we try it and see how it goes for a week or two? Besides, I can fix that weed whacker you gutted."

"Two weeks. If you can last that long." She held out her hand. "I'm Mandy Fielding."

Rocco looked at her small, long-fingered hand but did not complete the gesture. It was a handshake, for chrissake. A simple handshake. He didn't touch her. He couldn't risk it. She dropped her hand almost as quickly as she'd offered it.

"Tell me you're not afraid to get your hands dirty?"

He didn't answer her. She had no idea how stained his hands were.

"Right," she continued, nervously filling the breach his silence caused. She rubbed her palms on the sides of her thighs. "Well, I need some pastures mowed, old barbed wire removed, new fencing put up." She looked back to the cluttered garage. "And I need someone who can work magic with ancient farm equipment. That sound like something you're interested in?"

Rocco pulled a long draw of air. Wolf Valley Therapeutic Riding Center was way the hell off the beaten track. He cast a quick glance around them, seeing all the mindless, physical work that needed to be done—work he looked forward to tackling for the very reason that it was mindless. He glanced at Kit's sister. "It is."

"It pays $300 a week plus room and board."

He nodded, making no effort to negotiate. She cocked her head, studying him. He met her look with an unblinking gaze, his features shuttered.

"You know anything about ranching? You ever worked on a ranch before?"

"I grew up on a spread over in Albany County. Always thought I'd be one of the hands there one day."

"Why aren't you?"

He shrugged. "Army. Afghanistan. Been gone a long time."

"When did you get back?"

"A few months ago. I guess Kit didn't give you my dossier." He hoped she would take the bait, hoped it would distract her from drilling into the fact he'd been at Walter Reed until about a week ago.

It worked.

She crossed her arms and bit a corner of her mouth as she studied him. "No dossier, but it's not needed. Kit vouched for you. You've got two weeks."

Mandy turned and led the way to the older, smaller farmhouse. Four steps led up to a deep porch and a front door that opened into a small kitchen. "You're the only one staying here, so pick your bunk. The kitchen's stocked and linens are in the closet." She pushed the door open and stood back while he entered.

He did a quick circuit of the kitchen and living room, then turned down the hallway and looked at both of the bedrooms. Two twin beds were in either room with a bathroom between them that was entered by the hallway. The space was simple, clean. And a long, long way from the beautiful, jagged ranges of the Hindu Kush with its ancient, organic homes and enemies lurking in every shadow.

"You hiring more hands?" Rocco asked as he came back into the kitchen. A house this size would have slept ten or twenty fighters in Afghanistan, but after the fiasco at the shelter, he didn't feel like sharing the space.

"Not for a while. Not until we're closer to opening. I'm looking for a barn manager, but he'll eventually have an apartment in the stable."

Kit's sister sent him a measuring glance, and Rocco wondered what those big, green eyes of hers saw. When she backed across the threshold to the open space of the porch, he supposed he had his answer.

He was what he was and couldn't be anything else until he finished what waited for him. One more mission, one that was personal. When it was over, he would learn to be a civilian. Regular people everywhere managed to live normal lives. He could, too. He would have to.

Rocco took out his phone and dialed her number. "Kit gave me your number. Here's mine." He nodded at her phone, which had started ringing. "Save it. Don't hesitate to call me if something seems odd. I've got a pair of walkie-talkies in my truck. Keep one with you at all times so that you can get me anywhere on this ranch if phone reception is bad."

Kit's sister saved his number and put her phone

away. "Great. When you get settled, come get me."

"I'm settled."

She smiled slowly, still trying to figure him. He wished her luck.

"Well, if you can fix the tractor, I need to get those two pastures mowed. Then take down the old barbed wire and posts. I have new fencing being delivered in a couple of weeks. I'm going to be using these pastures as a quarantine area for new horses so that I can work with them before I move them down to the stable to be used in therapy. Several folks have horses to donate, but they'll need a fair amount of training before I can put a special-needs child or a disabled adult on any of them."

Rocco listened to her, feeling apart from her, from himself. Her words became muddled. It was too much talking. He could feel his mind shutting down, insulating him from being pulled out of himself and into her world. He had to stay separate, keep focused on his healing. While he was here, he would keep her safe, and he'd throw himself into the work, but he wouldn't let himself get caught up in the sweetness of her voice or the beauty of her eyes or the strange, melting sensation that being near her spawned inside him.

"Show me around your spread," he blurted before she elaborated further on a future he wouldn't be here to see. "And give me a run down of the problems Kit said you've been experiencing. Then I'll decide where I start working."

Chapter 3

Mandy stepped off the bunkhouse porch. "I shouldn't have told Kit," she said, more to herself than to him. "I wouldn't have except he caught me at an off moment and wouldn't let it go. There's nothing going on. Not really. Every construction project has problems. It's only that I'm up against a tight deadline, and nothing is falling into place. I wanted to open in August, but I don't think that's going to happen. I don't know when I'll be able to open. And if I can't start earning an income, this whole project is in jeopardy."

"Talk to me while we walk. I'll see for myself."

Mandy faced him, her hands on her hips. "I don't need a soldier, Mr. Silas. I need a handyman. Please don't look for trouble that isn't there."

"My name's Rocco. You've had to call the cops, true? How many times?"

"Twice. Several tools were taken from the construction site. Another time someone soaked the newly poured foundation in the stable. It froze overnight. Ruined it. Delayed work a week while the old concrete was removed and a fresh foundation was poured."

"Are your neighbors complaining of troubles? Burglaries? Vandalism? Stuff like this happening to others around here as well?"

"No."

"Kit said you've had a hard time keeping a handyman on staff. What happened with them?"

"You're the fourth I've hired. One needed extended time off to go help his daughter on her ranch. The next worked for a week, then never came back. The third went on a drinking bender. He kept coming to work either drunk or hungover, so I fired him—just this morning."

Rocco looked around the property. He wanted a handle on the trouble Kit was worried about. He would deal with the work piling up once the situation was secured. "Let's take that tour."

Mandy's property was on the upper slope of a steep ravine overlooking the town of Wolf Creek Bend far to the southeast. The terrain's natural terraces had been excavated to make the land useable.

Her home, the upper pastures, and the miscellaneous farm buildings that comprised the private ranch area were on the top level. The wide middle tier held the equestrian center buildings that were under construction. And the lower plateau contained several pastures. Mandy led him down the long driveway from the private residence to the first of two lower steppes.

The construction site was muddy from recent spring rains. They slogged across a thick road to a temporary construction trailer. Mandy climbed the steps. She stamped then scraped the mud off her boots as best she could. "George?" she called as she opened the trailer door and leaned inside.

"Right here. What can I do for you?" A slim man in his early fifties stood in the muddy road behind them. Rocco turned, taking a good look at Mandy's construction manager. His face was lean and gray. Shadows darkened his eyes, making him appear tired and haggard.

"George, this is Rocco Silas, a friend of my brother's. Rocco, this is George Bateman, the construction foreman. Rocco's going to be helping me up top."

George held out his hand. "Nice to meet you. Glad to see Mandy's rounded up some help."

Rocco glanced at the foreman's hand as his turned sweaty in his pocket. *Take it*, he urged himself. *It's a goddamned handshake. Take it.*

"He doesn't shake hands. War injury," Mandy answered for him.

Fuck. Now he was hiding behind a girl.

"Ah." George dropped his hand. "Iraq or Afghanistan?"

"Afghanistan."

"You boys did us proud over there. Thank you. So how can I help you?"

"Mandy mentioned some problems you've been having," Rocco said. "Mind if I look around, talk to your crew?"

"Not at all. I did a background check on every single one of my men. Besides a few traffic violations and some spotty credit scores, they had clean records. No drugs. No felonies. Maybe you can find something the cops and I couldn't."

"Credit problems bad enough to make them want to steal?"

"Nope. Just good men living through some bad times. Hasn't been as much work as we'd like lately. Some of their wives have been unemployed. Their families have been suffering. This job was a godsend."

"Where were the tools taken from?"

George nodded at a utility trailer. "We lock anything valuable up in the trailer every night. Found it busted wide open one morning when we came to work."

"You got some enemies, George? Disgruntled former employees? Angry competitors?"

A muscle worked at the edge of the foreman's jaw. "I treat my employees fairly. Pay them top wages. Hell, I'm barely making any profit on this job. I'm paying most of it to the men just so I can keep them. I would hate to get through these lean times and have no workers available for new projects. So, yeah. This job was competed, and I won it 'cause I bid it low. Maybe that was unfair, but it's survival."

"You didn't win on price alone, George. You have

a stellar reputation and you're local," Mandy added. "Those were important factors." She looked at Rocco. "The other companies were in different states. I doubt this job would have stirred much of an angry response from the losing bidders."

George gave them a tour of the buildings under construction, including an indoor arena, a pole barn, and a long stable with space for an office, a meeting room, and a small apartment at one end. Another crew was working on fencing for three pastures and a couple of smallish, round corrals in the lower terrace. It was an impressive setup.

When they finished the tour, Rocco asked to see the rest of the property. Mandy led him north toward a deer trail that led up a steep hill. The trail made a couple of switchback turns behind her house. At the top of the ridge, they could see all the way down to the town. To the west, the Snowy Range Mountains rose in jagged peaks of granite, hostile and forbidding like the steep ranges of the Hindu Kush, stirring an unexpected wave of homesickness in Rocco.

The wind that was merely a breeze below was blistering where they stood, clearing out the heavy clouds. The vista was breathtaking. Rocco filled his lungs with the crisp air. Twice. It smelled of snow and dust and sunshine.

He looked at Mandy, watched her peer across the view, her expression softening as she gazed at the land that she loved. The wind brought him a whiff of her soft scent. He pulled it into his lungs, secretly savoring it until a wave of guilt hit him. He didn't deserve to stand here in the warm sun and cold breeze, safe in the heart of America, enjoying the company of a woman. The ache he felt for what he'd left behind wasn't only skin-deep, it was bone deep. Soul deep, a MRSA infection in his spirit, consuming what was left of him.

Mandy made a quick braid of her hair so that it wouldn't blow, but her fiery mane defied restraint. She caught his gaze. He forced himself to look away and was relieved when she started down the other side.

He was about to follow her when a patch of white in the dirt caught his attention. He stepped over to it. Cigarettes.

"Mandy, do you smoke?"

She came to his side and looked at the ground. "No, but my grandfather used to."

"These are fresh. Have you had visitors up here?"

"No."

Rocco crouched down and looked at what he could see of the ranch the below. Some of the construction. The long drive up to the equestrian center. A similar drive into the residential section of the ranch. The back of the house. The toolshed blocked sight of the bunkhouse and the pastures beyond it.

"Do you ever see anyone up here?"

"No." Mandy crossed her arms and frowned as she looked around. "Maybe someone from the construction site comes up here."

Rocco doubted that. It would take a good ten minutes or more to get up here. It wasn't a convenient place to spend a quick lunch or smoke break. And if someone was coming up after hours, well, he had no business loitering up here, watching the ranch. Judging from the tension in Mandy's face, she'd come to the same conclusion.

"Let's move on," Rocco told her. "I want to see the rest of the ranch." They stepped down across a steep incline filled with boulders, sage, and scrub pines. Eventually the terrain leveled out and a path became visible.

Mandy waited for him to catch up to her. "We'll be widening some of these trails for our advanced students who are able to handle a trail ride. We've a thousand acres—plenty of space to provide an enjoyable experience for our riders."

He focused on the network of paths while she spoke. In Afghanistan, trails like these led to weapon and food caches, Taliban hideouts, and sniper nests. Standing here, unarmed and sheltered neither by body armor nor by the native garb of his undercover disguise, Rocco felt critically exposed.

The path they'd moved onto was well used—more than the others. "How often do you walk these trails?"

"Not very often. I made a couple of treks through here last month, picking the paths I wanted to have widened for our riders. Why?"

He shrugged. They were too established to have been used only a couple of times this spring. "Your land backs to Ty Bladen's property, doesn't it?" Rocco knew a skeleton crew was managing Blade's property.

They wouldn't be tracking through these woods—he'd sold off his herd when his father had died years earlier. His people would have no reason to come this way very often.

"It does. The Bureau of Land Management borders the other part. I don't know who leases it. We've never had problems with them. I don't pay much attention to it."

He'd followed too many goat trails in Afghanistan that led to insurgent hidey-holes to feel a warm fuzzy that these paths were just making themselves.

"Rocco, what are you seeing? You're making me nervous. Do you think someone has been coming through here?"

Hell. He lifted his hat and shoved a hand through his hair. Maybe he was seeing ghosts where there were none. The land here was arid. It needed irrigation to grow anything more than sage once the spring rains dried up and the summer heat came in. A little traffic now and then in this ravine would probably stress the vegetation enough to form semipermanent paths like these.

"No." He sighed. "I'm too used to looking for things that I'll never see here. Forget it." All the same, he decided to make a daily pass over the area, at different times, just to see what he might stir up.

When they returned to the ranch, they came out on the far side of the old barn. There was an old circular corral with a single occupant—an edgy, black-and-white Paint. The beast lifted his head, scenting them.

He moved to the far side of the ring, watching them with white-rimmed eyes.

"That's Kitano."

Rocco watched the Paint's skittish behavior. "What's wrong with him?"

Mandy shook her head. "They say he's gone loco."

Rocco didn't miss the look she flashed at him. He wondered if they were still talking about the horse. Damn Kit, anyway. Had he told her about Rocco's stay at Walter Reed? He shoved his hands in his pockets. "Has he?"

"I think so." She nodded. "I'm fostering him. I hope I can rehabilitate him. I don't know that I will ever be able to use him in the center's work, but I would be happy to settle him with a family who will love him."

"What happened to him?"

"He was part of a herd of horses used by a tourist's riding stable down in Colorado. His owners fell on hard times and couldn't feed their horses. They were put in a pasture where they slowly starved. Kitano didn't take a liking to that. He fought back, fought to free the herd. His owners beat him, then locked him up in a stall and forgot about him. I can't get him to go inside a building at all now. That's why I've got him in this corral."

Rocco cursed low under this breath. Kitano's hell was like the pit he'd been a guest in. The wind curled around the buildings, making a plaintive whine.

"How are you going to fix him?"

"I don't know. Time maybe. And patience. Plenty of food and water. Consistent handling. Basically starting over like he's unbroke."

She stepped on the bottom rung of the corral and pushed herself up to brace her folded arms on the top board. "My grandfather had a persistent belief that there was nothing sunshine, rest, good nutrition, exercise, and laughter couldn't cure."

"Horses don't laugh."

She looked at him. Her sharp, green gaze pierced the haze of his mind, the clutter of memories and heartache that rode him with razor-edged spurs. "I wasn't talking about Kitano."

He gave her a cold stare. She didn't fucking want to get into his head. It wasn't a safe place for any of them. "Thanks for the tour. I'm going to talk to George's crew." He touched the brim of his hat and headed back to the construction site.

Hours later, after meeting the guys working the construction site below, his gut told him George's assessment of his men was accurate. None seemed to be hiding anything. No one had seen any strangers around the site or up at the ridge.

Rocco sighed as he stepped into the steel toolshed. The building was an oversized workshop that had long ago been taken over as a storage area. Various farm equipment and household artifacts littered the space— mowers, tillers, attachments for the tractor, extra tires, tools, shovels, rakes, brooms, boxes, trunks, discarded furniture—all of it covered with a thick layer of dust, none of it in any order. The clutter and confusion of the space amplified the noise in his head, hitting him like a wall he couldn't pass through.

He looked behind him, back to the wide-open space of the ranch as a wave of impatience slammed into him. He was grateful for the job, for the place to crash. But holy hell, he didn't want to be here, fixing a goddamned tractor. He needed to be back in Afghanistan searching for his son.

Chapter 4

Alan Buchanan nervously crossed and uncrossed his legs. He'd been in this café for fifty-five minutes. Only five minutes to go. What a wasted day. He'd made the four-hour drive down to Denver only to now turn around and make the long drive home again. As usual. Over the past two years, he'd been summoned here at random intervals, several times a year. Until last month, he'd never once met with anyone.

For their part, his associates had kept their word. They'd erased his past, given him a new identity—complete with a wife and a kid, set him up in a new town with the capital to start a business. He'd missed only one of these meetings. One, and yet the consequence had been severe: his wife had been murdered.

He looked at his watch. One minute left. He got up to throw away his coffee cup, but immediately sat back down as Amir Hadad walked in and joined him.

"Hello, Mr. Buchanan. How have you been?"

Alan's mouth went dry. Amir looked like any other

affluent white-collar executive out for a coffee break that afternoon. A pinstripe suit. A neatly pressed white shirt. A perfectly knotted silk tie. His soft chin was well defined by an immaculately trimmed beard. His black hair was short. His dark eyes were alert. His friendly smile was contemptuous.

"I'm here. As requested," Alan answered, pleased that he didn't stutter.

Amir leaned back in his seat. "So you are. So you are." He waved a hand toward a waitress and ordered a double espresso. "You are aware of all that we have done for you? Yes?"

The memory of his wife's car accident flashed through his mind. They said she'd been drinking. It was a lie. The woman had been a teetotaler. "Yes. Of course."

Amir's coffee arrived. He did not touch it. "What is the progress on the construction site?"

"As you requested, it has been problematic. The girl is having a hard time keeping workers. The construction is taking twice as long as it should because of all of the delays."

"Very good. Very good, indeed. It's time that there should be a fatal accident, no? We need to speed things along."

"Kill someone? Who? How?"

"It matters not to me. If you can manage to do it without being caught, I will relocate you again when this assignment is finished."

"You're crazy," Alan hissed. Sending a surreptitious

look around the coffee shop, he leaned forward and lowered his voice. "That's insane. I'm not going to kill someone."

"Will you not? Has our time together been so onerous? One day of service here or there? You knew there was a price when you accepted the deal."

"I have already paid a terrible price. I lost my wife, thanks to you. I want out. Out for good. I will repay you what you have invested in me."

"There is no out, Mr. Buchanan." Amir took out a ten-dollar bill and set it on the table. "By the way, how is your daughter?"

"Don't hold her over my head. She isn't my kid. She was my wife's." He pretended indifference. "Do what you want to her, I don't care."

"Of course I was not threatening her. Do you think me a monster? But I do have your signed confession. I would not hesitate to turn it over to the FBI should you find yourself unable to complete your obligations to us."

Alan shut his eyes as he weighed his options. He couldn't cut and run, because he'd be right back where he was five years ago. He couldn't go to the authorities: they wouldn't believe him, and they'd throw him in jail for his past crimes. "I didn't mean I wouldn't do it, just that after I do it, then I'm out."

Amir smiled. "Good day, Mr. Buchanan. Always a pleasure to chat with you."

* * *

Fresh out of a shower, Rocco studied his duffel bag, trying to decide whether he should unpack it and stay awhile or keep living out of the bag and remain mobile. He'd waged this debate with himself for a quarter of an hour without any progress.

What the hell. He couldn't even decide something so freaking simple. It wouldn't take long to repack if he had to leave in a hurry. All he really needed was his shotgun.

He pulled his clothes out of the duffel and stacked them in the dresser. When he finished, he wished he hadn't. Everything he owned fit in two drawers. Almost thirty fucking years old, and what did he have to show for three decades of life? An old beat-up Ford, a shotgun he'd had as a kid, and two drawers of clothes.

He quickly tamped down on that line of thinking— it was a dark road that led straight to hell. His life had been so much more than the sum of his things. He was a father and a husband. A trusted warrior. A linguistic freak of nature, coveted by spec ops groups for the ease with which he could learn languages and emulate dialects. He had a dark complexion that let him infiltrate any indigenous people in the Middle East and the skills to survive on the lam in foreign, hostile lands.

At least he still had the languages, though there wasn't much use for a linguist in the wilds of Wyoming. Maybe that was a blessing.

He drew off his towel and stepped into briefs and a fresh pair of jeans. He laid out his toiletries in the bathroom, straightened the small bunkhouse, checked the locks on the doors and windows, and pulled the drapes. When everything was settled, he pushed an armchair into the far corner of the living room, facing the kitchen, moving it into the most defensible spot in the house. He set a box of shotgun shells next to it on the floor. With only the dim light from the bathroom, he settled into the chair for the night and reached for his shotgun. The hard, cold metal was all that passed for his backbone anymore.

It was after midnight. He'd spent the evening getting the toolshed straightened up. He'd found lumber in the old barn and made shelves for the boxes of household discards mixed in with the equipment. He set the implements that didn't fit the tractor off to one side for Mandy to decide what she wanted to do with them. Tomorrow, he'd tackle repairing the tractor— after another quick tour around the ranch.

He blinked. His eyelids were heavy. The nightmares couldn't take him if he didn't sleep, so he fought to stay awake. He hated nights the most. The dark was the perfect backdrop for the images his mind kept playing, a continuous loop of a B-Rated horror flick, except what he saw was real, a memory, and far, far worse than any movie. He held the sides of his head, wishing the images that taunted him were less fragmented. The wisps that played in his mind, in his dreams, were only teasers. The flesh of the story remained hidden behind a shroud, too terrible to recall.

The shrinks at Walter Reed had said he wouldn't

recover until he faced what had happened that day in Kasheem Baba. He didn't disagree, but the truth was locked away so deeply within him as to be impervious to drugs or nightmares, a secret that hid like a cancer, slowly killing him in its ravenous destruction.

* * *

Pale morning light eased through the windows. Rocco opened his eyes. Without moving, he looked around the quiet bunkhouse. He sighed and leaned his head back. He'd slept longer than he'd expected— longer than usual.

He changed into his running gear and jogged up the trails he'd seen yesterday, ending at the bluff overlooking the house. He counted the cigarettes. No new ones. He looked out over the vista. He'd catch the bastard who was watching Mandy. Sooner or later.

Rocco took the trail down from the bluff, through the construction site, and then down the long drive to the main road. Running when he was exhausted was a challenge, but going through the motions of being normal was all he had. The meds the shrinks gave him kept him too stoned to function, but without them, rage simmered just beneath the surface of his mind like a festering wound. He forced himself to rise with the sun, eat something—whatever little thing he could keep down—and breathe. None of it felt real. He could only hope that his brain would reengage, and he could own himself again.

And when he did, he was going back for Zaviyar.

He ran three miles down the road in front of Mandy's spread. The return trip was all uphill. By the time he came back to the dirt turnaround in front of the residential portion of the ranch, he was drenched with sweat. The sun was up and the day promised to be one of blistering heat. Spring weather here was as changeable as it was in the highlands of Afghanistan. Wintry one day. Blistering hot the next.

He looked up. Mandy stood at the ridge overlooking the construction site. Wind plucked at the edges of her hair, fanning it over her shoulders. Involuntarily, he turned in her direction, silently crossing the distance in the packed dirt. He lifted his face to the breeze, seeking her scent. It was faint, but he found it. Sweet, heady. He squeezed his eyes shut as a memory slammed into him.

Kadisha wore a long necklace of tiny jasmine flowers, warmed by her body and the heat of the summer evening. She laughed as she lifted it over her head and draped it over his, crushing the flowers against his chest to infuse the night air with the blossoms' sickly sweet fragrance.

Had she known, even then, what he was?

Rocco opened his eyes. Mandy watched him, frozen like a hunted animal, her coffee mug halfway to her mouth. Yet unlike prey, nothing about her was camouflaged. Her hair blazed like flames in the morning sun. Her green eyes matched her green fleece jacket, making her standout like a flower in the barren expanse of a desert.

He was breathing hard, and every draw of air

brought him her scent. He wanted to touch her, wanted to feel the smoothness of her cheeks against the palms of his hands, wanted it as he hadn't any human contact in a very long time. He couldn't risk it. He knew what would happen.

His hands curled into fists. He nodded at her, then pivoted and made for the house, hoping a shower would settle him. He had one and only one mission today: fix the tractor so that he could mow the fields. He showered, ate a boiled egg, then headed for the toolshed.

* * *

The sun was high by the time he'd cleaned the tractor's fuel filter and fuel supply hose, changed the battery, and flushed the radiator. He was rubbing the grease off his hands when Mandy came down to the shed with two glasses of something cold to drink. The tractor, which he'd moved to the dirt driveway, puttered next to them, releasing diesel fumes into the air.

"You did it! You got it running!" Mandy smiled at him as she handed him one of the glasses. He took it, careful not to touch her. It was against all reason that he was drawn to the sound of her voice. He looked at the tractor instead of at her, wishing she'd leave. He wasn't going to be here long. It was best not to form a friendship with her. They had no need to talk to each other.

He dragged his gaze up to look at her face. It was a

nice, open, American kind of face. She wore little makeup; nothing hid the freckles on her nose and cheeks. His gaze lowered to her chin and her long, thin neck, stopping at her collarbone. He forced himself to look lower, at the rest of her body. She wore a green tank top that clung to her body like a second skin. Rocco felt the heat of a blush warm his face as he looked at her body, a body she so carelessly exposed for his perusal.

He lifted his gaze to hers again. She gave him a tentative smile, her eyes wary. He glared at her. He didn't want to talk to her. Didn't want to talk to anyone. He wanted the silence to return. He needed to think. He stared at his glass, then took a sip. It was cold and sweet. Tea with big chunks of ice. Such an American drink, he thought, struck by another wave of homesickness.

He stared absently into the amber liquid, wondering what he missed, exactly? Living in a lean-to in the bombed-out skeleton of a building? A Bedouin tent? The beige, stucco walls and great arches that had been Kadisha's home?

His son.

He missed his son. Kit and Blade had said Zaviyar was dead. *Dead*. He couldn't fucking remember. And since he couldn't, he had to believe his son lived. Surely, one of the villagers who'd survived the explosion had taken him in. Rocco still felt a connection to him. A father would know if his son was dead.

Wouldn't he?

"When did you do all of this, Rocco?" Mandy's soft voice brought him back to the present. She was looking around the shed with an awed expression.

"Last night. It was too cluttered to work in. I hope you don't mind, but I took some lumber from a pile in the old barn for the shelves. The implements that don't fit the tractor are over there. You can decide what you want to do with them. If you don't want the furniture, I can take it down to the dump."

"I was keeping the attachments until I knew if that tractor would ever be functional again. Neighbors and people from town have been donating bits and pieces of equipment, hoping to help out."

"They're supportive of what you're doing here?"

Mandy frowned at him. "Why wouldn't they be? Wolf Valley has the potential to be a successful business, a good addition to the town."

"Just curious. Trying to make sense of what's happening."

Mandy looked at him with an assessing gaze. He doubted she liked what she saw. "Are you hungry? I can make a sandwich for you," she offered, gesturing toward the main house.

He shook his head. "I want to get the mowing done before I take a break."

"You are eating, aren't you?"

Rocco leveled a hard glare at her. "Kit tell you to babysit me? 'Cause I don't need a woman to look after me."

She took a step nearer to him. And another. The hairs rose on his arms, his neck. Was she as soft as she appeared? He ached to discover the feel of her. That very thought cooled his reaction. If he touched her, she would see, feel, wear the blight that infected him. He'll have made a leper of her, all for the fleeting relief touching her would provide.

Mandy stood barely a hand's breath away. Her voice, her scent, those were the only things he would ever know of her. Yet he couldn't resist taunting her, himself. He leaned closer, sucked in more of her lush scent. He did not touch her with his hands or his body or his face, just held himself close to her warmth. She should know what danger she was in if she tried to break through to him with food, or kindness, or laughter.

"Where I come from, Rocco, people treat each other with respect and kindness. I meant no insult by offering you a sandwich."

Dammit all, he *was* hungry. He'd kill for that sandwich, but he didn't dare eat—not a full meal, anyway. He kept himself in a constant state of deprivation. The hunger pangs gnawing at his insides were the only real thing in his world. As long as he felt them, he knew he was conscious and not hallucinating. It was his only landmark in what had become the crazy jumble of his mind.

And it wasn't just food he craved. He yearned for wild, unfettered sex. For a life lived with intent. For anything and everything that was Kit's sister. None of which could he experience until he had his son safely home with him. He took a step back. Glaring at her, he set his glass down and retrieved his hat, then made his way toward the tractor and the fields that needed mowing.

Chapter 5

Mandy drew a ragged breath as she watched Rocco walk away. She closed her eyes, picturing him as he'd just been, seeing his dark, brown hair, dark brows— one that arched a little higher than the other, lips bracketed by creases, hollows in his cheeks, his eyes consuming her.

She'd thought he was going to kiss her when he'd leaned forward. Her body still thrummed with anticipation. She forced more air into her lungs, then headed to the house, where she phoned Kit.

"Hi, Em," he answered. He'd called her by the first initial of her first name since their schooldays. There was something comforting in that old moniker. "How's it going?"

"You could have warned me."

The phone was silent awhile. "I didn't want to scare you. He needs to be there, you know. He needs what you're doing."

"He's so angry."

"Well, you would be too if you went through what

he went through."

"What happened to him?"

"War, baby, in all its ugly, scarring wretchedness. Just work your magic on him, ok?"

"I don't think he's eating. He looks so lean."

Kit sighed. "This is what I was afraid of. He's as stubborn as an ass, Mandy, but he has to eat. How's he sleeping?"

"I don't know. I don't think he is. He works late into the night."

"Probably still having nightmares. All you can do is work on one thing at a time. Get him to eat first, then we'll tackle the rest."

"I'll see what I can do."

"How's the construction? Anything new?"

Mandy told him about the cigarette butts and Rocco's concern over the paths in the back acreage.

"That's it. I'm coming out there," Kit said with some finality.

"There's no need for that. What would you do that Rocco won't? If there is something happening, he'll figure it out."

"I don't like it, Emmy. I want you to be safe."

"I am safe. Everything's fine, or at least, it will be soon."

* * *

That evening, Rocco took another tour of the property, looking for anything that jumped out at him, wondering if his instincts were misfiring or if something odd was really happening. Nothing seemed changed. No new cigarette butts had appeared.

As he came out of the hills behind the ranch buildings, he saw Mandy step into Kitano's pen. He watched from a distance, not wanting to distract her or alarm the horse. He had the advantage of being downwind from the corral, giving him the luxury of observing them unnoticed.

She started to walk slowly in a clockwise direction, moving with the confidence of a seasoned trainer, her posture neither one of aggression nor timidity. The Paint was facing her. He stomped the ground in warning. She kept moving forward as if she were merely enjoying an evening stroll. Kitano tossed his head, then moved a few steps away from her. She continued forward. Kitano moved as she moved, walking in a circle, staying ahead of her. His pace quickened.

Rocco's nerves tightened. What the hell was she doing in there alone with a mad horse?

Mandy stepped into the center of the corral. As Kitano moved in front of her, she raised her hand and made a few low, clicking sounds with her tongue, encouraging him to keep moving. She turned as he moved around the perimeter of the corral, clicking her tongue at him when he slowed. And when he grew a little winded, she dropped her hand and stood still. He eased down to a walk and then a full stop. She started walking toward him, this time in a counter-clockwise direction. Again, he moved away from her. When he sped up, she moved to the middle and repeated the exercise until he was fully winded. Then, and only then, did he let her approach him.

She took a rag out of her back pocket and touched it gently to his neck, behind his ears. Rocco could hear the low rumble of her voice as she spoke to Kitano but not the words themselves. Kitano tolerated her strokes until she reached his withers with the rough cloth. He tossed his head and whinnied, then rushed away. He stopped at the opposite side of the corral, watching her with a white-eyed glare, his sides heaving.

Mandy left the corral and waved at Rocco. "Thank you for waiting."

"I didn't want to distract him."

She nodded. "He spooks easily. He doesn't like men very much."

"Doesn't seem to like anyone very much." Rocco shoved his hands in his pockets as he looked down at her. The sun was low in the horizon, inching toward the jagged ridges of the Snowy Range, washing the land, the ranch, and Mandy in the warm orange hues of the long spring sunset.

"True. But he's letting me get near him, letting me touch him. That's big progress." She stepped up on a board of the corral and dumped a bucket of feed into his trough. She reached for the big bucket of water from the wagon she'd used to haul the feed and water out to the corral, but Rocco lifted it for her, pouring it into Kitano's deep water bucket.

"Speaking of progress, you did great with the fields.

Think you can get the baler to work?"

"Sure. I'll do it when the hay dries. Where do you want me to stack the bales?"

"I'd like them protected from the weather, but there's nowhere to put them right now. The barn isn't safe, and the pole barn isn't ready yet. How about stacking them up next to the toolshed?"

Rocco nodded. "Will do. I'll start on the old fencing tomorrow. What do you want to do with the wire?"

Mandy made a face. "Hadn't thought of that. Maybe we can find a recycler to take it."

"There's an artist in Cheyenne who uses scrap metal for her sculptures. She'll take it."

Mandy cocked her head, giving him a curious look. "How do you know her?"

The sculptor had come to the shelter looking for day laborers. He'd helped her out for a couple of days. No way was he going to tell Mandy that. He shrugged. "I just ran into her."

"If she wants it, then that would be great." Again, she gave him a questioning look. "Have you eaten today?"

"I'm not hungry."

"That's not what I asked."

Rocco leveled a hard look at her. "Giving Kit daily updates?"

She gave him a half smile. "If I don't call him, he calls me. He's like a mother hen. Worse, really." She met his gaze, her eyes searching his. "You must mean a lot to him."

Rocco sighed and shifted his gaze to the mountains behind her. "Tell him I had a good day. That's all that really matters, isn't?" He looked at her. "Day by day?" He nodded toward the garden wagon. "Need a hand with that?"

"No. Good night, Rocco."

"Night, Mandy." He started toward the toolshed, but looked over at her. "Hey—next time you talk to him, ask him when Blade's coming home."

She frowned. "I will. Is Ty okay?"

He shook his head. "Took a bullet in his leg."

* * *

Rocco got to work first thing in the morning instead of starting out with a run. It was best to vary his routine, especially if someone was watching the ranch. The sun was already burning off the morning's chilly air. Truthfully, he was looking forward to another day's hard work. After tinkering with the baler for a few hours last night, he'd actually gotten a few good hours of sleep before the nightmares came.

He fetched Kitano's feed from the bag Mandy stored in the toolshed, then refilled his water bucket. The Paint was hard to look at, thin as he was. Rocco didn't linger at the corral—Kitano wouldn't come near his food while he was there.

He was gathering the tools he'd need to work on the fence when Mandy came into the shed. "Oh! You're up early," she greeted him.

"So are you." He strapped on an old tool belt. Mandy's gaze dropped to the worn leather around his hips. Whoever had owned the belt previously was quite a bit heavier. Rocco had to tighten it several inches from the worn hole on the strap. "Hope you don't mind my using the belt—"

"It was my grandfather's."

Rocco went still, part of the strap in his hand as he looked at Mandy from under the brim of his hat. "I can use something else."

"No. It's fine. If you need it, use it." She went to fill Kitano's feed bucket.

"I already fed him."

She flashed a surprised look at him. "You did?"

He shoved a pair of pliers, a hammer, and pair of wire cutters into the tool belt. "Just doin' my job, boss." He grabbed a pair of heavy gloves, then touched a finger to his hat brim. Sunlight spilled over him as he stepped from the shade of the toolshed, heating his back and arms as he pushed the wheelbarrow over to the pasture.

Moving from post to post, he rolled the old rusted wire up, leaving the pieces as long as possible. The artist preferred it that way. When it became almost too heavy to carry, he cut the wire and bound the end, leaving the coil at the fence post. The work was simple and repetitive, yet he had to stay focused on it to keep from letting the barbs nick his skin.

At the end of the day, he'd barely made a dent in the amount of wire that needed to be removed. Even so, it felt like another good day. He was tired and sore, but he'd stayed present, stayed on task. He took the day's last wheelbarrow load to the back of the toolshed where he was gathering the coils and unloaded it, then put his tools away and wearily made his way to the bunkhouse.

He planned to take a shower, then open a can of tuna or something for dinner. He had no appetite, but he knew he needed to eat—and not only to appease Kit. He had to keep his strength up. If he ate small amounts, it wouldn't nauseate him. And it wouldn't remove him very far from the hunger he needed near at hand.

Mandy carried a tray with Rocco's dinner down to his cabin that evening with the same resolute determination she used in handling Kitano. She knew getting Rocco to eat would be a fight, but she was nothing if not stubborn. He never joined her for meals and very little had been consumed from the bunkhouse kitchen in the few days he'd been there. She crossed the porch and knocked on his door, the tray balanced on one hip. The door opened.

Rocco stood there in his white T-shirt and jeans. He'd taken his shirt and boots off. She'd probably caught him right before a shower. Embarrassment froze her tongue but didn't keep her eyes from wandering across his chest to the lean, well-defined muscles of his shoulders and arms. He was bigger than he looked fully clothed.

"Boss," he greeted her, no welcome in his voice.

"I brought your dinner." She pushed past him and set it on the table. When he reached out to lift the lid covering the plate, she saw the livid cut on his knuckles. "Good heavens! What did you do?" she gasped, lifting his hand for a closer look.

He pulled quickly away. "I cut it. No big deal."

"Did you cut it on the barbed wire?" The hostile look he gave her was her only answer. "Rocco! You might need stitches. And a Tetanus shot."

"I'm just out of the Army. All my shots are current." His cut was trivial. He'd been careless, letting a barb nick him. The damned thing had snagged in his glove and cut a trench across a couple of knuckles. He wasn't worried about it—he'd had worse.

She took hold of his arm and marched him toward the bathroom, which she'd stocked with a first-aid kit. She flipped on the faucet, then washed and rinsed her hands. She lathered up again, then drew his hand under the water and gently spread the foam over his skin.

Rocco watched her hands move against his. They were so much smaller than his, long-fingered, tipped with slim crescent moons for nails. He was touching her. Finally. He tried to savor the moment, tried to ignore the growing waves of nausea his fear of being touched caused.

Mandy turned off the water. She grabbed a towel and pressed lightly around his hand. When she pulled the towel away, fresh blood welled into the cut. Rocco watched the blood rise, red pooling in the gouged skin.

His hand seemed far away, as if he looked at it through a tunnel.

He could smell the smoke. Motorcycles and a truck were burning. As were the ancient homes of the village. Women were screaming. God, the wailing. Someone pulled at him, shouting something. The stench underlying the smoke curled into his nostrils, a sweet poison.

He yanked free of the hands gripping him. He shouted in Pashto for them to leave him alone. He tried to take a deep breath, but he couldn't get any clear air. He gulped for a breath again. He kept his eyes closed, refused to look around. Didn't want to see what he knew he would see. He covered his ears, blocking the screams, the roaring flames. His own sobs. Nausea hit him like a fist, blasting the air from his lungs. He doubled over. He couldn't breathe.

"Rocco?" A voice called to him. "Rocco? Are you okay?"

It didn't fit, that voice, that question. No one knew his real name. He looked up, letting his eyes focus briefly. An angel stood before him. A fucking angel. Shit. Was he dead? Bile rose violently. He made it to the toilet and retched dry heaves. He'd eaten some, but not much since he got here. There was nothing but spit to come up.

"Rocco? What's happening?"

He looked at the angel. She knew him. Had he fallen back to English? Had he blown his cover? Christ, where was he?

"Get out," he ordered, but the angel ignored him. She picked up a washcloth, ran it under the tap, then wrung out the extra moisture. She touched the cold fabric to his forehead, his cheek, his mouth.

Mandy. Not an angel. He heaved again, then swiped the back of his wrist against his mouth. "Get the fuck out. Get out now!" He grabbed her arm and shoved her through the bathroom door, then kicked it closed. He stumbled to the tub and turned the shower on, then climbed in, still clothed. The water's steady hiss filled his ears, cleared the smoke from his nose—along with the sweet stench of rotting flesh. He stared at the cracked white tiles. White. White was all that he saw. White was all there was. Whitewhitewhitewhite.

Mandy ran from the bathroom and out the small bunkhouse. She closed the door behind her, her heart slamming against her ribs as she stared at the raw wood. What the heck had just happened? What was wrong with Rocco? Tears welled in her eyes as she remembered the look of sheer terror on his face. What had he been seeing? Had he flashed back to the war?

She stared at the house a long moment, then decided she needed to wait for him. She sat in the old metal porch chair. Folding her legs in front of her, she realized she still held the first-aid kit. She dropped it onto the side table and wrapped her arms around her legs. The shower ran for a long time. Fifteen minutes. Thirty. Forty-five. The small water heater had to have run out of hot water long ago. At last, the faucet shut off. She heard footsteps.

The door opened. Rocco came out, peeling his wet

T-shirt over his head. He mopped his face with it, then leaned his forehead against a wooden support beam. His jeans and socks were soaking. He hadn't even removed his belt. Mandy didn't say a word. She held perfectly still, wishing she'd run home every bit as much as she knew she needed to stay.

Something must have alerted him to her presence. He turned abruptly. His nipples were puckered in the cold evening air. His skin had a bluish tint to it. Her gaze slowly lifted to his face and the rage rapidly gathering there.

"I told you to leave."

She showed him the first-aid kit. "I ran out with the kit. I still haven't fixed your hand."

"Fuck. You're not going to leave it alone, are you?"

Mandy unfolded her legs and crossed to where he stood. She didn't acknowledge his temper. She knew she had to work fast. She opened the kit, fished out two butterfly bandages, then stuck them on his ripped skin. "Now, go inside and put dry clothes on. When did you last eat?"

He shrugged, glaring at her.

"Go get dressed. You're freezing out here."

He entered the cabin, not bothering to close the door. Mandy stood with her back to the door, fighting the temptation to let her gaze follow him into the shadows of the bunkhouse. If he didn't dress and present himself in short order, he'd be in for a battle the likes of which he wouldn't be expecting. She folded her arms in front of her.

The porch creaked behind her. She saw Rocco standing there. He'd pulled a fresh T-shirt on, a dry pair of jeans and his combat boots. He propped a shoulder against the doorjamb. There wasn't an ounce of fat on his body. His face was lean, his cheeks unshaved, his expression edgy. He looked like a wolf after a long, harsh winter.

"What now, boss lady?"

"Now you're coming up to the house. I'm going to get some food in you."

"I'm not feeling much like company right now. And I ain't hungry."

"Neither am I. But you're going to eat, so help me God. If I have to grind up that supper and spoon feed you, I will."

His eyes narrowed. "I'd like to see you try."

"Don't put it past me." She waved him toward the stairs. "Get the tray and let's go."

He stepped inside the bunkhouse and came back with the tray, which he handed to her. "Run on home, little girl, and leave me alone."

Mandy held the tray in one hand and set the other hand on her hip. "Listen, soldier boy, I hired you to do a job, one you can't very well do if you're starving yourself. Now get out here and come up to the house with me."

He arched an eyebrow. "'Soldier boy?'"

"You heard me."

"No one ever teach you to cuss?"

"I don't think bad language improves a tense

situation." She pressed her lips together.

"You're wrong there, honey. Nothing expresses rage like a string of foul words."

"Rage?" She looked at him. "Or fear?

"Or that." He shoved his hands into his front pockets. She took his wrist and began leading him toward the main house.

He took one step, watching his arm where her hand touched his skin. Two steps. He didn't want her to see the blood and flesh stuck to him. The grisly debris would appear. It always did when someone touched him. She would see it. It would take her over, too. And once it did, she would never be free of it.

Three steps. He couldn't breathe.

He dug his feet in and stopped, pulling her around to face him. She had to get one thing real damn clear right now. "It ain't a good idea to touch me," he growled between clenched teeth. He bent over her, close enough to feel her breath on his face. Hot and sweet.

She was startled at the abrupt change in direction and almost dropped the tray.

"Why?" she whispered.

Why? He was warning her, and she wanted a discussion about it? "Because it's a trigger. I thought Kit explained things to you." She shook her head, her eyes huge. "I don't like being touched." He pulled free from her hold.

"You're sick, Rocco. You're not well."

"Now there's a newsflash."

She resumed her march toward the main house. "Maybe you should talk to a counselor?"

He followed her. A muscle worked at the corner of his jaw. Clearly, he couldn't pass for normal yet. He decided to lay the truth on the line. "I had three fucking months in the psych ward at Walter Reed. They determined I couldn't be rehabilitated and shoved me out the door with lifetime prescriptions of mind-bending meds." He looked at her. "I'm goddamned done with shrinks."

"You didn't have the right doctors, then. They should never have given up on you."

A slow breath hissed from his mouth. "I came back to Wyoming, looking for the pieces of my life that were here before the war. But they're gone. Just gone. There's nothing fucking left."

They had reached the house. Mandy walked up the porch to a side entrance that led to the eat-in kitchen area. Inside, she set the tray down on the counter and stared blankly at it a long moment, contemplating her next step. She looked at Rocco, considering him. He needed food—something, anything that would tempt him to eat. How long had he been starving himself?

She grabbed a block of chocolate ice cream, a carton of milk, a bottle of Hersey's syrup, and a banana, then filled a blender with the ingredients and ground it to a smooth, thick liquid. Pouring the milkshake into two glasses, she gave him most of the mixture.

He made a face, tension filling the lines of his face.

"What's in it?"

"You saw me make it. Ice cream, milk, chocolate syrup, and a banana. Nothing gross. Drink it." She sipped hers, watching him. He took a tentative sip. He held the cold liquid in his mouth as he stared at the glass. It was a decision point. She could see the battle in his face. The determination. He swallowed. He took another sip. He leaned against his side of the counter in the narrow galley kitchen and looked at her. She kept her face blank as she sipped at her glass, but she felt victorious.

"So what exactly is a therapeutic riding center?" he asked.

"It's a place of healing. We'll use interactions with the horses as a means of helping children and adults in lots of different ways. Some have disabilities from injuries or diseases. They need physical therapy to strengthen their core muscles to improve their balance and mobility. We'll work with children who have attention problems and adolescents who have anger problems. And it's not only our patients whose lives improve through their sessions here. The volunteers in this program from other centers report a significant improvement in the quality of their lives, too."

He studied her. "You're a regular Mother Theresa."

She gritted her teeth. "It's important work. And I'm proud to be doing it."

Rocco gave a harsh laugh. "I guess there's cosmic justice in that. I've spent a lifetime tearing the world apart. You'll spend a lifetime putting it back together."

Mandy watched Rocco, assessing him. Having a conversation with him was like licking a cactus. No matter what she said, she got a mouthful of thorns in return. She refused to sink to his level of fury.

Her gaze shifted to the floor, but his long legs filled her vision. His thighs were nicely formed. She dragged her eyes off his legs and absently wondered if Kit would come back as broken as Rocco. She tried not to think about Ty Bladen, the third member of their unholy trio. He'd always scared her. If he came home any angrier than he was when he left, he'd probably have to be locked up.

"How's your milkshake?" she asked Rocco, forcing her mind to different thoughts.

He looked at his nearly empty glass. "Cold." He swallowed the last of the thick drink and set it on the counter, then straightened. "Thank you."

"Sure. Listen, Rocco, I need you to take your meals with me from now on."

"That a condition of employment?" he asked, arching a dark brow at her.

"It is."

"I don't eat breakfast. And likely it won't be convenient for me to stop work when you've got lunch ready."

Mandy drew herself to her full height, which less than strategic given that he had more than six inches on her. And even though he was lean, he was all muscle. "What part of a condition of employment didn't you understand?"

"I don't need a goddamned mother. I can feed myself."

"And yet you don't." They stood almost chest-to-chest. This was so not good. She liked the way he smelled. Dark stubble shadowed his chin and jaw. His black eyes were utterly devoid of warmth. If he didn't yield, there was only one way she could force his compliance. "Don't make me call Kit."

His brows lowered. "That's a dirty trick."

She smiled. "But useful. We'll settle on suppers. Do you have any food allergies?"

"No."

"Any dishes you've been craving? Any requests you'd like to put in?"

His gaze moved over her face, lingering on her lips. It took him the length of a breath to answer. "No."

And of course, lacking any sense of self-preservation, Mandy asked one last question. "Are you a vegetarian?"

His lips parted on an inhaled hiss. He leaned close, bracing his hands on either side of the counter behind her, so close that she had to arch her neck.

"I. Eat. Meat."

Mandy closed her eyes, feeling the rumble of his voice as it left his body and entered hers. Oh. God. And then the air cooled around her. When she opened her eyes, the kitchen door was closing behind him. She stared at it, wishing she didn't feel what she felt.

Rocco was not the type of guy a rational woman would start mooning over. It was his eyes. They were so intense, so eloquent, that she couldn't help but imagine how he would look at her if they were ever to be intimate. It would be as if she were the only woman in the world, the only woman for him.

She crossed her arms, yanking herself from such foolish thoughts. Rocco was a long way from being ready for a relationship. He couldn't even touch anyone—how could the two of them be intimate? No, they weren't meant to be. But that didn't mean she couldn't be here for him. She owed it to her brother.

Chapter 6

Mandy forced herself to rise with the sun the next morning. She'd barely slept the night before; her dreams were so filled with a certain granite face and dark eyes. What would Rocco be like to kiss? Gentle and tender? Rough and edgy? Hurried and self-focused? Just thinking of him made her feel warm inside. She was definitely crushing on him. Not a good thing—she would never have carnal knowledge of him. Best accept that and move on.

She showered, then hurried to get breakfast prepared. He'd said he didn't eat in the morning, but she hoped that if she simply presented him with food, he'd take some of it. Besides, it gave her an excuse to run into him this morning.

Mandy loaded a tray with the morning meal, then started down toward the bunkhouse. Hearing someone inside the toolshed, she detoured that way. The big overhead door was open. Rocco was inside, loading up Kitano's feed and water buckets. He wore his running gear—loose pants and a T-shirt. She let her gaze roam over the muscles in his back as he filled the water bucket and carried it to the hand wagon.

As soon as he turned to her, she forced herself to look at his face. "Morning!" she greeted him cheerily.

He looked from her to the tray, then back again. He nodded at her. "What's that?"

"Breakfast. I didn't want to eat alone. I thought I'd catch you before you started on the fence." She set the tray on the counter where her gutted weed whacker had been. It now hung on one of the walls, next to several other farm tools.

He didn't come any closer. "We agreed on suppers."

Mandy shrugged. "There's more than I can eat here. Just have a bite. I have coffee for you," she offered, hoping to tempt him.

He frowned at her, clearly not pleased. He washed his hands at the utility sink, then walked toward her. Prowled toward her, actually. "Anyone ever tell you you're persistent as hell?"

Mandy handed him a cup of coffee. "Why would I back down when winning is important?"

"If I eat, what do you win?"

"Not what I win, it's what you win. You get your health back."

"What makes you think I'm not healthy?"

"Besides the day terrors? You're not sleeping. You're not eating. You work twenty hours a day."

He sipped his coffee, watching her over the rim. "If I eat, I'll be doing what you want. What will you do for me in exchange?" As he asked, his gaze lowered from her eyes to her mouth.

Mandy had to wait until her heartbeat slowed down before answering. "What do you want in exchange?"

"A secret. I want you to tell me something about yourself that Kit doesn't know, that no one else knows."

"I don't have secrets."

"Everyone has secrets. You broke a law. You cheated. You smoked pot."

"Can I lie?" she hedged.

"Hell, no."

"Fine." She filled a plate for him, loading it up with scrambled eggs, hash browns, and fruit. "Eat your breakfast. All of it. When you're finished, I'll tell you my secret."

He took the plate and glared at the food. "If you renege, you'll regret it."

Mandy bit her bottom lip. What the heck was she supposed to tell him? She really didn't have any dark secrets. She hadn't broken the law. And she didn't smoke pot. She'd never stolen anything. And she never, ever, cheated.

They ate in silence. She knew he watched her. Her face was flushed—she was uncomfortably warm beneath his silent perusal. Too soon, he set his empty plate back on the work counter.

He quirked an eyebrow. "Time to pay the piper."

Mandy had barely touched her meal. And now her stomach knotted. She looked up at Rocco. He crossed his arms, waiting for her answer.

"When I was a very young girl," she sighed, wishing she didn't have to tell him this, "I had a crush on Ty Bladen."

Rocco's brows lifted in shock at her confession. He barked with laughter. "Blade? You were hot for Blade?"

"I was a kid. I wasn't *hot* for him—he was much older than I was. But yes, I thought he was handsome."

He looked at her, studying her in a way that made her blush deepen. "All right, then." He didn't even try not to grin. "Thanks for breakfast. I'll see you at dinner."

* * *

Mandy was still stewing about their encounter when she walked into Ivy's Diner in town later that morning. Her discussion with Rocco had left her too disconcerted to make a normal start in her day. She needed to get some groceries, which was as good an excuse as any to stop in and have a cup of coffee with her friend.

Ivy was two years older than Mandy, but they'd been close friends ever since she'd started taking riding lessons from Mandy's grandfather while they were in grade school. She left town with her family after her sophomore year in high school—right after the scandal with Kit. They'd reconnected online a few years back. Mandy had been thrilled when Ivy decided to come back to Wolf Creek Bend and reopen the diner.

At ten in the morning, the diner had few customers. She'd caught them between the morning and lunch rushes. Celia was running the counter when Mandy sat down. She flipped the thick china mug over and filled it with coffee.

"What else can I get for you, sweetie?" she asked.

"Just the coffee. Is Ivy in?"

"She's in the office. I'll go get her."

Mandy looked around the cheery dining room. Booths with teal vinyl seats lined the walls. The tables and counter were edged in chrome. The look was definitely retro. Ivy had said she had an investor who'd funded the diner and its renovations. Having had to scrounge up funding for her own construction project, Mandy was happy Ivy had found the means to make her dream happen. It had been a big hit in town ever since she'd opened it almost a year ago.

"Mandy! I don't often get to see you during the day!" Ivy took one look at her and knew something was up. Mandy guessed her problems were written all over her face. She gave Ivy a poor attempt at a smile. "You know, I've got a ton of paperwork to do in the back. Why don't you join me? We can talk while I work." She picked up Mandy's coffee and headed to the back, clearly not taking "No" for an answer.

When Mandy walked into the neat little office, Ivy shut the door behind her. "Spill. You're face is flushed and it's not even windy outside. What's going on?"

Mandy covered her face. "Ivy, I'm in trouble."

"What kind of trouble?"

"Man trouble."

"So it's true! You do have a hot boy toy stashed at your house. One smokin' hot Rocco Silas, as I understand it."

"Who told you about him?"

"Officer Jerry's friendly with a couple of the guys working on your riding center. He's been complaining about your hiring yourself a man. I think he did a background check on him—for your safety, of course—but didn't find anything."

"Ugh. He's being vindictive because I wouldn't go out with him."

Ivy sat on the edge of her desk and waggled her eyebrows at Mandy. "So? Tell me. Everything."

"He's gorgeous. Tall. Dark. Mysterious. Moody. Angry."

"Mm-mm. How is he in bed?"

"I wouldn't know. We don't—we aren't—it's not like that. He's been diagnosed with PTSD. I think he has it bad, too. He won't eat. Doesn't sleep. He looks," Mandy paused, searching for the right word, "haunted."

Ivy sighed. "I'm sorry, Em. That's tough to deal with."

"I don't know what to do to help him. Kit says to tackle one thing at a time. He wants me to get him to eat, but Rocco seems to have an aversion to food." As soon as she saw the shadow that crossed Ivy's face, she realized she shouldn't have mentioned her brother.

"Why don't you visit Dr. Crowley? For a shrink,

he's easy to talk to. I've met with him a time or two. Or talk to the sheriff. He served in the first Gulf War. He might remember some of things he faced coming back to the States."

"You went to Dr. Crowley?" Mandy asked, shocked that her friend had been to see the town psychologist.

Ivy shrugged. "It hasn't been easy moving back here. So many memories. So many shadows."

Mandy took her hand. "Do you regret coming back?"

"No. Not at all. It was the right thing for Casey. And for me as well."

Casey was Ivy's twelve-year-old daughter. Ivy's and Kit's. "I think Kit'll be back soon. He's worried about the construction problems I've been having. That's why he sent Rocco over. They served together."

Ivy folded her arms. "That's nice," she said with a smile that held no joy. "So what happened that set you off today?"

"I had to tell Rocco a secret to get him to eat."

"Did you?" Ivy grinned. "What did you tell him?"

"I told him that I once had a crush on Ty."

Ivy's jaw dropped. "Ty Bladen. You did not."

"I was twelve, Ivy. I had a crush on everyone."

Ivy held up her hands. "No. I think you have good taste. Ty's gorgeous. He serves with Kit and your Rocco, doesn't he?"

"He's not my Rocco. And he did serve with them. I think he's getting out. Rocco said he was injured."

"Badly?"

"Shot in the leg. I don't know how severe his injury is."

"Wow. That's awful. I hope, for his sake, it's not too major." Ivy handed Mandy her now-cold coffee. "But I know just what you need to do about your hired man." Mandy eyed her warily. "We're going shopping. Then Friday night, you'll bring Mr. SexOnAStick to Winchester's for some drinking and hip grinding. He'll forget all about his troubles when he sees you in the outfit I have in mind."

* * *

Rocco made the short walk from the bunkhouse to Mandy's that evening. Hot dry winds had blown across the mountain all day, burning the new spring grass and sucking all the moisture from the ground. The air sat in place now, hot and unmoving, amplifying the growing sense of dread he felt in joining Mandy for supper.

He wanted to see her. He'd thought of little else since breakfast when she divulged her darkest secret. Every time he remembered the way she'd set her chin, her eyes looking straight at his when she told him, his whole body tightened uncomfortably. He felt an unreasonable wash of jealousy as he thought of Blade and Mandy together. She said she'd been a kid at the time, but she wasn't a kid now. She and Blade would be good for each other. Their lands backed to one another. They had something of a shared history having grown up in the same small town.

So why did he want to plant a fist in his friend's face? It made no sense. It's not like Rocco would be starting something with her when he would be leaving soon. No, this was only a dinner, a condition of his employment. He'd eat and get the hell out of there.

If he bungled the whole thing, she'd go back to bringing his suppers down on a tray so that she wouldn't have to deal with him. It wouldn't be the end of the world.

He walked up the steps to Mandy's porch. Taking advantage of the warm weather, she'd set a table on her front porch for their supper. Rocco felt his stomach clench at the explosion of color spread across it. The dishes were a noisy mixture of salmon, yellow, and green ceramic. The napkins were teal cotton. The tablecloth was a bright floral. The pitcher of iced tea was yet another color of blue. The salad bowl was a peach ceramic. The oversized salad servers were orange. He felt a cold sweat break out on his skin. He couldn't do this. He would break, he knew it.

The kitchen's screen door closed as Mandy joined him on the porch. He tried to calm his breathing. Her movement through the still air brought him her scent. It was faint. And pleasant. Against the warning of his shouting nerves, he drew her fragrance into himself. Sunshine. She smelled like sunshine and fresh air and the barest hint of jasmine.

It was dinner, he reminded himself. That's all. Only dinner. Nothing was expected of him. There'd be no repercussions if his behavior wasn't exactly normal.

He could get through this.

He looked at Mandy. She seemed made of shimmering light, backlit by the setting sun as she was. Unreal. He looked beyond her, down the rolling hills to the town several miles away. Maybe he wasn't really here. Maybe this was a dream.

A rare, good dream.

He set his hat on the porch railing, sending a glance toward the pasture he'd worked earlier. If this were a dream, he should be able to conjure up his Zaviyar, running toward him on short, toddling legs, squealing with the joy of seeing his father, his arms outstretched as he reached to be picked up.

The boy was precocious as hell. By the time he was two years old, he could speak in full sentences. Rocco wondered what more he'd learned in the time they'd been apart. God, he missed him. He blinked, then saw only the bare field. The space was silent and still. And empty.

A nightmare then.

Rocco sighed as the vision of his son evaporated. This was not a dream, but what had become his life. He sat woodenly in his chair when Mandy took her seat. She was talking, but he still didn't hear her. He wouldn't meet her eyes. He couldn't handle sympathy or questions or concern or anger or any fucking thing.

He had to go back to Afghanistan. Soon. He couldn't tackle the trip in the state he was in. He focused on his plate. He had to get better, get free of the cloud infecting his mind. If he didn't, he'd get himself and Zavi killed.

"Your boy's dead, Rocco. He died in the explosion," his doctor had told him at the field hospital where they'd taken him after the hit on the cave. *"You've got to accept that. He's gone."* Rocco couldn't accept it. He still felt him.

Mandy filled his salad bowl, then served him a wedge of lasagna and offered him the breadbasket. He looked at the basket but didn't take a roll. She set one on his plate, then filled their tea glasses before serving herself similar portions. She began to eat. He thought she was still making conversation, but he didn't look at her. His skin felt uncomfortable, like he'd put it on backward. There was no place about the table that he could rest his gaze, no place that it wouldn't get tangled in the loud, crazy colors.

Silence settled about them. He wasn't certain if it was the unnatural silence that clogged his mind, or if the grasshoppers had really stopped snapping about, the birds had stopped chattering, and Mandy had stopped talking.

He looked across the table. She'd set her silverware on her plate and was simply watching her hands in her lap, her shoulders a little slumped.

He sighed. This was such a mistake. He shouldn't have let her force him into this. She'd made a feast for him, and it would all be wasted. He sat as still and silently as she did, waiting for what would come next.

"What's going on, Rocco?" she asked after a moment.

He pushed his chair back and stood up. His napkin

was in his hand. When had he put it in his lap? He didn't look at her. "I can't eat. I can't. I'm sorry."

He took a step away from the table, but she was faster as she moved to block him from the stairs. "Why, Rocco?"

"Mandy, don't do this." He did look at her then, into her fresh, emerald gaze.

"You have to eat. Not much, but something."

"I ate this morning. I ate a lot."

"That was this morning. You jogged—what, six miles? And put in a long, hard day. Now it's this evening and you need to eat again."

"I can't."

She held her ground, waiting for an explanation. "Help me to understand."

"I need my hunger."

Mandy frowned. "Why?"

Rocco looked beyond her to the wide, circular parking area. He looked at the fields to his right and the town in the far distance to his left, looked anywhere but at her and her silent demand for the truth. Shit. She was going to make him say it.

He shoved a hand through his hair and faced her. "It's the only way I know I'm not hallucinating. It's the only thing I know is real."

She blinked, obviously expecting him to say just about anything but that. "If your mind is in a place where the real is unreal and the unreal is real, can't you conjure up hunger, too? How can you trust that your hunger is real?"

"Jesus, don't start fucking with my head. It's mangled enough."

"I know." She nodded. "So let's do this differently." She studied him. "I need you to trust me."

Trust her. What did that mean? He'd seen that same look in her eyes when she worked with Kitano, always calm, steady as a rock. Relief leaked in through the cracks in his wall, soothing the ragged parts of him. He wanted to trust her, trust someone, because God knew he couldn't trust himself.

He nodded.

"Okay. Sit here on the step." She sent him a look. "Please."

He did as she requested. She went to the table and picked up his salad bowl, plate, and glass, then sat next to him on the porch.

"I'm going to feed you. I want you to take as much as you can."

Rocco lurched to his feet, powered by the anger that flashed through him. "I'm not a goddamned baby."

She looked up at him from where she sat on the weathered, whitewashed boards. "I'm well aware that you're a man." A blush crept from her chest to her neck as she spoke. He watched the color blossom across her skin, feeling a corresponding heat in his body—but moving in an opposite direction. He gazed at her, wondering how to interpret what he was seeing, what he was feeling.

Curious, he sat back down. She cut a small bite of

lasagna and fed it to him. He chewed it as he watched her. When he swallowed, she gave him another bite. She smiled at him. "Do you like it?"

He liked the way she was looking at him. "Yes."

She gave him a bite of the salad. "Does it taste okay?"

"It tastes cold."

She fed him a forkful of lasagna. "And this? How does it taste? It was my grandmother's recipe."

"Warm."

"Those are temperatures, not flavors."

"Mandy," he sighed, "food doesn't taste like anything to me right now. Just temperatures and textures."

"Oh." She looked at the plate she held. "I suppose that's part of your not having an appetite." She served him another bite.

He took the fork from her. Cutting a small bite, he fed it to her, watching as her lips closed over the tines. He slowly drew the fork from her mouth, feeling the pull of her lips against the thin strips of stainless steel. Again, the warm flush spread across her skin. He swallowed, anticipating the next bite she would feed him. He suddenly realized he'd sit here and eat the whole goddamned lasagna with her if she'd keep looking at him as she was.

Mandy took the fork back and used the side of it to cut another bite. Instead of lifting it to him, she pushed it around on the plate as if she were preoccupied with a thought. He waited, knowing she would broach the topic that was bothering her once she found the right words.

"Rocco, what did you do in the war?" she finally asked.

"I was a linguist."

She lifted the bite of lasagna to him. "What does a linguist do?"

He watched her as he chewed. How would she judge him if he were to tell her how he'd spent the last decade. Three years in training, then seven in the field? "They do different things. Translate stuff."

She paused in feeding him another bite. "You were Special Forces, like Kit, weren't you? A linguist in the Green Berets doesn't just translate, does he?"

"I wasn't in the Special Forces." Nor was Kit, but she didn't have a need to know that. He considered how to explain to her what he'd been. There wasn't even a classification for it.

"How long were you over there?"

Rocco met her look. Her questions were making him uncomfortable. "A long time."

She smiled and lowered her gaze to the lasagna as she cut another piece and fed it to him. "Is it easy for you to learn another language? What did you speak over there?"

"Pashto, Dari, Arabic, Farsi, among others."

Her eyes widened. "You can speak all of those languages?"

"Fluently. And read and write them." And know the differences in hundreds of regional variations of each. He sighed. "Kit says I'm a linguistic savant."

"You're a Rosetta Stone. Was it always like that for you?"

"I think so. There were only two languages spoken on our ranch when I was a kid—English and Spanish. I grew up bilingual. In high school, I mastered French and German as well." He looked at her. "Both in my freshman year. That's when I knew I was different."

She gasped. "How do you do that?"

He shrugged. "I don't know. I was surprised to learn that most people can't do that. Language to me is simply vocalization of emotions. We all have the same emotions, the same need to communicate. We speak because we desire something or we're sad or angry or scared. We just use different sounds."

They'd finished his lasagna by then. She gave him the last bite of salad, then retrieved her meal from the table and sat next to him again, her hip against his thigh. It seemed to him that she sat closer, which he didn't mind. He took the loaded fork from her and carried it to her mouth. She was so wrapped up in feeding him that she wasn't eating any herself.

She chewed and swallowed. He cut a piece of lasagna. He figured he could keep her questions to a minimum if he kept her mouth full. It didn't quite work as planned.

"So you're a genius."

A breeze started up, tousling her hair, pulling a wide strand of it against her cheek. What he would give to be able to brush it away, run his fingers across her skin. Instead, he could only watch as she did it.

"More like an idiot. An idiot savant." He fed her the forkful and cut another.

"But you can read and write those languages, too. That's amazing. You are a genius. I wish I could do that."

Rocco closed his eyes as he considered how to explain it to her. "I think it's just that I don't tell myself I can't." He looked at her. "When I hear a new language or a new dialect, it first registers that whoever's speaking is communicating as any of us does. I don't hear them as being different. I hear the sounds of their emotions, and then I can speak those sounds. And once I can speak a language, deciphering its symbology is simple."

"I think you're amazing." He fed her another bite. She chewed and swallowed quickly.

"Do you?" What would she think if she knew what he'd done with his God-given talent, the enemies he'd killed and camps he'd infiltrated? She might see his work in the light of how many lives he'd saved— innocent civilians spared a death in crossfire and coalition troops spared from IEDs and gun battles. Then again, to her it might be merely a count of bodies.

A few minutes later as she gave Rocco the last bight of lasagna, a big drop of sauce landed on his thigh. She jumped, spilling a bit more. Rocco laughed, unable to stop himself when he caught her bemused expression. He took the fork that was still perilously suspended above his leg and finished off the bite on it.

"Oh! Sorry!" She wiped at the first spot with her napkin. She had to draw the material of his jeans taut to get at the second one. Did she notice the growing bulge only a few inches from her hand? The more she wiped, the harder he got.

His fingers dug into the edge of the old floorboards. He couldn't believe that she was touching him—even in so innocent a way as to dab at a stain—and it wasn't triggering the usual terrible reaction. Perhaps it was because she touched him through fabric.

And then, it wasn't just the stain she was touching.

She spread her fingers open on this thigh, looked at her hand on his leg, then slowly dragged her fingers down to his knee. Blood raced to his groin. God, he'd not had a reaction to a woman like this in years.

She rubbed her palm over his big knee, then stroked upward again, over the stain, to the top of his thigh. She moved to kneel next to him without lifting her hand from his body. He remembered seeing her touch Kitano, her hands slowly stroking over him like this. He closed his eyes, feeling like an idiot for thinking there was anything sexual in her leisurely exploration of him. When he opened them again, she was looking at him, waiting. The pink flush had returned to her skin, painting her cheeks.

Jesus. If merely touching him colored her skin, what would she look like when he was in her, thrusting, bringing her to a climax?

She ran her hand up over his hip, over his jeans pocket, to his waist. He could feel the heat of her skin through his shirt. He held her gaze now, daring her to stop, daring her to continue.

She edged closer to him as she ran her hand up his ribs, over his pec, to his collarbone. Her hand moved from his open collar to his neck, now skin to skin. He sucked in a breath, waiting for the smell of the ghost flesh, waiting to feel it sticking to him, drying, moving to her.

But it never happened.

He felt only the soft tips of her fingers on his throat, felt them stop at his jaw. She watched the path her fingers made along his jaw line before pushing them upward, over his chin, to his lips. She flattened three of her fingers and stroked from one side of his mouth to the other.

She was so close to him that he could feel the soft puffs of her breath on his neck. All too soon, far sooner than he wished, she drew her fingers across his cheek, down his neck, across his shoulder, and down his arm. When her hand cleared the cuff of his sleeve and touched his hand, he hesitated only a moment before pulling away.

"Don't."

"Why?" she asked.

"I don't like being touched."

"Liar."

He stood up, severing their contact, ending the moment. He'd been wrong. She never touched Kitano the way she touched him.

She came to her feet and met his look, but he was

spared further torture by the sound of a car pulling into the driveway far below. A sheriff's cruiser. It stopped in front of the house, not far from the steps. The deputy got out of his car but did not approach the porch. He looked at Rocco, then the flowered tablecloth, then Mandy.

"Mandy," he tipped his hat to her.

Rocco disliked him instantly. He felt his head clear in a flash as he became aware of the same animosity rolling off the deputy. He wanted to tell Mandy to go in the house while he dealt with the man, but that was totally whacked. He had no authority—he was only a visitor here. He crossed his arms and glared at the deputy.

"Jerry," Mandy greeted him from the top step.

"Heard you hired yourself a new . . . ranch hand."

"Yep. This is Rocco Silas. He served with Ty and Kit. Rocco, this is Deputy Sheriff Jerry Whitcomb."

Rocco gave a quick nod to the man. He hadn't missed the look that flashed through his eyes as Mandy mentioned Kit's name. What had that been about?

"Bobby know?"

"Does he know what, Jerry?"

The deputy looked at Rocco. "You hired yourself a man."

Rocco uncoiled his arms and took a step forward. Mandy stepped in front him, blocking him. "Are you up here on police business, Jerry?" she asked, ignoring his question.

The deputy made a face. "Curious about how

things were going with the construction, if you'd had anymore problems."

"No. Thank heavens. Things have been quiet."

Jerry nodded. "That's good." He puckered a corner of his mouth as he looked around the place. "That's real good. It was beginning to look like someone had a grudge against you, but I couldn't understand why. You never were a troublemaker like your brother."

He glanced at her and lifted his hat. "Well, you let us know if anything else happens." He looked at Rocco, a clear warning in his eyes, then got back into his car. Through the lowered window, he pinned Mandy with a look. "Good night to you, now."

Neither Rocco nor Mandy moved as they watched the cruiser move down her driveway and turn back onto the road. Rocco caught the shiver that passed through Mandy. He wished he could touch her, wrap an arm around her, pull her against his body. Instead, he offered the only comfort he could.

"I can kill him for you."

Mandy slowly turned to him. There was no humor in her face. "Rocco Silas! That is not acceptable behavior."

"It's what I do." He shrugged. "Don't worry, it won't look like murder."

"It's what you did." Well, heck. Where did that come from? she wondered, embarrassed to have implied she thought he was a murderer. "It's not what you did. I don't know what you did." God, she was rambling. "Jerry Whitcomb is not an enemy."

Rocco did not try to soften the threatening look he gave her. "Who's Bobby?"

Mandy crossed her arms. "A friend of Jerry's. We had an on-again off-again thing. We're off-again at the moment."

Rocco nodded. "Keep it that way."

"Bobby's nothing like Jerry. And I don't need you to tell me how to manage my personal life."

"I'll call Kit," he warned.

"That's not fair."

Rocco grinned. It was not a nice expression. "We're even then." He looked at the table. "Want some help with the dishes?"

"No. Thank you."

He set his hat on his head and jogged down the steps. Once in the drive, he turned around and walked backward, watching as she collected dishes. He felt strangely reluctant to move away from her.

"Em?" he called. She glanced over at him.

He stopped moving and hooked his thumbs in his front pockets. She walked to the edge of the porch, looking sweet and feminine as she leaned against the support beam.

"Thank you." He told himself not to notice the way the light hit her hair. "For feeding me." For the sunshine. The work. The place to be. Her eyes met his. "You sure I can't kill him?" He grinned at her.

Her eyes widened. "I mean it, Rocco! That's not funny."

Chapter 7

Rocco stood in the narrow shower stall two days later. Hot water sluiced down his back. It did little to ease the tension gripping his neck and shoulders thanks to the night's virulent dreams. He lifted his face into the sheeting streams of water.

Despite the sun and the work, the meals with Mandy, he lost a little more of himself every day. What pieces remained of his soul jangled against each other like the unglued shards of a broken pot, more apart than together.

A vision of wispy, gold-red hair sifted through his mind. Big, green eyes. Mandy. He couldn't see her or think of her without heat slashing through his body. The meals they shared in the evenings were a blessing and a curse. He ate because she would sit with him, chatting about lots of things. Nothing. The wind. Kitano. The progress of the construction. It didn't matter. Her voice flowed through him like a river. His source.

Thank God she wasn't a mind reader. His thoughts about her were never pure. He listened to her, watched her, all the while wondering what her voice would sound like as she straddled him. He would feel her laughter, her breathing. Her life would be a jumper cable to his, feeding it energy, strength. Life.

He ached to hold her, to draw her into himself. To pretend for a short while that he was whole. That he could feel something. Anything.

He opened his eyes through the streaming water. His dick stood at a right angle to his body, wide and thick, pointing straight toward the wall. He touched himself, felt his balls tighten even more. He slipped his fist over his rigid cock, slowly, imagining her mouth moving over him, those soft, pink lips parting, taking him deeper, deeper into her throat. He hadn't been blown in almost a decade. He'd lived the chaste existence of an unmarried Muslim while undercover. And once he was married, oral sex wasn't an acceptable practice.

Ah, God, Mandy. She would look up at him with those enormous green eyes, her mouth full of his cock. Rocco's nostrils flared. He shut his eyes, seeing her kneel before him. He pumped into his fist. In his mind's eye, he was easing deeper into her. Pulling back. He soaped his hand, making his grip slicker, moving faster. Harder.

He'd make her go to all fours, lifting her sweet entrance up toward him. He'd slip into her, easing in deep, feeling her sheath grab him. Then he'd take hold of her hips and slam into her, pumping, pumping until he felt her small muscles grab him, milk him, force him to release.

As he thought it, his semen shot out, sluicing in hot jets into the water that now ran cold. He leaned his head against the wall of the shower, feeling a long, long way from sated.

Nothing about him was right.

Wasn't that what had given him away? He'd been married for four years to the daughter of a powerful Afghan warlord tightly aligned with the Taliban. It had taken three years to infiltrate her people, but once there, it had been so easy to catch her eye, to find himself in her circle, to be accepted by her father. He'd paid the bride price of forty goats, ten cows, and five RPGs. They'd married in a long ceremony. He'd thrown himself into the act, giving her amorous looks and secret smiles. People saw what they wanted to see. He wanted them to see two people in love, a rare enough situation in a country so ravaged by war.

Kadisha had been promised to another before him. Ehsan Asir. Asir was a power-hungry zealot who'd worked hard to earn a spot on the Taliban's top leadership council, beneath Ghalib Halim. Asir was furious when Halim broke his betrothal to Kadisha in favor of Rocco. Had she shared Asir's feelings, Rocco would have found a different way to stay close to Halim. She hadn't though. She was over the moon to be the one to marry Rocco.

On their wedding night, he had been attacked by remorse. He knew he was stealing from Kadisha something he had no right to take—her innocence.

He'd taken his time seducing her, hoping to give her a memory to cling to when he was gone. He'd become a whore for God and country, all to slip into the sacred enclave her father inhabited, to join his inner circle and spy on him—and, when ordered, kill him.

His son was conceived on his wedding night. When Kadisha told him a few months later that she was pregnant, he'd been relieved. It meant he didn't have to bed her so much anymore—and that he could focus on the mission. After Zaviyar was born, Rocco knew his façade had begun slipping. He wasn't the happy groom, had never been the man he'd pretended to be. Kadisha, ever watchful, caught on. When Zavi was three, she told him she was pregnant again. And in the next breath, she said, "You did this. You killed us."

Rocco's fingers dug into the cold, wet tile, finding no purchase. *You did this*. He couldn't remember. His mind was a blank.

You killed us.

Perhaps he had killed them.

* * *

Mandy felt the first inklings of worry around 11:00 a.m. Rocco was gone. His truck was still parked next to the garage. His bed was made. His toiletries were still in the bathroom of the bunkhouse. She'd been tied up meeting with George down at the construction site for a while during the morning. She'd expected to find Rocco in the fields, as was his usual routine, but he'd done no new work on the fence line.

Had he gotten hurt during his run that morning? Would anyone have known to call her? She tried his cell phone again. No answer. She'd just retrieved her purse and keys when a sheriff's patrol car pulled onto the dirt road below. She watched it make the long drive up the hill, her stomach beginning to knot up.

Sheriff Tate put the car in park and rolled down the window. "Sheriff," she greeted him tensely.

"Mandy." He nodded at her. "You looking for your hired hand by any chance?"

"You found Rocco? Is he okay?" Why had the sheriff come out to tell her about him? Visions of Rocco having one of his fits in front of the whole town blasted into her mind.

"Hard to know. He's on First Street in some kind of a daze. He's just standin' there. Fred, at the general store, said he's been there since dawn."

Mandy gasped. "Is he hurt?"

"Nope. But he won't talk to anyone and he won't move along. He's scaring the natives. Can you get down there and see what you can do before Jerry Tasers him?"

Mandy shut her eyes. How had he gotten to town? Had he run the ten miles? "I'm on my way." She hurried to her SUV and followed the sheriff to town. Rocco stood on the corner of First Street and Elm, staring east down the two short blocks of Wolf Creek Bend's main corridor. Intersecting his line of sight was a state highway, railroad tracks, and then an abandoned grain elevator.

There was absolutely nothing of interest to look at, but he watched the far distance with an intense and unblinking stare. Mandy parked, then got out and stood beside her SUV, wondering what was going on with him, what he was thinking. Twice she looked where he watched, but could not see what held his attention.

A couple of pedestrians stopped to talk to him. News had gotten around town that a war hero had come back from Afghanistan and was working at her ranch. As Mandy watched, Rocco ignored the people, one of whom held out a hand as if to shake hands with him. He acted as if he didn't see them, didn't hear them. They frowned and walked away. Several people had gathered a little ways down the street and were standing about in small groups, surreptitiously watching him.

Sheriff Tate parked on Elm Street. He, too, got out and leaned against his car, his arms folded. The look he gave her made it clear that if she didn't resolve the situation in short order, he would.

"Hey, Rocco," she said in as calm a voice as she could muster when she came even with him. "What are you doing?" He didn't respond. She looked him over, checking to see if he'd hurt himself. Maybe he'd fallen on his run, hit his head.

"Are you okay?" she asked, touching his arm gently. No response.

She stood in front of him. He was taller than she was, so her position did not break his line of vision. He just kept staring out over her head. "Rocco, you can't do this." The sides of his jaw tensed, the only sign he was aware of her presence. "Please. You're scaring people. You're scaring me." His gaze dropped from the distant granary to her eyes.

Mandy couldn't stop a sigh of relief at the break in his concentration. "Hi." She smiled at him, uncertain how much of what she'd said he'd heard. "What are you doing?"

"I'm standing here."

"I see that. But you can't. You can't do this."

"Why the hell not?"

"You've been here for hours."

"So?"

"There are laws about loitering. How did you get to town?"

"Ran."

"You ran ten miles? While it was still dark?" she asked.

"I had to get here before dawn."

"Rocco," she sighed, "we have to go. We can't stay here."

"You go. I'm staying."

Before she could ask him why, another man walked up to them. He clapped Rocco on the back, then offered his hand and a friendly, "Welcome home. Thank you for your service."

Rocco turned and looked at the man with such animosity that the man dropped his hand and backed a step away before quickly moving along. Mandy sent him an apologetic look, but he never saw it. "You can't make trouble like this."

"Like what? I'm minding my own business. They should do the same."

She could see he was getting irritated, but he was watching her more and the granary less. "You ran down here in the middle of the night. You've stood here all morning. What you're doing makes no sense. You have to be hot and tired and hungry—"

His frown made furrows between his brows. The hard planes of his face became rigid. Something flashed in the back of his dark eyes. Pain. Memories she would never know, could never understand. "You don't know a goddamned thing about me."

"Hey, now. There's no call to talk to a lady like that," another good Samaritan said as he paused next to them.

Rocco flashed an angry look at him and snapped, "Fuck off."

Mandy sent the man a look and gave him a slight nod. He moved away to stand with Officer Jerry. "I don't understand why you're here like this," she replied to Rocco.

He spun her around, gripping her with an arm across her body, using his other hand to hold her jaw and point her face toward the old steel walls of the grain silo. Out of the corner of her eye, she saw Officer Jerry straighten and Sheriff Tate wave him back.

"What do you see?" Rocco asked her.

Mandy tried to draw a breath, but his grip was too tight to allow much air. She could feel the tension in his body. "I see buildings. People. A road. A highway. A railroad. The old elevator."

As close as he was holding her, she felt the long draw of air he pulled into his lungs, felt him press his face to the crown of her head. She wondered if he was aware that he was touching her. Maybe he only had issues when someone else was doing the touching.

"What are those things?" he asked.

"What things?"

"What you see. The buildings. The road. The people? What do they make?"

Mandy felt close to tears. In some elemental way, she knew her answer was pivotal, but she didn't know what the right answer was. "I don't know, Rocco."

"What do they make?" He shook her. "Look, Mandy. What are they?"

"It is my town."

"Yes. Yes, it is."

A small sob broke from her. He was more lost than she ever knew. "What is it that you see?" she asked, her voice barely a whisper.

"I'm not looking at the things."

She shut her eyes, praying for strength. Did he even know he was standing here with her, on the corner, in the heat of the midday sun? "Then what are you looking at?"

"The light."

The light? The sun was nearly directly overhead. The sky was a brilliant blue. Cloudless. The air was clear, no haze marred the view. "Why the light, Rocco?"

He let her go. For a minute, he said nothing as he stood silent and still, seeing something she couldn't. "There was an explosion in the village where I was working undercover. Taliban fighters captured me. They put me in a pit with wooden planks overhead. I had blood on me, debris from the explosion, all kinds of grisly shit. They didn't let me clean up. They didn't feed me. I got a cup of water a day. Five days I was in that hellhole.

"The last day, I stood as tall as possible. I was dying. I knew it. Facing east, I watched the light move over what was left of the village. I told myself I wasn't in that pit, hidden from anyone who might be looking for me, starving to death. I imagined being home, standing on Main Street in my town." He stopped speaking for a moment, his jaw pressed tightly shut as emotion threatened to overwhelm him.

"I promised myself that I would do this very thing. I would stand one entire day and watch the light move over my hometown, which looks so very much like this one."

Mandy dashed tears from her face. She straightened her shoulders and faced east as he did. "Then we will stand here, Rocco. You will watch the light, and I will keep people from bothering you." She said nothing else and looked neither to the right nor to the left.

A minute passed. Another. The silence thickened about them like foggy air. "Am I losing my mind, Em?" Rocco rasped.

She looked at him. Tears fell from her cheeks, but

she ignored them. "No. You are keeping a promise you made to yourself. You've earned the right to stand on this corner as long as you wish. And if I have to fight off every citizen of Wolf Creek Bend so that you can be here like this, then so be it."

A ghost of a grin tilted a corner of his mouth as he looked at her. "You should have been in Afghanistan. You would have been beautifully effective there, straightening up the bullshit nonsense from the elders in every village our guys cleared." He stared down toward the end of street. A minute passed. Another minute.

He sighed, still facing forward. "This isn't what normal people do, is it?"

"Normal is overrated." Mandy shrugged.

He bowed his head, rubbing his hands over his eyes. "I have to get back to normal."

"Why?" she asked, venturing a look at him.

He didn't answer her. "I've seen enough. I'm ready to go." He shoved his hands through his hair, then held his head. "Sorry—about this. About everything. You don't need a fucking headcase for a hired hand. What the hell was Kit thinking sending me to your ranch?"

"Forget it." Mandy smiled up at him. "How about lunch? My friend runs the diner in town."

He looked down at his T-shirt and running pants. "I'm not dressed for lunch."

She shrugged. "This is Wolf Creek Bend. No one dresses for lunch. Come on. They have the best milkshakes ever there."

He looked at her for a long minute. "I'm not sure that's a good idea."

"How badly do you want to be normal again? It would be a step in that direction."

He frowned down at her. "Fine. Let's go." They crossed the street. Rocco opened the door, sending a look around the street as she walked through it. What he was looking for, he didn't know. Habit, he guessed. Seeing who might be watching them, what the lay of the land was before he went inside so he'd have something to compare it to when he came out. It was an average day in a little American town. Nothing to worry about. He followed Mandy into the diner and immediately came to a stop.

The room was a riot of color—yellow and teal Formica, black-and-white tiling, chrome-edged fixtures, pop-culture memorabilia from the middle of the last century cluttering the walls. An ancient woodstove jutted into the room from one of the walls, home to a couple of potted ferns. A counter ran the length of one wall complete with metal stools covered in red padded vinyl. Glass stands of cakes and other treats stood at various intervals on the counter. The room smelled overwhelmingly of coffee and meatloaf and fresh bread, heavy and cloying.

The hairs lifted on Rocco's neck. Fuck average— something wasn't right, something that had nothing to do with the kaleidoscope of color used in the diner's décor. His instinct had never failed him in all his years in Afghanistan, not when it hit like this.

He grabbed Mandy, pulling her behind him as he glanced around the room. Someone had triggered his internal warning system. There was an enemy here. Someone who wanted him dead. He looked at every face of every man, seeing only ranchers, laborers, tradesmen, truckers. Good salt-of-the-earth types. The cops who'd been watching him outside were now seated at a table against the far wall.

"Rocco, what is it?" Mandy asked in a whisper at his side.

He took a step back, moving her with him. "There is an enemy here." He heard her loud sigh, but he didn't care. He wasn't wrong.

"There are no enemies here. These are just regular people."

"There is. I'm never wrong about this feeling, Em. Never."

Mandy moved in front of him, shielding him from the curious glances coming their way. "I know these people. They're friendly."

"One of them is not a friendly. We need to leave."

"No. We're staying. We're going to sit down and have a nice lunch like normal people."

"It is too dangerous. I don't know which one it is."

"It is none of them. I know them."

He looked at her, watching her expression. "You know all of them?"

She looked at the people seated at tables and booths. There was Sheriff Tate with Deputy Jerry, a couple of tables of farmers and ranchers, several local businessmen, two families she didn't know. The plumber and the family physician sat on stools up at the counter. Jerry and the sheriff, as well as a few others, were watching the small drama unfolding by the diner's entrance.

"I know most of them. The others I've seen around town. We're plenty safe. You're probably picking up on the vibe from the sheriff, who's about to head over this way. Just stop. Trust me. Please."

Rocco's heart was beating rapidly. He could feel a cold sweat break out over his body. He wasn't safe. He had no weapons with him, and his psych eval from Walter Reed had made it impossible for him to buy new. No matter. He could kill with his bare hands as easily. He would keep Mandy safe.

"We need to leave. We are surrounded," he told her. The smoke from the griddle took on a metallic scent. Blood.

The room shifted, flickered, became a courtyard filled with men in *shalwar kameez* wearing turbans and *khapol* caps, sitting about in small clusters, smoking, laughing, drinking tea. Hiding semiautomatics. A fucking viper pit filled with Afghan and Pakistani insurgents and village men who would as soon shoot an American as help one. And he stood among them in fatigues. Unarmed. It was his nightmare come true.

Ah, Jesus Christ. He was dead. Dead.

"Rocco, look at me. Look at me now." The voice of an angel whispered to him urgently. She touched cool fingers to his cheeks, cupping his face. His gaze shot to his arm. The blackened flesh was there, shrinking, drying. He tried to breathe. He wanted to vomit.

"There are no enemies here. You are safe. I am safe," the angel spoke, her voice so like Mandy's. Hot tears tracked down the clammy skin of his face. "Rocco, do you hear me?"

Please, God, kill me. Kill me, if you must, but don't touch the angel.

Mandy watched the sanity leach from Rocco's eyes as his body became rigid. She turned him and dragged him by his sleeve through the door, outside into the fresh air and sunshine, making a beeline for her SUV. She had no idea what just happened, but it was clear that Rocco was in over his head. She shouldn't have forced the diner on him. What had she been thinking?

He didn't resist as she settled him in her SUV. He said nothing as she reached across him and fastened the seat belt. She worried he might try to get out while she drove if he weren't buckled, or that the warning beep from the unfastened seat belt sensor would deepen his anxiety attack. She put the air-conditioning on full blast and rolled all the windows down, letting the movement of the air calm him as she drove back to the ranch. Halfway home, she heard him sigh as he leaned his head back against the headrest, finally coming back to himself.

At the house, Rocco jumped out of the car almost before she had fully stopped the SUV. He marched to the bunkhouse. She called to him, but he ignored her. He went directly to his bedroom and pulled his duffel out from under his bed. Jerking open the top dresser drawer, he pulled out his things and started shoving them into his duffel.

"What are you doing?" Mandy asked from the doorway. He should have known she'd follow him. He didn't waste a look on her. He had to leave. Had to run like hell.

"What does it look like?" he snapped.

"Stop this, Rocco." She took a handful of his clothes and brought them back to the drawer.

He glared at her hands on his clothes. "Why can't you leave me the hell alone? I'm not fit to be around people," he growled a warning as he grabbed his clothes and tossed them back into the duffel, most of them missing the yawning opening. "I'm dangerous, Mandy. I could hurt someone and not know it until afterward. I could hurt you."

His chest rose and fell, rage visibly building inside him. His face hardened. His nostrils flared. His lips pulled back from his teeth as a roar broke from him, shaking the walls of the little room. He backhanded the lamp from the dresser, swiping it against the far wall. The shattering sound fell short of the satisfaction he was looking for—it was far too little noise and destruction. He looked around the room for something else to destroy. Mandy had no doubt the dresser would have followed the lamp, along with several other pieces of furniture, had she not been standing in the room.

She didn't back away, didn't fold her arms. She held herself as absolutely still as possible. "You can't run from yourself," she said quietly, not as an indictment but as a simple statement of truth. "Where ever you go, you'll just end up there with yourself. You've got to stand and fight somewhere. Do it here."

He shook his head, glaring at the dresser. "What the hell was Kit thinking sending me here, a wolf into a lamb's home?"

"I'm not afraid of you."

His head lifted, his hard gaze leveling her. "You should be. I'm afraid of me."

"What is it that you fear?"

"Stay the hell out of my head, sweetheart. The shadows there have teeth. They will shred you as they have me."

She wasn't backing down. "Where did you go today, at the diner? In your mind, you saw something."

A muscle worked in corners of his jaw. "I don't know."

"Yes, you do."

"Leave it, Em."

"No."

Rocco sighed, his shoulders slumping. He looked at the wall in front of him. Tears pooled in his eyes, spilled down his rigid face. He thought, with some relief, of his shotgun and the cold metal of its barrel. He could put a shell in the chamber, put the muzzle against the roof of his mouth, and end the fucking hell festering in his head.

"Where did you go at the diner, Rocco?" Mandy asked again.

He shut his eyes. "There was a courtyard full of insurgents, resting from the midday heat. I saw them. They saw me. An angel was there. With your voice. I knew I was dead, knew there was no way I'd get out of there alive, but I begged God to spare the Angel."

He realized, in that moment, if he killed himself here, God would not spare her.

Mandy pulled a ragged breath. She forced her eyes away from Rocco, offering him the only kindness she could. Privacy.

"Put your things away. I'll go make you a sandwich, then you can get back to the work waiting for you in the pastures."

"I don't need a fu—"

"I know *you* don't, but *I* need to do this," she interrupted him.

He looked at her. "Why?"

"Because helping you is the only thing my brother ever asked of me. Ever," she answered, with more vehemence than she wished. The last thing Rocco needed now was more emotion. "Everyone here failed him," she said in a calmer voice. "I did. My grandparents did. His mother did. My parents did. His girlfriend did. The whole town turned its back on him when he needed them. This is the only thing I have ever been able to do for him. And I won't let you take it from me. You are important to him, and that makes you important to me."

She headed for the door but stopped at the threshold and glanced back at him. "Look, Rocco. Not all wounds are physical, but they all take time to heal. Cut yourself some slack. You had a setback today. Big deal." She shrugged. "It's not your first and it won't be your last. I don't care what the town thinks of you or us or me. I never have. So don't start arguing that you should leave." He said nothing, which seemed the best of all mercies.

She'd taken two steps before he stopped her. "Em?" His face was pale. Lines of fatigue showed around his eyes, his mouth. "Make it two sandwiches. And a milkshake?"

She smiled at him and nodded. "Coming up!"

Chapter 8

The next few days were blissfully uneventful for Rocco. He worked. He ate. He ran. The shadows held less and less of him. Maybe there was something to Mandy's grandfather's philosophy.

He spent his evenings sitting on his porch, tending her second-hand tack. Area residents had donated most of it, like much of the center's equipment. Some had belonged to her grandfather. All of it needed cleaning and maintenance.

He worked in phases with the leather items, cleaning, conditioning, then mending. Tonight, he was preparing to stitch a cinch buckle back on a child's Western saddle when Mandy came down the hill toward the bunkhouse. He looked her over from her feet up, letting the distance camouflage his interest. Her boots were made of soft leather that hugged her slim calves. She wore a short jean skirt that flared at her bare thighs. Her shirt was a short-sleeved, blue gingham confection scooped low at her neck with thin ribbons of elastic that made it fit tightly around her slim waist. Her hair was loose. The streams of her copper mane were topped with a straw cowboy hat.

She looked good enough to eat.

He picked up a lump of beeswax and drew it down the length of saddle thread, then turned the thread and waxed the other side. He didn't look up when she stepped onto the porch.

"Hi!" she greeted him.

"Evening."

"Rocco, you're amazing! These pieces look new! I didn't have the heart to tackle them yet." She ran a hand over the child's saddle. "We may not have to buy as much tack as I'd feared."

"Mm-hmm." He still didn't look at her, though he knew she watched him. Her voice and her scent were as seductive as the sight of her. All he could think was how useful that bare stretch of wall behind him could be. That short skirt would be no impediment—he could have her legs wrapped around his waist in seconds flat.

Did she know how close he was to breaking? What the hell was she doing out of the house dressed like that?

"Rocco—do you dance?"

He pricked his finger with the thick needle and swallowed an oath. "Not unless my life depends on it."

She leaned restlessly against one of the porch supports, her hands behind her, a knee bent as she braced a foot against the wood. "Do you think you could make an exception tonight? I thought we could go into town and meet my friend, Ivy, at Winchester's. They do line dancing there. It'll be fun."

About as much fun as standing in a field of rattlers in mating season. The thought of a crowd of people made him break out in a cold sweat. A person couldn't move through a barroom thick with people without touching some of them. What if he had one of his freak-outs in the middle of Winchester's? That would be a grand start to the work she was doing here, just top off his little performance earlier in the week. People would avoid her riding center for fear of running into him.

"That ain't my thing." He shoved the needle through the next hole, playing for time as he flicked a glance at the smooth, pale expanse of her thighs. "You goin' out dressed like that?"

"What's wrong with what I'm wearing?" Mandy asked, looking down at herself. She smoothed a hand over her denim skirt, pressing the short hem of it against her raised thigh.

He locked his eyes with hers. "Your legs are showing."

She laughed, spilling that tinkling, joyful sound across the porch. Goosebumps rose on his arms. "What century are you from?" she teased him.

He dropped his gaze to the leather strap he held. He'd been in Afghanistan too long, most of the past eight years—seven of them deep undercover. He was used to much more conservative behavior from women. He stabbed the needle between the two sides of leather he was sewing and tossed it on the table. "Then I guess I better go with you. Make sure no one mistreats you."

She grinned. "Yes, you'd better."

* * *

Rocco backed his old Ford into one of the last parking spots in the section farthest from the bar entrance. Neon signs listed their draft beers and made a wagon wheel appear to be turning. He regretted his decision to come as soon as they walked through the small crowd of people who milled around the entrance. He opened the door for Mandy even as he cast a glower over the crowd, daring any of the men to look at her.

He stared at her back as they walked through the long entranceway, focusing on her as if she were a lifeline. They passed the coat checkroom, restrooms, offices, and kitchen entrance. The place was low ceilinged, paneled in pine, lined with posters, prints and sculptures. Benches made of halved logs sat along the hallway. As the entranceway opened to the main bar area, the crowd thickened.

Mandy seemed to know where she was going. He followed her, his gaze focused ahead of them, making eye contact with the men, claiming her in an ancient way of silent communication between men, one that worked in any culture, anytime. It was brief, subtle, and harmless unless ignored—wholly effective in opening the crowd so that they could pass.

Long rows of tables bordered the dance floor. Large booths lined the walls on three sides, forming a horseshoe around the band and dance floor. Mandy drew Rocco to a corner booth with a circular seat where a woman was sitting between Officer Jerry and another man Rocco had not yet met.

Instantly, Rocco wanted to get Mandy out of there. There was only room for one of them at either end of the half-circle table—he wasn't going to be able to sit next to her. If he made an issue of it and asked them to scoot around, he'd still have to let Mandy sit next to one of the men. And if he didn't, she'd be open to approach from men outside their group.

The woman between the two men noticed the situation and quickly pushed against Jerry to get him to move down so that they could both squeeze in beside the other man. Rocco let Mandy get in first, choosing the lesser of the two evils. When they were settled, Mandy performed introductions.

"Ivy, this is Rocco Silas. Rocco, Ivy Banks." Rocco looked at the woman sitting with them. She had dark hair, black maybe, and blue eyes. She was petite in stature and very pretty. He could see why Kit had fallen for her. It felt odd sitting here with the woman who'd made his friend's life a living hell. Did Kit know she was back in town?

Rocco had to pull himself out of his thoughts as Mandy introduced him to the men. "You remember Jerry. This is Bobby Gallahan. Bobby, this is Rocco. He's a friend of Kit's."

Rocco met Bobby's friendly gaze, feeling no warmth for the bastard who had been Mandy's lover. The man leaned across her to offer a handshake. Jesus. Not that. Not here. He couldn't do it, couldn't risk what might happen. He reached for the menu that was lying in the middle of the table instead, ignoring Bobby. The silence that met his rudeness was deafening. He ignored it, too.

A waitress came by to take their order. Rocco asked for an iced tea while Mandy ordered a micro-brew from a local brewery.

"So, Rocco—Jerry says you're recently back from the war. Thank you for your service," Bobby said.

Anger flashed inside Rocco. He held still, trying to let the feeling wash through him, but all it did was sit and fester. This stranger thanked him for his service— service that cost him his wife and son and unborn child. Thanked him for becoming more Afghan than American. Thanked him for losing his mind.

He ground his teeth to keep from saying something that would upset Mandy. She must have felt his tension. She put a hand on his thigh. He forced himself to nod at the man, trying to take the comment in the spirit it was intended. He pulled a long breath to calm himself. He knew he shouldn't have come here tonight.

"Bobby turned pro on the rodeo circuit this year," Mandy said, providing Rocco a welcome distraction.

Rocco looked at Bobby. "Congrats. What's your event?"

"Steer wrestling."

"He rodeoed all through high school and college," Mandy told him. "He was always hitting up local businesses for sponsorship money before he started earning some nice prizes."

"They'd see him coming and just take out their wallets," Jerry added with a chuckle. "Then he struck gold. Found a first-class operation to sponsor him—a bank out of Jackson Hole. Bought him his pretty new rig."

"Glad to see it's worked out for you." Rocco offered, though he couldn't help but think that while this guy was wrestling steers and dreaming of the PRCA tour, Rocco was navigating the deadly Nangarhar and Kunar provinces in Afghanistan to infiltrate the Taliban's upper echelon. Christ, how the hell was he going to make a life that held any meaning for him after having spent so many years on a razor's edge?

"How's the construction progressing, Mandy?" Ivy asked, moving the subject away from Bobby.

"It's progressing, but slowly. You know the foundation had to be repoured for part of the stable. Nothing bad has happened since then. Maybe whoever was messing with us has moved on to other mischief. The pole barn is nearly finished. The fencing crews are making good progress in the lower pastures. Rocco has removed most of the barbed wire from the old pastures up by the house.

"Fingers crossed things continue smoothly now. I'm going to bring the horses over in a few weeks, once the upper corrals are finished. After I've worked with them a bit, maybe Casey could come over and help me put the horses through their paces. I train them with sacks of hay to get them used to unstable riders, but it would be good to get an actual child in the saddle to play that role."

"She would love it!" Ivy accepted for her daughter.

The waitress returned with their drinks and took their meal orders. The DJ played a popular slow song that had couples leaving their tables and taking to the floor.

The plaintive chords of the music echoed inside Rocco. He realized how much he'd missed American music—Country especially. He hadn't heard this song before, though it was obviously an old favorite with the crowd.

Mandy took his hand. He looked at her fingers bending across his knuckles and knew she was asking, oh so sweetly, if they couldn't please dance. He looked at his hand, his forearm, his other forearm. All he saw was his blue chambray sleeves. No blood. No burned flesh. He'd come this far with no repercussions. Perhaps he could risk a dance.

He got out of the booth and offered Mandy his hand. The feel of her soft palm in his was almost more than he could bear. They moved around the tables and joined the swaying crowd on the dance floor.

Multicolored Christmas lights hung off suspended wagon wheel chandeliers, casting a festive glow across the dancers. The room was warm, filled with heated

bodies in motion. The music was loud. The scents of
food and liquor were strong in the air. Yet, when he
faced Mandy on the floor, it all receded. It was as if
he'd ducked under water, hearing things only through a
dense filter. She smiled at him. He did not smile back.
It took every ounce of his concentration to keep
control of himself.

He'd wanted to hold her, to feel her in his arms, for
the longest damn time. He knew her skin would be like
velvet. He placed his hand on her waist, starting the
dance with a respectful distance between their bodies.
Somehow, on the crowded floor, she ended up against
him, soft, curvy. Her naked legs forked his, her leather
boots making shuffling sounds against the grainy floor.
When she laid her head against his shoulder, he
couldn't resist pressing his face against her silky hair.
He breathed her scent, faint, elusive. Its sweetness
reminded him of jasmine. But not of Kadisha. Never
her.

Heat pooled in his groin, intensified by the pressure
of her belt buckle against his cock, every movement a
stroke against his arousal. His hand traveled upward
over her back, holding her tighter against him, pinning
her breasts against his ribs. Others were dancing as
close. No one noticed the liberties he was taking. He
pressed his lips against the crown of her head. She
moved slightly. He kissed halfway to her temple, and
then touched his lips to the bare skin of her forehead.

He wasn't even aware the music had faded into
another song with a faster tempo. She looked up at

him, her body fully against his, her eyes dark like a secret forest, promising him the tranquility he sought. This, this was what he'd needed, what he'd craved.

A man tapped him on the shoulder. "Mind if I take this dance?"

Rocco's left hand flashed upward to grab the intruder's Adam's apple in an instantaneous reaction before realizing it was Bobby. Mandy straightened and pulled at his hand before he could close his fist and crush the son of a bitch's windpipe.

"Rocco, stop. It's only a dance."

Rocco frowned down at her as he let the rodeo star go. "You *want* to dance with him?"

Rodeo didn't give her a chance to answer. He took hold of her and moved her deeper onto the dance floor. Rocco folded his arms, standing where she had left him, glowering at the man who now held her. The couples had to move around him on the floor. A low buzz began in his ears. Out of the corner of his eye, he saw Ivy leave their table and approach him. The movement of the dance brought Mandy and Rodeo past him as Ivy came even with him. Neither one looked at him as they danced by.

"What's goin' on, Rocco?" Ivy asked. He didn't answer, just kept his eyes on Mandy. She followed his gaze. "Oh. Ooohhh! C'mon back to the table. He'll bring her over when the dance ends."

Rocco didn't move.

"Would you like to dance with me?" Ivy offered.

Rocco did look at her then. He wondered when Kit

had last seen her. She didn't wear a wedding band. Would that please or torture his friend?

"I can't dance with you."

"Why?" she asked.

"It's complicated."

"Then come back to the table. If Bobby bothers Mandy, I promise I'll kick his ass for you so that you don't have to."

"No you won't. That pleasure will be all mine."

She smiled at him, and he felt some of his disdain for her melt away. As they headed back to the table, he wished Kit were here, having this evening with her.

When the song ended, Rocco got out of the booth to let them in. Mandy's cheeks were rosy, her eyes shining. Rocco hated that another man had given her that glow. Mandy scooted in next to him, pushing her body up against his, touching him from thigh to hip to shoulder. He looked down at her, trying to see if her closeness meant Bobby had insulted her in some way. She met his gaze and smiled, the look in her eyes meant for him alone.

The waitress came with their food, temporarily interrupting other treks to the dance floor. He took a couple of bites, mostly so that no one would make a big deal of his not eating. Officer Jerry and Rodeo were having a heated debate about baseball pitchers—a subject he couldn't contribute to having been out of the country for so long. He hadn't kept up with any of the teams or their star players. He pushed the food around on his plate until Mandy's hand squeezed his thigh.

He looked at her. She was making a show of biting the food off her fork. She nodded toward his plate. He didn't take the bait. Instead, he watched her chew, watched her swallow, waited for her to take another bite, all the while remembering their first dinner together when she'd fed him. As soon as she realized what he was doing, a blush slowly stole up her neck. He grinned, pleased that the color was for him and not Rodeo.

"Hey, guys—I need to make a run to the lady's room," Ivy announced a short while later when everyone had finished eating. "Can I bother you to let me out?" Rocco scooted out of the booth with Mandy and Rodeo to let Ivy out. She grabbed hold of Mandy's hand and pulled her along with her. Once inside the restroom she faced Mandy. "What are you doing here?"

"In the restroom? Or at Winchester's? You wanted to meet Rocco, remember?"

"Yes. And God, he is sex on a stick. Why are you still here? That man can't take his eyes off of you."

Mandy shrugged. "It's not what you think."

"Yes, it is. Go home and get laid."

"Ivy! You're incorrigible!"

"No, I'm not. It's been a long time since a man looked at me the way Rocco does you. Don't waste that. You saw him stay on the dance floor after you went off with Bobby, didn't you?"

"Yes." Mandy smiled. "He looked really angry."

"He was really angry. You should put that energy to

use—take him home and soil the sheets."

Mandy sighed. "It won't work. He doesn't like to be touched. You saw he wouldn't shake hands with anyone when we got here."

"You've had your hands all over him tonight. He didn't seem to mind."

Mandy thought about that for a minute. "He didn't, did he?"

"If I were you, I wouldn't be wasting another minute here when I could be home alone with him."

"I don't know, Ivy. I haven't been with anyone in a long time."

Ivy squelched that argument. "Silly girl, it all still works the same."

Rocco pulled the truck to a stop in front of the main house a short while later. Mandy gave him a smile, but did not move to get out. She'd had two beers—surely not enough to incapacitate her, was it? he wondered. By the time he came around to her side, she'd opened her door and had pivoted to sit with her boot heels braced on the door's ledge. "Did you have fun tonight, Rocco?"

"I enjoyed our dance." That had been the only thing he'd enjoyed. He wasn't up on recent sports news and teams, so he couldn't contribute to the guys' conversations about baseball or basketball. The only politics he was familiar with were the bad decisions coming out of Kabul and policy fluctuations in Washington. He didn't have plans for the summer, other than keeping Mandy safe and then going back for his son. He'd been a lousy addition to their party.

"I enjoyed that, too," she agreed.

He reached for her waist, carefully lifting her so that she wouldn't bump her head as he helped her from the truck. He didn't release her. "I didn't enjoy that bottom-feeder, Bobby."

"He's not a bottom-feeder. And we're not seeing each other anymore. What about you? Is there a special girl waiting for you somewhere?"

Only Kadisha, who likely was waiting in hell for him. He dropped his hands and stepped back, setting a little space between them. He shook his head and shoved the truck door shut. "There's no one."

"How long has it been?" she asked in a voice that had gone low, husky. God, was he hearing her correctly? Was she asking what he thought she was asking?

"How long since when? Since I had a woman, or had one I wanted to have?"

"I didn't think there was a difference."

Kadisha had been expecting their second child. How long ago he'd been with her? He'd run out of excuses to avoid their marriage bed last summer. The women in the village were talking about his lack of interest in his wife. He'd been so focused on her father. Perhaps that had been his undoing. He'd made Kadisha love him, then cut her loose, thinking the ruse was in place. He'd never thought it needed care and feeding.

"There is when your life isn't your own."

Mandy stood in front of him in the bluish moonlight, waiting for a sign from him. His hand shook as he lifted it to her face. He'd touched her a few times tonight without repercussions. He knew he was pushing his luck, touching her one more time, but he was unable to deny himself the pleasure. He drew his fingers down her cheek, feeling the downy soft skin at the side of her face. He caught the stray strands of her hair and pushed them back with the others behind her head.

"Do you want me, Rocco?"

Jesus H. Christ, did he want her. It was as if she, alone, brought him the air he breathed. If he stepped away from her, he would suffocate. He forked his hand through her hair until he cupped the back of her head. He drew her closer to his body, close enough that he could feel her warmth, almost sense the percussion of her heartbeat in the air between them. He bent toward her, low enough to catch the breath from her parted lips against his mouth. He waited, hovering close, feeling the rhythm of her life force.

"I want you," he whispered against her mouth. "I have since I first laid eyes on you." He looked into her eyes, moving his head so that the moonlight fell across her face. Her eyes looked black. A trick of the light, no doubt. A trick he felt in his groin. Her hands touched his waist, then moved slowly, cautiously, up his chest. He was barely aware he and Mandy were moving in a slow rotation, circling each other, letting the light from the moon play against one, then the other, as if they danced to silent music that hummed between them.

Her hand moved up to his shoulder, across his collarbone, to his neck. A muscle in his jaw bunched as his dick responded to the feel of her palm against his skin. She caressed his jaw, his cheek, his temple.

"Your eyes are unbelievably sad, Rocco. Why?"

"Don't ask me questions I can't answer."

"Make love to me."

Words failed him. He could only nod.

"I'm going to change," she said, smiling. "I'll come right down." She slipped free from his hold and trotted to her porch. Rocco made his way to the bunkhouse. He tossed his hat on the table.

It hit him then, the answer to the question he'd asked himself earlier.

Nine months. He'd last been with his wife *nine months* ago. A cold sweat dampened his arms and chest and face with its stink. Their second child would have been born this month.

"You did this. You killed us."

He ripped at the buttons of his shirt, tearing it from him, checking his arms for the ghost flesh that he felt sticking to him as tears made hot tracks down his cheeks. He kicked his boots off and stripped out of his T-shirt, jeans, briefs, and socks, leaving them where they fell in the hallway to the bathroom. He flipped on the shower, feeling the burned flesh drying, shrinking, pulling at his skin. The smoke choking his lungs.

He lunged into the shower stall. Grabbing the soap, he fell to his knees, swiping the bar over his arms, building a thick, white lather to wash away the burned flesh. He reached for the washcloth and began scrubbing the dead skin from his arms, even as his mind gave in to the screams that had haunted him since that day.

Mandy took a quick shower, dried her hair, and pulled on a sexy babydoll. It was sheer white, with satin push-up cups and lacy briefs that matched. She'd bought it a couple of years earlier, but had never worn it—hadn't even removed the tags until tonight. She started out of her bedroom, feeling very naked walking through the house in something so revealing. At the door, she paused. What if she stayed the night there? She couldn't walk back to the house in the daylight dressed as she was.

She slipped into a pair of flip-flops, then grabbed her raincoat and shoved her arms through the sleeves as she hurried from her house down to the bunkhouse. She knocked on the door. No answer. She cracked it open and realized Rocco was taking a shower. She stepped inside, feeling suddenly very shy. She took her coat off and wandered into the bedroom that he used, wondering which was his bed. Neither of them looked as if they'd been used lately.

It seemed terribly bold waiting for him in one of the bedrooms. She went back into the small living room. One of the armchairs had been pushed into a corner. She sat in it. His shotgun and a box of shells were on the floor next to it. That seemed odd, but she didn't give it much thought. Sitting still seemed to highlight her nervousness so she went to stand in the shadows by the kitchen. That was best. She felt better standing up.

Still he showered. From her vantage point, she could see the clothes he'd stripped out of on his way to the bathroom. His space was otherwise very tidy. She smiled, imagining his haste to get showered before she came over.

The water kept running. Like before, when he'd taken that long, freezing cold shower. Something wasn't right. She ventured down the hall and knocked on the bathroom door. No answer.

"Rocco? I'm here." No answer.

She poked her head around the door, expecting a room full of steam. It was cold, like a grave. Rocco was in the shower, washing himself with a red washcloth. She pulled back, realizing he hadn't heard her. No sooner had she shut the door than it dawned on her that she hadn't provided any colored linens. The towels and sheets she'd stocked the bunkhouse with were all white.

She hurried into the bathroom, and pushed open the sliding shower door. "Oh, my God. Rocco stop!" Cold water lashed across her back as she reached inside and grabbed hold of Rocco's hand, stilling the white terrycloth that was red with blood.

Chapter 9

Rocco looked at her with unfocused eyes. Mandy wasn't certain he saw her.

"I have to get it off."

"Get what off?"

"The blood. The skin. I have to get it off."

"Rocco, you're making yourself bleed. Come out of the shower. Let me look at what you've done." She kept the cloth pressed to his forearm as she helped him to his feet and out of the stall. Lowering the lid on the toilet, she had him sit there. Kneeling before him, she prayed he hadn't slashed his wrist as she peeked beneath the cloth. He hadn't. The blood was from an abrasion farther up his forearm.

His knees bounced nervously as his feet jiggled against the cold tile floor. His face was pale, his lips blue, his breathing uneven. She was afraid he was going into shock. She grabbed his free hand and wrapped it around the bloodied cloth, squeezing his grip to hold it tight. She pulled a couple of thick towels from the shelf and covered his shoulders and legs with them. She flipped on the hot water tap in the shower, thinking that would heat the little room quickly—unless he'd already emptied the hot water in the tank. Fortunately, he hadn't. Steam began to fill the room.

Finally, she turned her attention back to him, easing his hand away, murmuring low, soothing words as she would to a spooked horse. "Okay. You're okay. I'm going to take a look. Turn your head away. I don't want you to see this."

He looked at one arm, then the other. "I know it isn't there." She straightened the towel over his shoulders. His eyes were still dilated.

"What isn't there?"

"The black flesh. It sticks to me. I see it. I can feel it. I can smell it. But I know it isn't there."

Mandy couldn't make any sense of that at all, so she didn't respond. She needed to see how bad his wound was before she could begin processing his strange words. She peeled the washcloth away. He'd rubbed his skin raw on both sides of his left forearm. It bled freely but wasn't deep.

"It's going to be fine, Rocco. It's only a scratch. You're going to be fine."

"No, I'm not. I'm too goddamned fucked up to be fine."

She brushed a thick, wet lock of hair from his face, then pulled his forehead down for a kiss and held him against her mouth. "I'm not lying. You're going to be fine. Don't get up. I'm going to grab some Neosporin spray and bandages. Close your eyes. Focus on breathing."

She hurried to the medicine cabinet and took out the items she needed. She gave his scrapes a quick spritz of the Neosporin, opened a couple of packages of gauze pads, then covered them with a sticky wrap that would keep the whole works in place on his arm.

Still kneeling on the hard tiles, Mandy smiled up at him. "All done." The room was feeling comfortably steamy. Her gorgeous babydoll clung to her like a second skin, limp and dull. "What happened here?"

He shrugged. "This is why they kicked me out of the Army."

She let out a short huff of air. "Hallucinations have a funny way of freaking people out. Suppose you tell me why you're having them?"

"If I fucking knew, I could get it to stop."

She stroked a hand over his chest, beneath the edge of the towel. "Do you see the flesh now?"

He looked at himself. "No."

"Do you smell it or feel it?"

"No."

"That's good. Neither do I." She rubbed her hand up his uninjured arm and back down. "You know, I don't scare very easily. Maybe you could trust my eyes, for now, just until you can trust your own again. If I see flesh sticking to you that isn't yours, I'll tell you. And unless I do, you can know that it really isn't there, that you don't need to get it off of you, okay?"

He didn't answer, but he didn't refuse either. Tears welled in his eyes. She felt them pool in her own eyes as she stroked her hands up and down his arms. "When did this start happening?"

He shrugged. "Landstuhl—the hospital in Germany. I was out of my head. I had to be restrained. I'd been speaking Pashto for so long, I forgot to speak English. No one understood me."

"Were you injured in Afghanistan?"

He nodded. "Remember that explosion I told you about?"

It all clicked for her. "Ohhh. That makes sense."

"Does it? Because it fucking doesn't to me."

The long hours he worked would leave him little time for sleep. She remembered none of the beds had been slept in, and the armchair was in an odd place in the living room with the shotgun and box of shells close at hand. "You aren't sleeping, are you?"

He shook his head. "Not much."

Kit said he'd been having nightmares, but these hallucinations were day terrors. "After my parents' death, when I first moved in with my grandparents, I had a lot of nightmares. My grandfather said my mind was trying to tell me something, a message that I was not allowing myself to hear when I was awake. He said we have nightmares because there's something going on inside of us that we don't want to face so we close ourselves off from it—but when we do, it stalks us in our sleep. Were you given sleep meds at the hospital?"

"I was, but I quit taking them when they discharged me. Left me too hung-over to function in the morning."

"And then these hallucinations kicked in when you quit sleeping?" Again, he nodded. "Rocco, it's your same nightmare, but now it's a waking one. You're trying to tell yourself something, but you're not listening." He looked at the wall behind her. "What happened in that explosion?"

"I don't remember."

Mandy studied him. "How were you injured in the explosion?"

"I don't know. I blacked out."

"You have to try to remember that day, remember the explosion."

"No."

"This won't stop until you do."

He looked down at her. Tension distorted his face, like a cable drawn too tight. "I'm going back to Cheyenne. You don't need to deal with this crap."

She sat back on her haunches. Her hands were still on his knees. He'd stopped jiggling his legs, and his breathing had calmed, but his eyes were still wild.

"Good," she agreed with his decision. "Do that. Because this war injury is shameful and should be hidden. You should have to deal with it alone."

Anger flashed across his eyes at her sarcasm. He stood and lifted her in one smooth movement, pinning her against the wall, his hands under her armpits. She could barely touch the floor with her toes.

"I'm out of my fucking mind. What if I hurt you? What if I black out, mistake you for the enemy?"

Mandy set her palms against his cheeks, willing him

to look at her. "Have you ever mistaken a friendly for an enemy?"

No, he hadn't. But he'd mistaken an enemy for a friendly, an error that had cost his second child's life and had put Zaviyar in so much danger. "When I flashback, I lose track of myself. I'm not aware of what I do."

"I'm not afraid of you."

"*I'm* afraid of me. I'm afraid for you."

"Rocco, I don't want you to go. I think this is where you need to be."

He stared at her. He looked at the hold he had her in—if he needed more proof, he had it right there. Shaking his head, he eased her to her feet and pressed his hands flat against the wall on either side of her head. His towels had dropped away when he stood up. His penis leaned against her belly, a hard rod throbbing to life. The feel of her body against the head of his cock sent a shiver through him.

She lowered her hands from his face to his chest and rubbed in small circles. "Please. Stay. Strangers won't understand you. They will make things worse. And Kit will be here soon, I know it. He'll be able to help, too. And you said Ty's coming home. This is where you need to be."

He sighed and slowly lowered his forehead to hers. His nose was next to hers. She could feel his breath on her mouth. "I'll stay. For a while. Unless this gets worse." He pulled back to look at her. His face was shuttered. He wasn't letting her in and he wasn't letting himself out. It was her luck, Mandy thought, to have a man she could be crazy about walk into her life, only to have him walk right back out again. She lowered her gaze to stare blindly at the light furring of dark hairs on his chest. Tears spilled down her face. She didn't want him to leave. Ever. But it didn't matter. Clearly, she wasn't enough of a reason for him to stay.

Rocco swiped his thumbs across her cheeks. Her tears robbed him of words. He pulled her against his chest, holding his arms loosely around her. Her arms wrapped about his ribs, her hands flat on his back, her face pressed into his chest. He tightened his hold about her. He could feel the slippery moisture of her tears on his skin, feel the cool pull of her breath.

His dick was throbbing, alive, aware of her in a way he tried futilely to ignore. He tried to calm the deep breaths he drew, but every slight movement he made brought his body in contact with Mandy's in new and exciting ways.

If he didn't pull away now, he would be lost. There was nothing gentle in the way he desired her.

Mandy's hands eased around his sides, moved up over his chest. Her tears had stopped—for that, he was grateful. Her lips pressed against his sternum. Her tongue, hot and moist, tracked up, then across his collarbone. She lifted her face to his neck. He kissed her temple, drew the sweet scent of her hair into his lungs. She smelled like Mandy, not Kadisha. His relief was intense. Grounding.

His hands cupped her shoulder blades as he drew

her up against himself. He kissed her cheek, followed the line of her jaw to her lips, and there he paused. "Tell me you want this as much as I do. I want you to be sure about this. Very shortly, I won't be able to stop."

She smiled against his lips, and breathed, "I want this."

He nodded. "Good." He felt a wave of possessiveness—something he had no right to feel. She was not his forever, only his for now, this moment. He eased her down to her feet and stepped back. Fishing through his shaving kit, he found a couple packs of rubbers. He ripped one open and slipped it down over his cock, which helpfully, was standing at a rigid right angle to his body.

Mandy watched him. She licked her lower lip. Her eyes met his, green eyes gone black with desire. He reached into the shower and shut off the water, which had long since turned cold. He pulled the shower door shut. Lifting her hands, he pressed one to the grip on the shower door, the other to the towel bar on her other side. "For support," he said, grinning.

He parted the damp sheath of her babydoll top. His fingers stroked the velvety softness of her belly, his hands dark against the paleness of her skin. "You are beautiful." And she was—amazingly, breathtakingly beautiful. He traced the top edges of her bodice. Satiny cups covered her breasts. He ached to pull them down, to reveal what they covered. He pushed his dick downward, between her tight thighs, rubbing himself between her legs, against her panties.

He kissed her neck, moving down to the curve of her shoulder and slowly back up. His lips paused over the pulsing vein in her neck, feeling her frenetic heartbeat. His mouth touched hers, hovering briefly, lips to lips, letting her acclimate to him before he moved across her lips, drawing her mouth open with his. His tongue slipped into the sweet darkness of her mouth even as his dick pressed between her legs.

She moaned. Her tongue touched his, rubbing, pressing. He drew the backs of his fingers down her shoulders, over the upward swell of her breasts, then eased the fabric of her bodice down, dragging it beneath her breasts. Pulling back, he looked at her bared skin. Her dusky nipples were puckered. He rubbed his open palms against the sensitive nubs. Around. Up and down. She held tightly to the bars where he'd placed her hands as he cupped a breast and suckled on the peaked nipple. She gasped, arching into him. His cock jerked in response. Christ. He could come just sucking on her. He rolled her wet nipple between his thumb and forefinger as he moved to her other breast.

He felt the ragged breath she drew, responded by drawing a long draw of air through his teeth as his tongue flicked her tight nipple.

"Please—" she begged.

"Please what?"

"Please end this."

He grinned. His fingers left her nipples, easing

down to her hips. He went to his knees, hooked his
thumbs in her panties, and drew them slowly down her
lean legs. He kissed her belly button, her hipbone.
"Lean back against the wall." He lifted one leg and laid
it over his shoulder. She had shaved all but a band of
red-gold hair over her mound. He nuzzled it, hungry
for a taste of her.

"You might want to keep holding on," he supplied
helpfully as he drew her other leg over his other
shoulder, opening her sex to him. Supporting her with
a hand beneath her bottom, he leaned forward to
stroke her with his tongue. He swept across the
sensitive folds, circling her clitoris, pressing against it,
starting a rhythm her body instinctively responded to.
He rubbed his free hand over his dick. He was hot,
hard, his cock standing upright, waiting. He shoved his
tongue into her opening, tasting her sweetness.

There was nothing conservative about her response
to him. Her chest and neck were flushed with passion.
Short, breathy gasps escaped her parted lips. Her hips
bucked against his mouth. Her knuckles were white as
she gripped the bars.

He turned his attention to her sensitive nub, laving,
pressing, sucking. He speared her with two fingers. In
and out, until he felt the first convulsions of her
orgasm take her. He pulled back before the waves of
pleasure could fully engulf her. She cried out a protest,
tightening her legs around his head.

He grinned up at her, offering a last sweep of his
tongue before he cupped his hands under her buttocks.

He drew her legs off his shoulders, lowering her onto his erect cock, fast, hard, seating himself to his balls in her wet sheath.

She threw her head back and screamed. Her inner walls pulsed over him, pulling him with her into an explosion of ecstasy. He gripped her hips, lifting and slamming her down on top of him, spearing her until he found his release.

When they both returned to reality, Mandy felt limp, drained. Completed in a way that she'd never known was possible. He was breathing as hard as she was. There was an edge in his lean face as he watched her, his big hands still on her hips.

It was sex, pure and simple. There was nothing more to what they had shared, she knew that. But it had never been like this for her. She wanted him again. She wanted him to take her all night long. He left her feeling dazed. Drugged with desire.

She had no business yearning for more. He'd given her what he could. She shouldn't ask for more. She rose and straightened her bodice, then pulled her panties back on. He turned and removed the rubber.

She opened the hall door, felt the cool air clash with the heated, steamy air from the bathroom. She moved down the hall, feeling adrift, without an oar. Without a compass. Without any means of finding her way back to who she was before Rocco.

She retrieved her coat and was tying the sash when Rocco joined her in the front room. He'd drawn a pair of jeans on. They were zipped but unbuttoned and rode low over his bare hips. He leaned against the opening of the hallway, his hands in his pockets.

"You don't have to go." *Please, don't go.*

She stepped into her flip-flops. Decision made.

"Right. Then I'll walk you back up to the house." He lifted his jacket off the pegs by the door and slipped into it.

They walked from the bunkhouse to her home in silence. Outside her porch, he caught her hand, twined his fingers with hers.

"Thank you for patching me up." He looked down into her eyes. A lazy breeze blew a bit of hair over her eyes. He moved it back. He wished he understood her silence, the things her big eyes were saying. "You are an angel, the only light in my very dark life." She blinked. He thought the dim porch light revealed a pool of moisture in her eyes, but he couldn't be sure. "Did I hurt you tonight?"

He hadn't imagined it. A tear slipped down a cheek when she looked down and shook her head. He pulled her into a hug, feeling an impossible sense of rightness standing there, holding her, having nothing to offer her but himself.

Perhaps he could convince her to wait for him. As soon as he found Zaviyar, or his grave, he would come back. He would begin again—with her, if she would let him.

* * *

Sun beat down on the fields the next day, baking

the ground, the air, and Rocco. Even the barbed wire he was taking down was hot to the touch. He wore his hat and T-shirt, but had removed his long-sleeved shirt midmorning. His white bandage was smudged and torn in places. He lifted his hat and wiped his forehead on his shoulder. He'd be glad to see the last of the wire. His hands and arms were filled with dozens of nicks from the little metal prickers. Tiny tears with frayed edges dotted the thighs of his jeans.

He took a wheelbarrow full of the discarded wire up to the pile he was building by the toolshed. His stomach reminded him that he'd heard Mandy ring the chow bell a while earlier. When she'd talked him into taking suppers with her, he hadn't planned to eat three squares. Now he looked forward to each and every meal. He washed up at the utility sink and pulled on his shirt.

Mandy was talking to someone as he came even with the porch of the main house. A man. Rocco started up the steps. Bobby, the rodeo king, sat across from Mandy at a table set for two. Either he'd taken Rocco's spot, or Rocco was a third wheel at their lunch.

Mandy looked up and smiled. "Rocco, you remember Bobby," she said.

"Rodeo." Rocco nodded at the interloper.

"Rocco." Bobby nodded back.

Rocco swept the table with a glance. "Am I interrupting? Thought I heard the chow bell, but I could have been mistaken."

"No—you're fine! Sit down. I saved you some.

Bobby came over for a visit, and I asked him to stay for lunch." Mandy handed Rocco a plate and silverware from a stack of items on the far side of the table. "Hope you don't mind a cold pasta chicken salad?"

"Looks great," Rocco said as she passed the serving bowl. "Taking a break from the circuit?" he asked Bobby as he filled his plate.

Rodeo nodded. "Last night was my first one back in town. Thought I'd swing by and visit my gal."

Rocco arched a brow. "Your gal?" He looked at Bobby, then at Mandy. "Didn't know you were seeing anyone." Was it his imagination or did her expression tighten?

Before she could answer, Rodeo spoke for her. "We've got an on-again off-again kind of thing."

"That a fact?" Rocco asked, sending Mandy an angry look.

"And right now, we're off again," Mandy said, shooting a dark look at Rodeo.

"I told you I'd overlook what happened last night. I get that he came back not quite right and needed your attention."

Silence blanketed the porch. Rocco stared at his food, wondering if Mandy had said something about him, about what happened when they got home to Rodeo.

"I don't even know what that means, Bobby. Why would you say something like that?"

"Oh, come on. It's all over town, his fit on Main Street earlier this week, his meltdown at the diner, the way he was at Winchester's last night?"

Rocco stood up, pushing his chair away with the back of his calves. "Time for you to go," he said to Rodeo.

"I'm trying to talk her into a weekend away," Rodeo continued as if he hadn't spoken.

"She's putting in eighteen-hour days trying to get the center open. She doesn't have time to play with you. And I'm not sure you heard her earlier, but I did. She said your on-again off-again thing is off. For good."

Rodeo stood up. "I know she's been working hard. She needs a break. And I won't be able to spend much time with her over the summer, so I thought we should have our weekend sooner rather than later."

Mandy stood up and began gathering the serving dishes. "Rocco's right. I can't take any time off right now. In fact, I need to get back to work. Thanks for stopping by, Bobby. Good luck at your next event. I'll be rooting for you!"

"That's it?" Bobby looked from her to Rocco and back again. "Because he said so we're done?"

"No. We were done long ago. Maybe before we even began. I'm sorry, Bobby."

He retrieved his hat and shoved it on his head. He gave her one last reproachful look before heading down to his brand-new Ford Dually Crew Cab. Ivy said his horse trailer matched his truck with his name boldly lettered on the side. He had to be doing well on the rodeo circuit to afford a rig like that.

She'd enjoyed their time together, but it never had the depth she truly needed. He'd only been a diversion—as she'd been for him, probably. And now that she'd had a glimpse of what she really wanted, everything else paled in comparison.

The porch grew silent again as she and Rocco watched Bobby's truck drive away. She turned slightly and caught Rocco's gaze. She should have looked away, should have hurried about her business. She should have done anything other than let her gaze linger with his, watch the anger leave his face, to be replaced by the dark hunger that filled the void. She crossed her arms in front of her.

"Is it over between you and Rodeo?"

She sighed. "It's not as simple as that."

"Then break it down for me."

"We went to school together. He was a few years ahead of me. A while back, we ran into one another again. We were about the only ones who still lived in the area who hadn't settled down. He was busy with his touring. I was busy with my studies and working on my plans for this center. Our relationship was convenient. It worked. Neither of us was ready to commit to a permanent situation. I never saw him as selfish, but I guess that's because I was as self-centered as he was. We both got what we wanted and gave nothing of ourselves in return. It's kind of sad, really."

Rocco stepped closer, moving at an angle. She backed up until the banister stopped her. "So is it over?" he repeated.

"Yes."

"I don't share my toys. And I don't play nice with others."

Mandy lifted her chin. "I'm not a toy."

Something changed in his expression. Hardened. His eyes went glacial. The planes of his face grew rigid. He bent down close to her and spoke through clenched teeth.

"No, you're not. You know what you are?" he asked in a quiet voice. She braced herself for all the cutting things he would say, shocked by how much his opinion would affect her.

"You are sunshine and moonlight, laughter and joy, a life lived entirely without fear. You heard the call of a dream and made it a reality. You are everything I believed I was fighting for all those years."

He straightened. His features had once again aligned themselves into his standard, implacable mask. Mandy's heart skipped a beat. No one had ever said anything so lovely to her. She reached up and took hold of his face.

"You are a beautiful man, Rocco Silas."

He drew her into an embrace. Mandy wrapped her arms around his waist and pressed her face to his chest. This was like their dance last night. He did not take from her, but gave to her—his strength, his courage.

"I will not share you, Mandy. But if you prefer him to me, or prefer any other to me, I will step aside."

She drew back to look at him. "I don't prefer him." Or any other, she added to herself.

He looked at her for a long moment. She could see shadows in his eyes and wondered what thoughts he had that he couldn't—or wouldn't—share with her.

Chapter 10

Rocco came to a full stop in Mandy's kitchen that evening. She wore a short skirt of layered ruffles and a button down white shirt. And those same damned short boots she'd had on last night. Her legs were bare. He knew how soft they were, and he ached, instantly, to run his hands along their smooth, velvety length.

"You going out tonight?" he bit out.

She sent him a look as she brought dishes to the table. "No."

He crossed his arms. "Then who's coming over?"

"No one." Her face was guileless, which heightened his suspicions.

"Then why are you all dressed up?"

She faced him. Christ, that was unnerving. He'd rather be out in front of a hidden Taliban sniper than Kit's sister standing so close, so soft, so open.

"Rocco," she said with a little, feminine laugh that raised the hairs on his neck and shot blood to his groin. "You really know nothing about women, do you? Sometimes, for no reason at all, we like to look nice. To feel pretty. Are you hungry?"

Belatedly, he realized she was gesturing toward the table. Fuck yeah, he was hungry. But not for dinner.

Rocco took a step, and then another, stalking forward with only one intent in his mind. When he stood before her, he still moved in, forcing her to step back until her hips met the edge of the counter.

He lifted her up to the cold surface. Her breathing was fast and shallow, matching his. Her eyes were wide and dark, like a forest beckoning with its hidden paths and secret treasures. He spread her legs and stepped between them. When she lifted her hands to his shoulders, he pulled them down and set them flat against the counter, giving her a slow shake of his head.

He bent slightly, nearly touching the curve of her neck as he stroked her calves. Christ Almighty, she was luscious. He knew his hands were rough, calloused from his work. He should worry that it offended her, but he didn't care. He stroked slowly, slowly upward. She was the only one he could touch. He'd missed having physical contact with a woman. His mind was fucked, but he trusted hers—if the phantom flesh showed up for real, she would tell him. And unless she said it was there, he was safe. He could trust. Could indulge.

He drew his hands up and over her tiny knees, so little they fit in his palms, so different from his bulky joints. He spread her legs a little farther, watching as his hands smoothed up over her thighs. His skin was dark against her pale skin. He pushed the edge of her skirt higher, up to her hips, revealing the delicate white panties she wore, more lace than garment.

He dragged his gaze up to meet hers, watching her face as he stroked his hands slowly back down to her knees, letting his thumbs drag against the soft inside of her thighs. Her lips parted. She arched toward him. He leaned in, feeling her rise to meet him like a magnet connecting with its other half. He did not let their mouths touch. Instead, he dipped his mouth down to the corner of her jaw, almost close enough to touch her. He drew a deep breath, scenting the perfume of her skin, sweetened by nothing other than her natural scent and the barest hint of jasmine. He knew she felt the draw of air against her cheek, for she sucked in a sharp breath and pushed against him, nuzzling him, aching, as he did, to consummate their kiss.

He lifted a hand to stroke her core, touching her only through her panties, teasing her with what they both wanted. The fabric was damp with her desire, her clitoris swollen. He stroked and rubbed, playing her body. She pressed against his hand.

"Rocco, please—"

"No. You get no say in this. It is my time, my joy to give. You just have to take it." His nose was against hers, his lips hovering above hers, their words a fevered breath shared between their mouths.

She grabbed hold of his face, her fingers splayed against his cheeks. "I want you. Now. All of you! Please!"

He smiled as he deepened the pressure against her.

"Later. This is only an appetizer. Come. Come for me. Let go." And she did. Crying out. Aching for more.

When Mandy's screaming nerves slowly settled down, she was still starved for him. And judging from the size of the bulge in his jeans, he was in a similar condition. She stroked him. A muscle bunched in his jaw. "I want you. Now. I want to finish this."

He took her hands and kissed her knuckles. "Soon. We've dinner to eat."

"I don't care about dinner."

"I do. You worked hard on it."

Mandy looked at the table, feeling absolutely no appetite for the meal. "Please, Rocco."

"The best things in life should be savored, slowly." He stepped back and lifted her off the counter. She stood before him, completely at his beck and call. "Take your panties off."

"But we're going to eat—"

He arched a brow at her. He had something delicious in mind—she could see it in his face. Unable to resist him, she drew the lacy underwear down her legs, kicking off her boots to step out of them.

"Put your boots back on." Again, she complied, leaving her panties on the floor. He smiled at her, then led her to the table.

"Oh! The iced tea!" She grabbed the pitcher from the fridge. He sat while she poured his glass. He stroked her thigh, moving his hand up to cup her bare buttock, watching her with eyes that had gone dark with hunger.

She sat at the table and helped herself to a portion of Salisbury steak, mashed potatoes, and green beans. He did the same, and for a moment, neither spoke. She felt naked sitting at the table without underwear. She ventured a look at him, only to see that he was observing her chest. She watched him until he raised his eyes to hers. He took another bite of his food, chewing it slowly. When he swallowed, he didn't take another.

"Unbutton your shirt and push it to your waist."

A heated blush stole up her neck. "We're at the dinner table." If she did what he asked, she knew she would never think about a meal at this table the same way again.

"We're alone. Do it."

Her fingers shook as she unfastened the first button. This was cruel and unusual punishment. He continued to eat while she undressed, watching, savoring the skin she revealed. She pulled her arms free of the sleeves and pushed it down, sitting before him in her lacy bra. She ventured a look at him. His eyes lifted to meet hers. He smiled.

"You are an amazing cook."

"I learned from my grandmother. She was definitely old fashioned in her ideas. She felt there was nothing more important than a family meal at the end of each day. Except, maybe, for breakfast and starting each day with a full stomach." She was rambling now, chattering to keep herself from attacking him. Mandy cut a piece of meat and shoved it into her mouth.

"Kit told me you lost your parents before high school. I'm sorry about that. You were lucky to have such wonderful people to take you in. They would be proud of you now."

She nodded. "My grandfather was a foreman on Ty's father's spread. He always wanted to make a living off this ranch, but he was never able to. He and I had the same dream."

"What was Blade like in those days? And don't tell me 'hot.'"

Mandy looked at her plate as she dipped back into her memories. "He was a lot older than me. I didn't really know him as a kid. I saw more of him once I met Kit. Truthfully, he always made me nervous. His father was a cruel man who delighted in tormenting anyone and everyone. I do remember one story my grandparents told me. Ty had broken his leg while his father was in one of his frequent, drunken stupors. He beat Ty up for crying. Nearly a week later, when he sobered up, Ty's leg was still untreated and had become infected. He spent a month in the hospital and had to have several surgeries. My grandmother visited him every day. When he got the cast off, my grandfather worked with him to help him regain his mobility. He had Ty doing certain chores around the ranch here to build his strength, then got him riding again.

"When Mr. Bladen learned that his son was working on his foreman's ranch, he became unhinged. He fired my grandfather. But Mr. Bladen's other hired hands had had it with him by then. They threatened to quit if he didn't hire him back. My grandmother cried for a week. They all could have lost their jobs. But there was more work available in the area in those days, so they were bold. Every one of them told my grandparents they would rather work in the coalfields than for Mr. Bladen. He took my grandfather back, but was worse than ever to him. And Ty didn't come over anymore after that."

"I knew his dad had been a son-of-a-bitch, but I didn't know how bad he was. Blade thrived in the Army. I hope he'll adjust easily to being a civilian again."

"Has it been an easy adjustment for you?"

Rocco met her glance. "No."

"Why?" she asked, her voice a mere whisper.

Rocco looked at his plate as he considered his words. "I knew what I was in the Army. I knew my mission. My life, even as an irregular, was structured. I had a purpose. I have none of that now."

Except, he did have one last mission. He'd made progress here. He was eating regularly and sleeping more. Soon, he'd be ready. Soon.

When they were both finished eating, Rocco stood and started to clear. "Leave these." Mandy stopped him. "I'll do them."

"Nope. You cooked. I'll clean."

Mandy stood up and started to pull her shirt back on. He stilled her hands and shook his head. "We'll have dessert as soon as I finish the dishes." He led her to the counter beside the sink and lifted her up. "Keep me company." He leaned forward and kissed the soft skin beneath her collarbone, ran his lips over her collarbone and up her neck. Nibbling on her jaw, he grinned as he looked up into her eyes.

He made short work of putting the food away and washing up. When he was finished, he turned to her, looking her over from head to toe as if trying to determine where to start his dessert feast.

He touched the back of his knuckles over the curves of her breasts, tracing the soft skin above her bra.

"Want coffee?" she offered a little breathlessly.

"No. I want you." He drew her hips closer to the edge of the counter, kissing her throat, her jaw, making his way over her chin to her lips. His tongue swept inside her mouth.

"Am I allowed to touch you?" she whispered.

"You can do anything you feel moved to do. Or sit back and let me do you." He kissed her again, his mouth feasting on hers, forcing her surrender, melting her bones. When she was breathless and clutching at him, he dropped to his knees and mouthed her core.

Shoving his hands up her thighs to cup her buttocks, he pressed her soft folds to his mouth. His tongue stroked, wandering where it wanted, tasting her desire. She cried out when he entered her with two fingers, and again when he sucked her clitoris. He looked up at her as his fingers stroked inside her, his mouth wet with her dew. He pulled one side of her bra down, exposing her breast.

Gently, he took her nipple and rolled it back and forth, watching as it tightened into a hard nub. And then, still holding her nipple, he mouthed her again. Mandy nearly arched off the counter. When he sucked her, spasms started. She bucked against his face, helpless to do anything but surrender.

When her body grew still, he rose and kissed her, letting her taste her own passion on his lips. He pushed her bra down, freeing her other breast. Mandy reached to his sides and drew his T-shirt up over his head. He'd run things the entire evening. Now it was her turn. She wanted to see him lose his control, wanted to drive him as mindless with passion as he'd made her.

She pushed him back away from the counter and slipped to her feet, then her knees. Unbuckling his belt, she opened his fly and spread the sides of his jeans against his lean hips. He wore no underwear. His rigid cock stood at the ready for her, deeply veined and heavy.

Mandy smiled up at him as she drew him toward her mouth. His eyes became hooded as he watched her mouth cover him. He was big. It was hard to fit her lips around him. He let her take him at her own pace, watching her intently, the tension deepening on his face. As she eased him deeper into her mouth, her tongue stroked the sensitive underside of him. His cock jumped involuntarily. She sucked and licked at him. Her hand reached into his jeans and cupped his balls. She massaged him, licking and squeezing until his hips were pushing him deeper and deeper into her mouth.

"Yeah. Like that. Like that." He threw his head back and cursed. Then suddenly he pulled free. Bending, he scooped her up and set her up on the counter again, then shoved inside her, sheathing himself to his balls. He began to pump inside of her. God, she'd never felt anything so wonderful.

"Wait—a rubber!"

Rocco paused, shuddering against the control he imposed on himself. "Right, a rubber." He dug around in his back pocket and pulled one out. Before he could open it, she put her hands on his and held him still.

"Or not. I'm on birth control. And I don't have any STDs. I haven't been with anyone since my physical, except you, last night."

Rocco hissed, drawing a long breath into his lungs. He took her hips and started pumping again. "The Army gave me a clean bill of health, too. I haven't been with anyone since my wife." And no one for years before that.

"Your wife?" Mandy pushed on his shoulders. "You're married?"

Ah, Christ. Not this discussion. Not now. "No." Shit, he was going to come trying to hold himself back.

"You're divorced?"

"No."

"Who is she?"

"She was part of my cover in Afghanistan."

"Was? Is she dead? Was she undercover like you?"

His ardor cooled in an instant. *You did this. You killed us.*

Rocco withdrew from Mandy. He pulled her skirt down and buttoned his fly, then picked up his T-shirt and pulled it over his head. There was no way he could answer her questions. He wanted no secrets between them, but there were big chunks of his memory missing. And his mission wasn't something he was willing to talk about. There were no answers he could give her.

What the hell had he been thinking to pursue this with her? He was too messed up for a relationship. Nor did he plan to stick around. And if she had such a visceral reaction to the fact that he'd been married, what would she say when she learned of his son?

He crossed his arms and leaned against the opposite counter. "I completed my mission. That's all I can tell you."

Tears filled her eyes. She righted her bra and pulled her shirt up, slipping her arms into the sleeves with jerky, angry movements. "You completed your mission," she ground out. Reality hit her like a bucketful of ice water. What did she really know about Rocco, besides the fact that he was a passionate and generous lover?

He'd been in Afghanistan, undercover. He'd been in an explosion of some sort. And he'd been a prisoner of war. Those were all random facts. She didn't know him at all. What was she thinking leaping into a sexual relationship with him? If she let it happen now, it would be the Bobby situation all over again.

Granted, she'd never come close to letting Bobby

break her heart. But Rocco could. She cared for him enough to want to go slowly, let their relationship build from the ground up.

Her gaze crossed the chasm that had opened between them. "I'm sorry, Rocco. I can't do this. I can't do this now."

Chapter 11

Static ripped into the silence of the bunkhouse. Rocco jerked awake, his heart slamming. He looked around the room, not recognizing where he was. "Rocco? Rocco, can you hear me?"

The walkie-talkie. A long, relieved breath eased out of his tight lungs, until he realized something had to be wrong up at the house. He grabbed the yellow plastic device. "Go ahead." He was out of his chair and jamming his feet into his boots as Mandy's whispered response rushed into the room.

"Someone's in my house."

He grabbed his shotgun, then ran out the door, glad he'd slept in his clothes. "Where are you?"

"In my room."

"Is the front door unlocked?"

"It is now."

"Lock your bedroom door. Don't come out until I tell you it's safe." He clipped the walkie-talkie to his waistband and reached her porch in record time. On the porch, he eased the front door open, shotgun at the ready. He made a visual sweep of the living room, then turned down the hall leading to the master bedroom. He moved silently through the dark, a shadow in a house of shadows, all his senses engaged. This danger he knew. It was comfortable. Search and kill. He checked the bedrooms, their closets, the bathroom. All was clear. He knocked on the master bedroom door. "You okay?"

Mandy ripped the door open. There was enough moonlight to see her pale, tense face, her enormous eyes. She nodded.

"What did you hear?"

"There was banging somewhere out there. Someone, something was walking around. The floors creaked. I know I heard something."

Rocco nodded. "Stay here. Lock your door. I'll check out the rest of the house."

"No way. I'm coming with you."

He frowned down at her, but didn't want to waste time arguing. It was probably a raccoon or something that had climbed in through a window. "Stay behind me, then." Two cold hands slipped between his back and waistband as she gripped his pants and leaned close to his back. She peeked around his shoulder, stepping in the shadow of his steps. They moved down the hall as tightly as sack racers in slow motion.

Her arms wrapped around his waist, and she buried her face in the middle of his back as they went through the dining room, the kitchen dinette area, the galley, across the hallway to the laundry room, a storeroom, and at last, to the back door. It was closed and firmly locked.

"Nothing. Let's go downstairs." He reached a hand behind him, needing distance between them to take the stairs safely. She threaded her fingers with his. He moved slowly, in no hurry to lose this time with her. They'd barely talked for the last few days. She'd been sending him supper on a tray. God, he'd missed her.

They moved through the rooms downstairs. Three bedrooms, a bathroom, a utility room, a storeroom, and a large, open rec room. It was a big house for one small girl. Did its emptiness haunt her? She'd probably dreamed the noise. Or perhaps one of the cottonwoods towering over the house had dropped a branch.

They made their way back upstairs. At the top of the steps, he pulled her in front of him into a light hug. She was ice cold. He rubbed her arm. "There's nothing here, babe. The house is clear."

"I know what I heard, Rocco."

"Tomorrow, I'll take a look around the house and see if maybe something fell on the roof."

"It wasn't the roof. It was by the kitchen. In the hallway. It was coming toward my room." She stood next to him, so closely that they touched from calves to shoulder. He glanced around at the shadowy living room. Nothing was out of place. He didn't know what she'd heard before, but there wasn't anything suspicious now.

He looked down at her, seeing the tension in her face. "Want me to stay here tonight?" he asked before realizing what it sounded like he was suggesting. "I mean, not with you, but here. In the living room. Alone."

Before Mandy could answer him, they heard a bang in the hallway by the kitchen. Her hand tightened on his. "See? That's what I heard!" she hissed.

There was a clattering of items from the kitchen, then the sound of nails skittering across the wood floor as an animal rushed toward the backdoor. A low growl set the hairs at Rocco's neck on edge. He flipped on the light switch in time to see a gray animal push out through a small access flap in the back door.

Rocco cursed. "You've got a coyote coming in."

Mandy slipped free of her death grip on Rocco's back. "I don't think that was a coyote. It was too small, and it had no tail." She flipped the outside light on and jerked open the door. Two dogs stood a few yards from the last step, a little one and a big one. The little one was standing guard. It growled when it saw them.

Rocco had seen plenty of pariah dogs in the Middle East. Often, they were vicious predators, always hungry, always hunting. "Go back inside, Em. You don't need wild dogs stalking the ranch. I'll take care of them." He stepped in front of her.

"Wait! Rocco, they're just strays. They're hungry and lost."

He pushed her toward the door. "There could be a whole goddamned pack. Get back inside."

"Rocco. Stop. You're not going to shoot them. They belong to someone. You can't kill them."

She slipped out of his grip and moved down the back steps slowly, eyeing the ghostly forms of the dogs in the distance. She sat on the bottom step and called to them in a friendly voice. Neither came to her. The larger one was eating something. She walked toward it slowly, talking in a cheerful voice. When she was about six feet from them, she knelt down and patted her thighs, calling the strays over. The little one, a Blue Heeler, stood stiff and growled. The larger one, a Golden Retriever, wagged his tail but didn't look up from the sleeve of bread he was munching. Both of them were reed thin.

Mandy talked to them for a while as the Golden fed on the stolen bread. "Look at you, you little fierce thing. You stole food for your friend," she said to the Heeler. "You can't be all bad. Come in the house. I'll cook some rice and eggs for you."

That must have sounded appetizing to the Golden, for he gave the empty bread bag a last swipe with his paw, then came over and nuzzled Mandy. She laughed, and stroked him, feeling for injuries. The Blue Heeler sniffed the breadcrumbs, then came over, keeping a safe distance from Mandy. She reached a hand toward him, but he shied away.

She slowly came to her feet, then picked up the remains of the bread bag, chattering with them to follow her inside. The Golden stayed close to her, but the Heeler was hesitant. At the steps, the big dog took a step and cried out.

"Rocco! He's hurt! Please, carry him inside. I need

to look at him."

He made a face but did as she requested. Shouldering his shotgun, he gently lifted the old dog. Seeing Rocco up close, the little Blue Heeler ran fast for the shadows behind the house.

"Take him to the kitchen," Mandy directed. Rocco set the beast on the floor near the table. He ran his hands over his back, his belly, his legs.

"Nothing broken. Just some minor scrapes. And he's malnourished as hell. They're lucky the coyotes didn't get them."

Mandy set a bowl of water near the dog, then busied herself mixing up a batch of scrambled eggs and a big pot of rice.

"What are you going to do with them?" Rocco asked, watching her work.

"Someone must be worried sick about them. I don't see any tags on this one. I wonder if he has a microchip. I guess I'll take him into the vet in town tomorrow. Get him checked out. Hopefully, I can catch the other one too."

Just then, there was a noise at the back door. Mandy grinned at Rocco, now recognizing that sound. "I knew his buddy would be back." The other stray fussed at the door a bit more, then came inside. Mandy didn't look at him, forcing her attention on the food she was preparing. He walked around the house once, then sniffed at Rocco and checked on his friend. Apparently satisfied, he went back around to the other kitchen entrance and sat in the hallway watching

Mandy. When the eggs were ready and cool enough to eat, Mandy put two bowls on the floor. One near the old retriever, one a short distance away for the other dog. She kept the rice for their breakfast.

She walked over to Rocco, ignoring the dogs while they ate—though all of her senses were keyed in on them. Eventually, she became aware of the fact that she and Rocco leaned against opposite sides of the kitchen entrance. His arms were folded across his bare chest as he watched her with a frown.

"How is it that we all seem to find you?"

"What do you mean?"

"Abused horses, disabled children, starving dogs, broken men."

She wanted to step into his arms, to feel them wrapped around her. To listen to his heartbeat. The look he was giving her said he would welcome it as well. But she was the one who had put the brakes on. And really, the situation between them hadn't changed. She didn't know enough about him to be intimate with him. If they were going to have a relationship, they'd have to move more slowly than they'd started out.

Her eyes watered. "I want the world to be perfect and everyone in it to be healthy and happy."

He shook his head. One step brought him to her. He cupped the back of her head and kissed her forehead. "It never will be, honey. But people like you make it a whole lot better." He stepped back. "You okay with these mutts tonight?"

She nodded. "Thanks for rescuing me. Come up

for coffee tomorrow morning. Maybe I'll cook some eggs for you, too."

He grinned. "Lock the kitchen door behind me," he said as he went to check the locks on both the back and front doors. "Tomorrow I'll look at the doggie door, see if I can cut a scrap of wood to cover it." He took up his shotgun and slipped out into the night, waiting by the kitchen door until he heard her lock it.

* * *

By the time he went up to the main house for breakfast the next morning, he'd done a three-mile run and had made a circuit of the ranch. All looked quiet. Things had settled down since his arrival. Perhaps it had been a prankster making mischief for Mandy. But why? He didn't like questions he couldn't answer.

The kitchen door was open. Two dogs stood at the screen door, both barking viciously at his arrival. Mandy shushed them and called for him to come in. She was cooking up a feast. The room smelled of coffee, hash browns, bacon, eggs and cinnamon rolls. He realized how hungry he was.

She brought the last platter to the table, sending him a welcoming smile that stole his breath. Her hair was braided, and the golden-red rope hung in front of her shoulder. She wore jeans and a long-sleeved, plaid shirt opened in the front to reveal a white tank top. An apron covered most of the front of her, but he'd seen her sweet, round ass when she was at the stove.

"Morning," she greeted him.

His mouth was suddenly, strangely dry, his tongue stuck to his teeth. He was barely able to nod at her. She poured him a cup of strong, black coffee and handed it to him.

"Hungry?"

His gaze moved over her mouth and chin, to the patch of skin between her open collar and the tank, to the ripe swell of her breasts and her tiny waist. He forced himself to look at her eyes. "Starved."

She smiled. "Then sit, before it gets cold."

"How did the mutts do last night?"

"Fine. I made a pallet for them to sleep on, but in the middle of the night, they were both up on the bed with me."

"After breakfast, we can take them into town to be checked out. If they were chipped, their owners can be contacted."

"That's what I'm hoping," she said without conviction.

"You want to keep them."

Mandy sighed. "I do. My grandparents always had dogs. I've been too busy to take one on. But Yeller and Blue are so sweet together. They need me. I think I'm settled enough to handle them now."

"Yeller and Blue?" he asked, wondering where she got those names.

She rubbed the Golden Retriever. "Yeller because he was too scared to come into the house and steal his own food." She reached over and patted the little tan and gray-spotted dog. "And Blue because he's a Blue

Heeler."

"Don't get too attached yet," Rocco warned. "If it can't be these two, then we'll find one from the shelter. There's no shortage of dogs needing homes."

Mandy smiled at him, her eyes filled with a warmth he had to be misinterpreting. She was happy at the thought of adopting dogs, not that he'd said he'd help her adopt them.

A short while later, they'd rigged up leashes and were loading the dogs into Mandy's SUV when one of the construction workers hurried over to them. His face was tense. He pushed his hat back a bit and scratched at his forehead.

"Mandy? We got ourselves a situation."

"What kind of situation?" Rocco asked the man.

"George is in the hospital."

"Oh, no! Is he okay?" Mandy asked.

"They said he and his wife will make a full recovery. They're suffering from carbon monoxide poisoning. His house was full of it. His wife was able to dial 9-1-1 before passing out. His dog died."

"What happened?"

"Don't rightly know. He had the detectors in his house, but they must have failed. And he'd had routine maintenance on his furnace not too long ago." The man looked at Rocco. "Anyway, don't know if we should keep working, with him offsite and all. What's your call?"

Rocco glanced at Mandy then back at the construction worker. "You his second-in-command?"

"That I am. Name's Tom Mason." He held his hand out to Rocco, who looked at it a second, then took it in a brief clasp. He could feel Mandy's surprise. Hell, he felt his own surprise.

"Then put yourself in charge and keep the crews going. I'm going to run into town with Mandy, but I'll be back in a little while. If you need me, call me." They exchanged phone numbers.

The man nodded before heading down the hill to the construction trailer. Rocco cautiously met Mandy's stunned gaze. He grinned.

"You touched him. You shook hands." Mandy was shocked.

"How about that? You said I could trust your eyes. Since you didn't react or warn me, I figured the blood wouldn't get on him. I didn't even feel it move on my skin. Maybe it's gone, Mandy."

She jumped forward and wrapped her arms around him, burrowing her face in his neck with a triumphant laugh that filled him with a warm contentment. He pulled her in tighter, feeling every curve of her body against his. He buried his nose in her hair, loving the faint scent of jasmine that drifted about her.

He pulled free as soon as he realized what he was doing. She'd made her preferences known. She wouldn't appreciate being mauled out here in the driveway, in the bright morning sun. Aw, hell. He couldn't even think about not touching her without getting hard.

He cleared his throat, then sucked in a few calming

breaths of air while Mandy got the dogs settled in the SUV.

Once in Wolf Creek Bend, he saw that the vet's office was across the street from the police station. "Mandy, will you be all right at the vet's by yourself? I'd like to have a word with the sheriff."

She gave him a curious look. "About George?"

"Yep."

"Sure. We'll meet back at the car when we're both done."

Rocco crossed the street and entered the police station. Jerry was at his desk in the front area. He looked up and gave Rocco a distinctly unwelcoming nod. "How can I help you?"

"I'm looking for the sheriff."

"Come on back." He opened the gate to the desk area and walked Rocco back to an office. "Sheriff, you've got a visitor."

Sheriff Tate looked up from his desk. "Rocco! Good to see you. How can I help you?" he asked, getting to his feet. He carefully kept his hand to himself, Rocco noticed. Briefly, he considered offering a handshake, but thought better of pressing his luck. He needed info out of the sheriff—info he would not get if he had a meltdown here.

"Did you hear about what happened to George Bateman?"

"Mandy's construction manager? No, what happened?"

"His house was flooded with carbon monoxide.

Almost killed him and his wife—they're in the hospital."

"Wow. That's bad news."

Rocco watched his reaction closely, but could read nothing in his expression. "Don't you think it's odd to have yet another inexplicable thing happen? He'd had his furnace serviced not too long ago."

"I'm not following. You saying there's a connection between something at his house and the construction site? 'Cause I don't see it."

"I'd like you to look into the situation. It's too coincidental."

"Look, Rocco, not to get you upset or anything, but you ain't fighting insurgents here. Accidents happen. Sometimes a whole darn string of them—"

"And sometimes they aren't accidents at all."

"I've got nothing to go on with this and no call to go askin' questions. I'm sorry. There's nothing I can do for you or Mandy."

Rocco put his hands on his hips. "That a fact? How about I get you some evidence? Will you take it seriously then?"

"If you find something, you bring it to me, you hear me? I don't need you going off half-cocked, stirring up trouble, scaring people. Bring me some facts, evidence, proof, something, and I will look into it. I'm fond of Mandy. I've known her her whole life. Everyone in town likes that gal. We don't like what's going on out at her place, but none of it adds up to anything." Rocco took his leave, frustrated with the sheriff.

He was leaning against Mandy's SUV, his arms crossed, when she brought the two dogs out of the vet's a few minutes later. "What's the verdict? Did the doc recognize them?" he asked as he helped her settled them in the SUV.

"He didn't. Neither had a chip. He gave me some diet suggestions to help them gain weight back. He said someone might have driven out to the country to drop them off. And then the poor things have been wandering about. That happens more often than you think. I'm not sure we'll ever know."

"You gonna keep them? Or do you want to take them down to the shelter in Cheyenne?"

She flashed a look at him. "I'm not taking these boys down to a shelter, Rocco."

He looked at her, feeling something inside him twist. With hope. Was she this possessive of everything—everyone—she rescued? "Then keep them it is."

Chapter 12

Rocco sat on the top step of Mandy's porch after supper. The evening was slowly rolling toward night. The construction site had been secured for the day. Kitano was happily munching his evening meal. The strays, full and sated from yet another small meal, lounged in the last vestiges of sunlight.

Mandy joined him on the stoop, handing him a cup of black coffee. All around them was peace and tranquility, but Rocco couldn't shake the feeling of a storm brewing, as if what had happened to George was just the first stacked domino in a line of them.

They'd learned from a phone conversation with George's wife earlier in the day that their furnace had been serviced by the same company that currently was providing plumbing and HVAC services on Mandy's equestrian center. It was, at last, a link, but Mandy refused to see that there was any connection at all. In fact, they'd argued about it earlier. He didn't want to continue their discussion, so he stood and walked to the ledge that looked down to the construction site and sipped his coffee in silence.

The accuracy of his instinct was an immutable truth he'd learned long ago never to doubt. Even when his mind was fucked all to hell, his gut held true. And right now, it was screaming a warning he could not ignore.

Mandy could not see the danger—nor could he, for that matter. But it did exist. So how was he to keep her and her dream safe?

He looked where she was sitting on the stairs and sighed. She smiled at him, a gesture he did not return. The world had gone mad, and he alone saw it happening.

"Okay," she said over the rim of her coffee mug. "Let's go through it again."

"It makes no sense, I know."

"But it's eating at you, so let's step through it."

"Who benefits if you fail to open the center?"

"No one. Not our therapy clients. Not the town that would have gained visitors for restaurants and gas stations and hotels. If I shut down construction until we figure this out, the crew and tradesmen would definitely not benefit."

Rocco sipped his coffee. A minute passed. A cold feeling settled in his stomach. "We're looking at this wrong. Instead of who might benefit, tell me what happens if things continue on the path they're on, with escalating issues and even violence."

"The cops will have more work to do. The emergency clinic in town and the hospital in Cheyenne will have more clients. My customers will not have a convenient place to come for hippotherapy.'"

"Keep going. What else will happen?"

"I will lose this ranch because I'll have construction loans I cannot repay."

Christ, it was all right before them, had been all along. "Before that. What will you do before that?"

She gave an exasperated sigh. "Call Kit and cry. I'll feel like such a failure." She set her coffee on the step and folded her arms about herself.

"Right. And what will Kit do?"

"He'll come out, thinking he can make everything right. He hates this town, Rocco. He once said he'll never come back—when we met over the years, it was never here. But for me, because of this, he would. I know it."

Rocco looked at Mandy, waiting for her to catch the implication. When she frowned at him, he explained. "This isn't about you. It isn't about the town or the center. It's about Kit."

"How can it be about Kit? True, this is his hometown, but this ranch has never been his home. My successes or failures do not spill over into his world, except in their emotional impact, perhaps."

"If you fail, he'll come home. Your failure is the bait luring him back here."

Mandy gasped. Her eyes widened as the impact of what he was saying settled in. "I don't know how much you know of what happened before he left, but he didn't leave on glowing terms. He'd made a stupid teenage mistake. He can't have enemies here from that—still—can he?"

"No idea." Rocco shrugged. "Someone is forcing him to come home. I don't know why." He thought of Ivy, Kit's high school flame. She was a poster child for a woman scorned. She'd only recently come back to town. And now this mess was happening.

"What are you thinking?" Mandy asked.

"What about Ivy? She and Kit don't exactly have a peaceful background."

Mandy looked at him. "No. Absolutely not. She did not come back to start trouble."

"Stranger things have happened, Em."

"Not Ivy." She wondered how much he knew, if it would be violating Kit's trust to tell him the whole sordid story. "He told you what happened, didn't he?"

"Some of it."

"Ivy was fifteen and Kit seventeen when they began dating. Kit was planning to go into the Army to get the tuition assistance the GI Bill offered for college. They—they were intimate. Ivy got pregnant. That news came out the day Kit turned eighteen. Her father accused Kit of statutory rape. He wanted him thrown in jail, wanted his life ruined. It was a big scandal in town.

"Sheriff Tate managed to intervene. He had Ivy's father agree not to press charges if the sheriff personally oversaw Kit's enlistment. No sooner did Kit graduate and walk off the stage with his diploma, but Tate took him in his patrol car and drove away. Ivy and her family moved away that summer. None of us knew what had happened to her or the baby. She never wrote. She never visited.

"I heard, several years later, that she'd kept the baby. And then, she reached out to me online. It was wonderful to hear from her. We reconnected as if there'd been no lost time.

"I was thrilled that she came back to town, with her daughter. I can't believe that she would wish Kit harm. You met her. She is lovely and cheerful and well-adjusted. She adores her daughter. She's excited about the diner and their future. She would not do something so evil."

He'd once thought Kadisha incapable of evil, too. A memory moved through his mind, there and gone before he could capture it. What had happened the day of the explosion? Why couldn't he remember?

"Evil has a heartbeat all its own, Em. It may be Ivy. Or it may be someone who was hurt by the whole scandal. Or it may yet be something or someone else. Whatever it is, Kit can't come home."

He took out his phone and dialed Kit.

"Hey. What's up?" Kit answered.

Rocco looked at Mandy, wondering how to break the news to his friend that someone wanted him dead. "There's a problem."

"I know. I was about to call you."

"The accidents here are no accidents. Someone is trying to draw you out."

"That's what I picked up on. Remember that chatter I mentioned? Well, it's gotten clearer. I'm coming out there. I'll talk to you tomorrow."

"No. Don't come here."

"Too late, bro. Blade and I will be in Denver tomorrow. We'll be up to Wolf Creek Bend before dinner."

Rocco cursed. "Don't bring Blade into this. Tell him convalesce somewhere else."

"Negative. The chatter's from a Taliban cell operating out of Denver. They've figured out where we live, and they're gunning for Blade and me. And now that you're there, you're a target, too. Shit, they hate you more than they hate either of us combined. You're probably why they're targeting me and Blade."

Holy hell. "This ranch is nearly impossible to secure. It's wide open and sits inside a bowl of higher ranges. Perfect ground for sniper attacks," Rocco warned.

"I'm bringing up a team and some equipment. Have Mandy clear us some space in the basement. See you tomorrow night. Keep my sister safe."

When Rocco lowered the phone, he couldn't escape Mandy's worried look. "He's coming home, isn't he?"

Rocco drew a breath. His lips pressed together in a thin line, he nodded. "Yep. And Ivy is not the problem."

* * *

The house was silent. Rocco had checked all the windows, upstairs and down. The doors were locked.

He looked around at the shadowy interior, dreading the battles to come. Mandy had kept her grandparents' 1960s reproduction Americana furniture, electing to reupholster the worn pieces rather than replace them. The pieces were large and comfortable, made for the big-framed bodies of Western ranchers. The woven, oval rug looked like the only new addition to the room.

This ranch was her home. It was supposed to be a safe place. He had to do whatever was needed to keep the war from getting any closer. He suspected Kit's assessment was correct—that just as the enemy had attacked Mandy's ranch to get to Kit, they would have attacked Kit and Blade to get to him. He was the biggest threat.

He'd moved invisibly through various Afghan villages and camps, blending in with the native population. He'd heard firsthand the whispered rumors about himself, the Gray Ghost—an American commando who'd infiltrated the Taliban. Tactical errors experienced by the insurgents—errors that benefited the Americans—were blamed on him. Women manipulated his legend, horrifying their children with fiendish tales of what would happen to them should the Gray Ghost come to their village, warning them to behave and to beware of strangers.

His mission hadn't been to kill any of the first tiers of Taliban officers. It had been much more focused than that. He'd been ordered to gain the trust of Ghalib Halim. Observe, learn, document, and report—learn what he could of the Taliban's internal leadership structure.

In addition to the years of Red Team training that he, Kit and Blade had undergone, he'd had a full year of specific training for his assignment. It had taken one year to establish his cover in Afghanistan, a year to move ever closer to Halim, and four years to wait and observe. The hardest fucking years of his life. His fellow soldiers were being targeted by snipers, IEDs, and ambushes every day while he moved among the enemy with the mind-bending speed of a threatened chameleon, helpless to protect them with anything other than the info he fed to Kit and Blade.

There were others like him, still embedded with the enemy, other linguistic savants. The forward eyes and ears—and sometimes guns—of secret American Red Teams.

And yet now, his team had become the targets here, on American soil. If the bastards were successful in Wolf Creek Bend, who would be next? Other retired warriors? Their families? Was this a testing ground? Or was this more personal? God, he wished he had answers.

"Can't sleep either?" Mandy's quiet voice seeped into his thoughts. He didn't answer her. He hadn't even been aware she'd come into the room. Some guard he was right now. He'd moved an oversized armchair back against the wall, in the corner, giving him a line of sight to the stairs, the kitchen, the hallway, and both front and back doors.

Mandy sat on the sofa. In the dim light of the

room, he could see that her back was upright and rigid, her hands tucked between her knees.

"What's going to happen, Rocco?" she whispered.

He'd like to tell her everything would be okay, that the good guys always won. But that was a pack of lies, and it was never a smart thing to lie to an angel.

"We're trained professionals, Em. We'll take out bad guys."

"But who are the bad guys? There have been no strangers in town. This is not an operation that can be run from a distance, is it? So they have to be here already. How will you know who to target?"

"We'll know."

Mandy got up and started pacing, rubbing her arms from the chilly night air. The skimpy tank top did little to provide warmth. Or cover of any sort. Every now and then, she'd pace in front of the wide bay window, silhouetting herself against the porch light.

Rocco uncrossed his legs, tried to ease the pressure on his groin. "Want me to tuck you back in bed?" *Please, please, go back to bed and quit torturing me.*

She stopped and faced him. "Only if you'll come with me."

"I won't."

"Then, no." She made a few more passes around the room.

"Mandy," he sighed, "come sit beside me."

For the space of a breath, she did not move, and then she was a flash of motion. She grabbed the quilt from the back of the sofa and folded herself up next to him in the wide chair, almost lying on top of him. The armchair was large, but it wasn't meant for two people. He set his gun down, then helped settle the quilt over her shoulders and wrapped his arm around her.

"Why did you move the chair over here?" she asked. He looked down at her but didn't give her an answer. He was able to see very little of her expression, but he felt the slight stiffening in her posture. "This is how you slept, even down at the bunkhouse, isn't it?" Again, he didn't answer. "Why?"

He kissed her forehead. He doubted she could see much of his face in the dark, but he didn't want to reveal more than was safe. "Because nightmares make bad bedmates."

She sighed and lowered her head to his shoulder. He could feel more questions brewing in her mind.

"Tell me about your wife, Rocco. What was her name?"

He sighed. This was bound to come up some time. Best answer her questions once and be done. "Her name was Kadisha Halim. She was the daughter of the village leader, a warlord we needed our eyes and ears on. His poppy business sent hundreds of recruits to Pakistan for training and founded terrorist cells across the world, even here. His village was a key stop on the many trails between Pakistan and Afghanistan, high in the Hindu Kush, so remote the coalition forces patrolled it only rarely and could never hold it. Marrying Kadisha was like getting the golden key. I had free and complete access to the village and its leaders, fighters, and their plans.

"Your brother and Blade were my handlers. For a few years, I was able to stream valuable information to our guys." *Tell her about Zavi. Tell her now,* a part of him urged. But he couldn't. He would have to tell her his command was convinced his son was dead, and those were words he could not speak.

"What happened?"

"The explosion." He shrugged. "Ended everything."

She moved slightly so that she could look up at him. "Have you remembered more of what happened that day?"

"No. I wish I did."

She settled against him once more, fitting into his side like his other half, a perfect match. Unable to stop himself, he touched the tips of his fingers to the soft skin of her chest, stroking along the rim of her flimsy tank top, up to her collarbone, and then to her neck. Reversing direction, he stroked downward, letting the backs of his fingers have the pleasure of touching her.

"When the others come, you will properly cover yourself."

Mandy smiled, unconsciously dropping the quilt away as she stretched like a cat. "When the others come, I will parade about in my bra and panties."

Rocco growled as his gaze took in her arching curves. "I don't want them looking at your skin." *It's mine alone to view and savor.*

"We aren't in Afghanistan, Rocco. You don't get to

tell me what to wear, or do, or think. A woman likes men to admire her. *I* like it. It makes me feel pretty."

Anger slashed through him at the thought of men touching her with their eyes. He cupped the back of her head, tangling his fingers in her hair as he leaned over her, drawing her back against the arm of the chair. "I will not have men ogle you."

"Why does it matter to you?"

Because you're mine. He pressed his face into her neck, letting his mouth discover what his fingers already knew—her skin was god-awful soft. He palmed a breast, knew his erection was like a metal pipe pressing against her hip. She wore no bra. Gripping her hair in his fist so that she would not move, he lifted her shirt, exposing a soft mound and its pebbled nipple.

Moonlight slashed across her face and chest. He held her gaze as he bent to taste her breast. His nostrils were flared, and he felt the tension in his face, in his whole body. He did not take her nipple. He nuzzled at the wide underside of her breast. She moaned. His cock hardened even more, throbbed painfully.

He cupped her soft flesh, pointing her hardened nipple toward his face. He stroked it over his open lips in a slow, terrible circle.

"This is why, Mandy. A man cannot look at your body without envisioning his hands, his mouth on you." His cock in you. "It is disrespectful. Of you. Of himself."

She arched against him as if hungry for more touching. "I cannot control what foolish thoughts men think."

"We have important work to do. Do you want us distracted beyond all reason, too far gone to help you?"

Mandy wrapped her arms around his neck. "There is only one man I want distracted beyond reason. Only one, Rocco. I will beg if I have to. I am not proud."

Rocco shifted upward slightly as he smoothed his hand over her cheek. "Forget me, Mandy. *We* cannot be. Not now." Perhaps not ever.

"Take me back to bed. Please."

He lifted her, and carried her to her room. When he set her on the bed, she took hold of his hand before he could pull away.

"Stay with me. I won't touch you. You need to rest before Kit and his men come. You can avoid sleeping as easily here next to me as you can in that chair in the living room."

Rocco stroked a finger down her temple. He shook his head. "Good night, Mandy."

Back in the living room, he sat in the armchair. Alone. The fabric was still heated where her body had been. His skin burned from her touch. Her taste. It would be like this the whole night, he knew—the specter of her nearness as terrible as actually holding her.

Hell. If he were going to burn, it might as well be for the flesh-and-blood woman as for her memory. He took up his cell phone and shotgun, then joined her in the bedroom. "Move over," he grunted, irritated as much with his weakness as his need.

He settled his shotgun on the floor and set his phone on her nightstand, then lied down on top of the covers. She curled into him, propping a knee on his thigh, her breasts against his ribs, her head on his shoulder.

"Is this you not touching me?" he asked.

"Hm-mm." She wiggled a bit closer. "It's already too late, you know. We already are something."

He reached a hand under her shirt, moving upward to capture her breast. "I know." And it hurt. Wanting her. Touching her. Leaving her.

Chapter 13

Late the next afternoon, Rocco put away the post-hole jack and the metal stakes he'd pulled from the old fence line. He'd continued with his normal work that day, after they had rearranged things in the basement to make the rooms ready for Kit and his team. George had been released from the hospital but wouldn't be allowed to return to work for another few days. The construction crew continued as usual. Mandy had worked with Kitano. Despite the shadow that hung over the riding center, she had a schedule to keep and there was still much work to be done.

A black SUV turned up the drive.

Rocco shoved his leather work gloves in a back pocket and picked up his shotgun, watching from inside the toolshed. He expected it was Kit, but wanted to be certain. He couldn't see inside the vehicle with its dark tinted windows, and that made him nervous.

He didn't have long to wait, however. Kit jumped out of the driver's side and hurried around to the passenger door. Rocco shouldered his gun and went to greet them.

"Back off, Kit. I'm not a goddamned toddler," Blade groused as Kit tried to help him get out of the SUV.

Rocco smiled. Some things never changed. "You sure about that? 'Cause you needed big, bad Kitten to bring you home," Rocco teased.

Blade's piercing gray eyes lifted to Rocco. For a moment, Blade studied him, missing nothing. It was uncanny how he could look at a man like that, peel all his protective layers off, and see the truth of what lay beneath. "You look good, Rocco. Kit had me thinking you'd taken up cutting yourself or some such bullshit."

"Hell, you know better than to listen to him," Rocco admonished as he held out a hand. Blade hooked his thumb around Rocco's and pulled him close for a shoulder bump. "I'm glad you guys are here," Rocco told them, "but I don't like it one bit."

Kit slapped him on the shoulder, then handed him a duffle bag. "Thought you'd keep all the fun to yourself?"

"Something like that. Where's the team you mentioned?"

"They stopped for dinner at the diner in town. Wanted to make it real obvious that the game had changed." Kit smiled.

Blade looked at Rocco and grinned. "You've heard of the subtle and patented 'Guns Blazing' approach?"

Rocco laughed. "You staying here or at your place, Blade?" he asked as he took up another duffle bag.

"Here, for now," Kit answered for him.

Rocco led them through the front door into Mandy's house. No sooner had the door closed than Mandy came running from the kitchen.

"Kit!"

"Hi, sis," Kit said, catching her up as she launched herself at him.

She pushed free and looked up at him, cupping his hard chin in her hands. "Wow. Look at you."

"What do you mean?" he said with a frown.

"You're all buff. And you've got that flat top. You look scary."

"I am scary."

Blade scoffed that off, stealing Mandy's attention. He stood inside the door, leaning on his cane.

"Hi, Ty," she greeted him, somewhat cautiously.

"What? No hug for the man who watched after your brother's ugly hide all these years?"

Mandy smiled and gave him a hug. Watching Blade's arm wrap around his woman, Rocco felt an unfamiliar tension ratchet up his nerves. He had the absurd drive to rip her out of Blade's hold—until he caught the look in his friend's eyes, the look of an orphan at Christmas time. Blade had no one, nothing to go home to. There would be no welcome home dinner for him. No one to weep tears of joy at his return. Rocco knew what that hollowness felt like, for he'd experienced that very thing not too long ago. He met Blade's gaze and watched him shutter away his emotions.

Blade straightened and looked down at Mandy. "Well, little sister, you sure filled out in all the right places," he said with a grin.

Rocco made a warning sound. Mandy moved to stand in front of him and leaned back against him.

Kit frowned, glaring at Rocco. "What the hell is this? I sent you to protect my sister, not take advantage of her."

"Dial it back, Kit." Rocco pushed Mandy behind him. "I don't like what you're implying."

Kit moved closer, his face dark with anger. "Implying, hell. I'm stating full out. You overstepped yourself."

"You got an issue with me, then let's take it outside. 'Cause, yeah, I got a thing for your sister."

"A 'thing?' What the hell does that mean?"

"It means I care for her."

"Shit. I care for her, too, Kit," Blade interjected helpfully, "but you aren't tearing me apart."

"Stay out of this, Blade." Kit was face to face with Rocco now. He was built heavier and had a few inches on Rocco, but such differences mattered little to either of them. "What are your intentions? My sister deserves better than a wham-bam, thank-you ma'am."

"Oh, for heaven's sake, Kit." Mandy leaned around Rocco's arm to speak—he blocked her from coming forward. "I'm not a child, so don't you two dare have this conversation without me. And what Rocco meant was that we're still discovering what it is we're feeling. Don't crowd us. Now, why don't you all go wash up?

I've got dinner ready."

Blade laughed. He clapped a hand on Kit's shoulder and steered him toward the bathroom. "Nice going. Would have been better if you two had come to blows, splattered some blood, broken some furniture. Next time, try harder, okay?"

Rocco had forgotten what a smart ass Blade could be. He rolled his shoulders, then followed his two friends. It was going to be interesting having them here.

Dinner was an event Rocco could have passed on. He didn't like sharing the table with Mandy and two other men, despite the fact that one was her brother. Mandy sat opposite Rocco, as she had for many meals. Unbidden, the memory of her sitting before him in her bra, laughing, being serious, being Mandy, popped into his mind—the night he'd driven her to put the brakes on their relationship.

"It's great that you haven't changed the place much, Mandy. I can still feel your grandparents here," Blade said. Rocco narrowed his gaze on the man, trying to read beneath his statement. Blade was an expert in manipulative psychology. He knew, always, what to say and when to get the results he wanted. Exactly what was he after here?

"I didn't want to make many changes. I liked that homey feeling. It's as if they've just stepped out for a little bit and will be right back."

Blade smiled at her. Rocco lost his appetite. "Your grandfather was a big influence in my life. He stood strong against my dad. He's the only one who ever did,

I think."

"What he did for you when you broke your leg, getting you to stretch it out by riding and doing all the different chores he had you do inspired me to go into hippotherapy. I noticed your injury's in the same leg. I can massage it for you, if you like."

"Sure. That'd be great."

"No," Rocco growled. What the hell was wrong with him? Blade was like a brother to him. Rocco should be glad that Mandy could help him, but all he could think of was her hands on his friend's thigh.

"I'm a trained physical therapist, Rocco. It's what I do. Or what I was meant to do, before all of this." Her voice broke, and it was that thread of emotion that made him relent.

"Then you aren't doing it alone."

Blade sighed. "Fine. Rocco can join us, because if he doesn't, I won't get the massage. And if Rocco comes, Kit has to as well because he's too damned curious to be left out."

Kit frowned as if he were no more pleased about Mandy treating Blade than Rocco was. "We've got the other guys coming shortly. Let's get them settled first. Besides, I need to talk to both of you. Rocco, if you have gear down at the bunkhouse, bring it up here. You can bunk with me." He looked at his sister and added in a grim voice, "Or Mandy."

Kit's phone rang. "Bolanger," he answered.

"Hello, Mr. Bolanger. Glad to see you arrived safely," came a smooth voice on the other end.

Kit hit a couple of buttons on his phone, triggering the voice recorder. "Who is this?" he asked, though he knew the answer. Amir Hadad, lieutenant to a powerful Afghan druglord.

"I am disappointed that you don't recognize me. I know your name, where you live, who your friends are, what your sister is doing. I know so very much about you, yet you know nothing about me."

"So enlighten me," Kit urged.

"My name is not important. What really matters is that I am going to destroy your life as you did mine. First, I will kill your friends, who themselves are guilty of heinous war crimes. And then I will terrify your sister, a process that has already begun. Perhaps I shall offer her protection as only a strong and intelligent warrior can—"

"Well, that eliminates you then, Amir." Kit interrupted the man's diatribe.

"Ah, so you do know me. I will destroy your village, as you did mine," the man continued, his voice strident. "It is the will of Allah that justice be granted. An eye for an eye. *Allah akbar*, Mr. Bolanger." The call ended. Kit stopped the recording.

Kit looked at Rocco and Blade. "*Allah akbar*, my ass." He played the call back. "Amir Hadad is here, in town. He's watching us."

Mandy gasped. Rocco reached across the table and took hold of her hand. He could feel her trembling and tightened his grip. "Amir started it, but we'll end it."

"Mandy, do you mind if I talk to Rocco and Blade

for a few minutes? We'll go outside."

Reluctantly, she let go of Rocco's hand. "Not at all.
I'll get some coffee started."

Rocco and Blade followed Kit as he moved across
the porch and walked into the middle of the wide,
circular dirt driveway. Rocco shoved his hands in his
pockets and glanced at Blade to see if he knew what
Kit was up to. Blade's face revealed nothing, which
meant he knew exactly what Kit was going to say.

"What's going on, Kit?"

"I want to talk to you about joining Tremaine
Industries."

Rocco had mixed feelings about Kit's new
endeavor. The Army's Red Team Program produced
assassins—the coldest, deadliest killers in the service or
out of it. Going into business with any number of other
sociopaths wasn't something to take lightly. "Who else
is in?"

"Blade's in."

Rocco looked at his friend. Blade smiled and
shrugged. "What can I say? I like guns."

"You know Max Cameron, Val Parker, and Kelan
Shiozski," Kit continued. Those were names Rocco
hadn't heard in years, guys he'd completed the Red
Team training with. "The others finished the program
before Blade and me or came after you. You'll meet
them tonight. Tremaine Industries is a sanctioned
company that's well funded and equipped. Their work
led them to the group behind Mandy's problems.
Owen Tremaine wants you, too, because while

collectively we know several languages, none of us has your linguistic capabilities."

"I'm done, Kit. I'm fried," Rocco told him.

"Don't decide yet. We'll talk more about it later, with the rest of the guys." He looked at each of them. "I think it may be the only way to keep Mandy safe. And we'd be able to complete something we left unfinished in Afghanistan."

Rocco frowned. "What's that?"

"Take down Abdul Baseer al Jahni and his little flunky, Amir Hadad."

* * *

Mandy waited with the guys for the rest of Kit's team to arrive. Rocco was pacing, which heightened her nervousness. She jumped when Kit's phone rang.

"They're here," he said as he went to open the front door. The dogs started barking when the first of the six men crossed the porch. Each of them was carrying large black equipment cases and heavy duffel bags. When they were all in the living room, the space shrank to half its size. Every one of them was tall, wide, and built for fighting. Though they were dressed in civilian clothes, no one could mistake them as anything but warriors.

Three of them came forward right away to greet Rocco. They grabbed hands and bumped shoulders, pounding each other on the arm.

"Damn, it's good to see you again," a tall, black-haired warrior said. He had warm, olive-colored skin with dark brown eyes and arching black brows. His high cheekbones gave him the look of an American Indian. "When we didn't hear from you, Max and I checked in with Kit. Heard you'd taken a long-term assignment in Afghanistan."

"Yeah, you were under, what, seven years? Sure took you long enough. But you always were the slow kid in class," said a man who looked like a Viking warrior.

"Slow kid? What the hell, Val? He smoked your ass in training. He smoked all of us," the third man clustered around Rocco said. He looked like a pirate with the red bandana he'd tied around his head like a skullcap and his bushy beard and moustache. Blue ink covered his arms in a complex pattern that looked Celtic.

Val grinned. "I'm glad you're okay." He paused and gave Rocco a searching look. "You are okay, aren't you? You look like hell."

Rocco shook his head and gave them a sheepish grin. "Never could hide anything from you."

Mandy reached over and slipped her hand into Rocco's. One by one, the men became aware of her. It was unnerving having all nine of them turn their focus on her. Rocco wrapped an arm around her shoulders. She felt an odd thrill at the thought that he was staking a claim.

Kit glared at him, still unreconciled to the fact that they were together. He made the introductions. "This is my sister, Mandy Fielding and that's Rocco Silas," he said for the benefit of the men who hadn't yet met Rocco. "You guys know Blade. We'll go around the room." He thrust a thumb toward the man leaning against the wall. "That's Owen Tremaine, founder of Tremaine Industries." His light, blond hair was shaggy and had a slight curl to it. His tan face was weathered and clean-shaven. The fine lines about his ice-blue eyes told a story his mouth would never reveal. His cold gaze met Rocco's for a long, assessing look before he glanced at Mandy and nodded.

"Mandy, that's Max Cameron, Tremaine Industries' systems expert," Kit said as he indicated the man with the bandana. Shadows darkened his hazel eyes as if he'd seen more of life than he'd wanted to. He looked like a knot of energy. Mandy wondered how he could sit still and be focused enough to be their tech guy.

Next, Kit nodded to the man whose rich butterscotch hair fell in waves from his forehead—the Viking warrior in the trio who'd greeted Rocco. Thick brows framed Caribbean blue eyes. A trim beard and moustache wrapped around his mouth in a way that didn't quite obscure his dimples. "That's Valentino Parker, sniper extraordinaire."

Kit gestured toward a man who appeared to be Puerto Rican, with warm mocha skin and black eyes. "Angel Cordova, Tremaine's engineer and demolitions expert." He was built like a wrestler, with arms as wide as her thighs. He had a great square jaw, a mobile mouth with large, white teeth. His hair was thick and wavy, cut close to his head.

"Kelan Shiozski," Kit continued, pointing to the next man. "He can move like a shadow," he told Mandy. Kelan, the third member of the trio around Rocco, had inky, black hair that was straight and fell to his shoulders. He looked like a tribal warrior from long ago.

"Greer Dawson is a systems guy, too." Greer looked like an all-American suburban athlete, lean and clean-shaven with silky brown hair that curled about his ears. Thick brown brows arched over whiskey-colored eyes.

Mandy looked at each of them as he was introduced. She tried to associate each name with a face, but feared she'd get it scrambled for a while. She'd never seen such a large group of fierce men. She did notice that, except for Owen, each of the other men had acknowledged Rocco with a demeanor that was neither assessing nor judgmental. He was one of them—nothing more needed to be said.

"It's nice to meet you all," Mandy greeted them. "Thank you for coming out to help. I don't really understand what's going on, but if Kit brought you here, it can't be a good situation." She looked at Kit. "We've cleared out the basement for you. There are three bedrooms down there, two with double beds and one with two bunks. Then there are two more bedrooms with twin beds in the bunkhouse. Put your team where you want them."

Kit had them move the cases into the basement and their duffels into the bunkhouse and the bedrooms downstairs. He and Blade were going to take the bedrooms upstairs.

While they were getting settled, Mandy looked up at Rocco. "Have you decided who you're bunking with yet—me or one of the guys?" she asked with a saucy smile.

He looked at her, surprised at her invitation. "You ready for that? 'Cause I've been doing fine in an armchair."

"No more armchairs. You need to sleep."

"Then I better bunk with one of the guys."

She put her hands on her hips and glared at him. He laughed and lifted her up into a tight embrace, holding her captive so that his mouth could take hers. She surrendered in his arms, circling his neck with her hands as her lips parted beneath his. Her acceptance of him was the most seductive thing Rocco had ever experienced. Their tongues stroked each other, gently, slowly. Reverently.

He drew back and looked down at her, touching a hand to her face, shocked by the changes she'd wrought in him in such a short time. Good Lord, he was falling hard for this woman.

"Well, it's a true fact that you're a hell of a lot easier on the eyes than any of the team. If you have room for me, I'll stay with you. I can sleep on the floor."

She smiled and slowly shook her head. "My bed or nothing. Your choice."

He frowned down at her. "There is no choice, then."

"Get a room, you two," Blade growled as he slung his duffel over his shoulder and claimed one of the bedrooms down the hall. "We've got a war to conduct not a porn flick to film."

When everyone was settled and the equipment had been set up, Owen convened a meeting in the downstairs rec room. As the men moved downstairs, Kit pulled Mandy aside.

"Can you give us a few minutes? Owen and I need to bring everyone up to speed. We'll have you brief us about what's been happening afterward. Gather up your files covering the construction project and bring them when I call for you. Greer and Max will start digging through them tomorrow."

"No problem. I'll be ready when you are." Mandy collected her files and stacked them near the stairs. She poured herself a cup of coffee in the kitchen and discovered the new team had brought in a ton of food supplies in coolers and bags. She stored what she could in the freezer, fridge, and cupboard, then boxed some of it to take down to the bunkhouse in the morning. It began to feel as if they were preparing for a siege. The whole thing was terribly unnerving.

Downstairs, the guys settled around the room, some sitting on either of the two sofas, some leaning against the walls. Greer and Max turned their desk chairs to face the room instead of the long, white tables loaded with equipment. Owen closed the basement door. "Did you sweep the basement for bugs?" he asked Max.

"We're clear," Max said.

Owen nodded for Kit to begin the briefing. "Tremaine Industries provides security and intelligence services to various U.S. government agencies," Kit said to Rocco. "They've been contracted to work on a case out this way involving an Afghan druglord whom Blade, Rocco, and I know quite well—Abdul Baseer al Jahni—and the Wyoming-based organized hate group he's aligning himself with." Kit looked at Rocco and Blade.

"Is al Jahni in the country?" Rocco asked.

"We think so. And his hate group of preference is the White Kingdom Brotherhood, or the WKBs."

Kit sent a look around the room at the rest of the guys. "At the beginning of this year, the three of us, Blade, Rocco and I, executed a kill order to take out a warlord named Ghalib Halim. Rocco had been positioned to collect intelligence on him. Halim wasn't merely a village elder, a fierce general, and a Taliban officer, he was also a pivotal link in Abdul Baseer al Jahni's drug trafficking infrastructure. al Jahni replaced him with Amir Hadad. Amir's a graduate from the University of Colorado. He is the one facilitating al Jahni's partnership with the WKB to distribute al Jahni's heroin here in the U.S."

"What do we know about the WKB?" Kelan asked.

"They're a white supremacist gang that's thriving—in prisons and out—in Wyoming and nineteen other states including California, Florida, and Virginia,"

Owen answered. "They have about ten thousand members nationally who are not currently incarcerated. They're making alliances with any criminal group of any racial mix that helps them grow their power network, including the Mexican drug cartels and Afghan druglords."

"I gave you the identities of the WKBers who got through to Ghalib Halim," Rocco reminded Kit. "They bragged to us about getting men in their squad killed while on patrols so that they could be taken by Halim's men. They caused some of the friendly fire incidents that hit the news. The bastards knew being captured was the only way to get close enough for a meeting with Halim. Their allegiance was only to the WKB, never to their units or their country."

Rocco looked around at the team. No point telling them how easy it was to assume a false identity—they were all masters of that art. "I had the traitors branded before they left Halim's hospitality. I wanted to be able to find them again if needed. And I made it clear that they were to make a similar mark on their brothers and associates—anyone Halim and al Jahni could trust once they came stateside."

Kit slowly smiled, holding Rocco's gaze. "What's the mark?"

"A crescent moon and star right here," Rocco said, pointing to the area below his left ear.

"It'll be interesting to see how pervasive that's become among the WKBers." Owen said.

"We believe al Jahni is retaliating against the three

of us for the damage we caused his supply chain. He's learned who we are and where we live, and he's sending a message to his associates—allies and enemies—that he'll recoup an eye-for-an-eye if anyone dares move against him. At anytime. In any country. He may be building this into a *fatwā* targeted against anyone with military connections here in the U.S. in order to grow his power network back home.

"This situation is a Pandora's Box. If it isn't quickly contained, there could be a flood of retaliatory actions taken on our soil against our troops, peace officers, and even civilians—families of our warriors. Our warriors' identities are concealed during missions, but not on base, not from the public, and not from the Afghan askars working with us. Once an enemy knows our name and our point of origin, they have everything they need to hit us hard here at home."

Kit sent another look around the room, waiting for the full impact of his words to settle in. "Tremaine Industries has been retained to discover who al Jahni's operatives are, how he manages them, how he put his team together, how he's funding it. When we have our information, we bring them in for further questioning. We do not, and I repeat—we do not—have kill authority. We take the motherfuckers alive if it's a kill or capture situation."

Owen gave Rocco an assessing look. "So now you know what we're up against. Before we go any further, I need to know if you're in or out."

Kit nodded, his expression grim. "Rocco, you met

some of the key White Kingdom Brotherhood liaisons. You speak the languages of all the warlords in al Jahni's network. You're intimately familiar with their culture, their thinking, and their strategies. We need your knowledge and expertise."

Rocco met Kit's hard gaze. Truthfully, he knew he didn't have what it took to do another long-term undercover assignment. "I'm done, Kit. I can't go under again like I was."

"We won't be sending you overseas," Owen told him. "We need you here working with us—stateside. I need you to stay in the game."

Rocco looked away. It was no fucking game. Men's souls were at stake. But Mandy was also in danger. So were these men and others like them—and their families. He looked around the room at the men Kit had assembled.

Val, Max, and Kelan were men he considered brothers, as were Kit and Blade. The others had to be made of the same steel, forged in the same fire. They had all survived the Program to become Red Team members. Every one of them was a well-honed killing machine. He glanced at Blade, who started to grin.

"Aw, hell. I'm in," Rocco caved.

Kit came over and shook his hand, pulling him in for a bro hug. "I never thought you were out. Let's get Mandy down here to go over what's been happening."

Mandy walked through the basement door that Owen held for her. She looked around the space that had served various purposes to her family since she was a child, but none this terrifying. In the short time they'd been here, the new team had assembled an entire war room, with maps, white boards, and computers lining the circumference of the rectangular space.

The old rec room, which was large enough for two suites of living room furniture, seemed to shrink in on itself with nine very large warriors in it.

She set her folders on one of the folding tables the team had brought, then went to stand near Rocco. He reached over and took hold of her hand, providing an anchor in a world that had gone crazy.

"Mandy," Owen started, "as you may have surmised, the problems you've been having here aren't the work of mischievous kids. It's intentional sabotaging by some enemies of the United States, enemies your brother, Blade and Rocco faced overseas. It's a big deal, and it's why we're here. Those enemies have brought the war stateside, and they're using it as a distraction to cover their real purpose—growing their drug network."

Mandy couldn't hide her shock. She looked from Owen to Kit, then Rocco. Their serious faces drove home the fact that this was a major issue.

"The people in question are teaming up with the White Kingdom Brotherhood. You may have heard of them?"

The WKBers had a big spread less than fifty miles from the ranch. "Yes. Everyone here does. They keep to themselves up at their compound," she said.

"They've been there since before I was born. They've had a few clashes with the town and the law here and there, but none in a long while. They sometimes go to Winchester's. Hal, the owner, has had some run-ins with them. But generally, they don't give us any trouble, and we leave them alone."

"They aren't a benign biker gang," Kit told her. "They're colluding with Afghan criminals to take their drug network global. They're still active, still lethal, still spreading hate, and they need to be stopped."

Mandy looked around the room. "So that's what this is about, then." Rocco squeezed her hand, worried about how this added stress would affect her.

"Why don't you bring the guys up to speed on what's been happening here," Kit prompted.

When Mandy finished, Greer asked, "What contractors has George brought onsite?"

"There were several bids, but I think he ended up going with just one who could handle the plumbing. He has an electrician on staff. And there was some flooring work, but he decided to keep that in-house as well. I brought my files so that you can look through them."

"Wait a minute," Rocco stopped her. "The sheriff said that plumber was the only plumbing and HVAC guy in town. He's the one who worked on George's furnace, too. And didn't you say he was at the diner that day I felt an enemy?"

Kit frowned at him. "Whoa. What happened at the diner?"

"Mandy and I went there for lunch one day last week. I felt an enemy in the room. Triggered a nasty panic attack." Rocco sighed and glanced at Kit, who exchanged a look with Owen.

"Look man," Kit told him, "we all know you're working through some shit. Your instincts are probably spot-on. They always were. We'll look into the plumber."

"It can't be him," Mandy argued. "He's been here for two years. He bought out the business from its old owner. Everyone knows him. He's not a stranger. And he's not a drug addict."

"It's a place to start, Em. Nothing more. Nothing less," Kit told her.

Rocco went to the maps and showed the team the areas where he could tell patrols had taken up observation positions. "These are the ridges where we're vulnerable from sniper fire," he said, pointing on the topographical map to a few high points that overlook the property. "In the morning, I'll give you a tour."

When the briefing concluded, Owen speared her with an intent look. "This is a sensitive operation, Mandy. You've been brought into it because you're already in the middle of it. What we've discussed here is not to leave the premises. Is that understood?"

"Of course."

"If anyone asks what the team is doing here, we've come for some R&R and to give you a hand getting the center open. Given the problems you've had, no one except the bad guys should doubt the cover. Under no circumstances are you to have visitors over or bring anyone down here."

"I understand." She crossed her arms to keep herself from surrendering to a burgeoning sense of terror.

* * *

It was late that night before Rocco, Kit, Ty, and Mandy gathered in the upstairs living room. Ty was absently running his fist over the knotted muscles of his thigh. She retrieved a towel and her massage lotion, then faced him.

"Let's do that massage. The lotion I have contains a mild heating and numbing agent. It should help ease the pain. Tomorrow, I'll massage it again. And I'll give you some exercises you can do to help stretch and strengthen your leg."

Ty leaned back against the sofa, spreading himself open for her as he gestured for her to begin.

"I need you to take off your jeans, please," she asked quietly.

He stood and grinned at her. "Sure thing, sweet knees." He dropped his pants, exposing the black boxer briefs he wore and his raging hard-on.

Kit cursed. "Cover that thing up, would you?"

"Mandy—" Rocco growled, warning her away from Ty.

"Enough you two. Leave the man alone." She handed Ty the towel she'd brought.

"Yeah. I haven't had any since before I was shot, you know. It's not like I can control my reaction when a beautiful woman tells me to get naked."

"Blade, I don't think you need to be conscious for the massage," Rocco warned.

Mandy knelt on the floor beside his leg. "The wound looks good, Ty. You had some excellent surgeons work on it. It will take a while to build up your muscle strength again. You're favoring your thigh, which is throwing you off in other areas—your back, your hips, your shoulders. Let's get this thigh a little more relaxed."

She poured the oil into her hands and rubbed them together to heat it up. The light scent of flowers perfumed the air. She knew Rocco watched every stroke she made, but she forced herself to close her mind to his reaction.

"Mandy, how are you funding the construction?" Kit asked.

"Grandpa left me some money from his life insurance policy. And the town has held a couple of fundraisers for the center. I have two grants, one federal, one from a private investment firm."

"Who was the private firm?" Rocco asked.

"RKT, Inc.," Ty answered.

Mandy looked at him. "How did you know?"

"We invested in it?" Kit asked, a surprised pleasure in his voice.

"We needed a tax deduction. She needed the money," Ty answered.

Mandy frowned at Rocco.

"The three of us started an investment company years ago," he told her. "I had all that income from my salary that I wasn't using. Blade started investing it for me, then we used it as seed money for larger investments. He's got an instinct for it that neither Kit nor I have. He and Kit bought in. None of us needs to work another day if we don't want to. We can live off the interest the fund makes. It took a hit a few years back, but it's already recovered that loss and then some."

She looked at Ty, then Rocco and Kit. "I don't know what to say. I wouldn't have been able to do this without your grant. There was one other donation, but I don't know whom it came from. I found five thousand dollars in cash in an envelope on my doorstep one morning. There was a note that it should be used for the center, but no signature."

"Do you still have the note?" Kit asked her.

"I do. It's in the files downstairs."

"Good. I'll send it off for fingerprints. See if we get anything."

As Mandy finished working on Ty's leg, she heard Kit ask Rocco, "So what's with the beard, man? Thought you said once you were stateside, you'd never have a beard again?"

It wasn't so much the question that caught Mandy's interest as the silence that followed it. She looked over at Rocco, waiting for his answer, disliking the changed tension in the room. She nodded at Ty, then straightened.

Rocco's face was taut, his eyes bleak. "I'm going back."

Kit cursed.

"Rocco, he's gone," Ty said as he drew his jeans up and fastened them. "We looked everywhere, talked to all our informants, and had our female translators question women from several villages. There was no hint, no whisper, not even any misinformation. No one took our bribes or payments or tried to swap favors. There was nothing."

Had someone been left behind? Mandy wondered.

"And that didn't seem like odd behavior? Didn't make you suspicious?" Rocco asked. "They're afraid. Terrified. They know something. Someone has him. He did not die."

"What are you talking about?" Mandy asked Rocco.

His gaze slashed her way. She could tell he did not want to answer. "My son."

Mandy felt the room spin. He had a son. First, a wife he didn't think to mention, and now a son. How many more surprises was he keeping? She'd lost her heart to a man who did not trust her and would not share his life—his past or his future—with her.

He could give her only the now, and God knew, if that was all she could get, she'd take it.

Kit stood up. The cold glare he gave Rocco chilled the room. "You'd go back knowing they'd send one of us after you? You're too dangerous to be allowed to go rogue. Your death would be sanctioned. You'd make one of us, your brothers, kill you."

Rocco gave a dry laugh, an empty, humorless sound as he, too, came to his feet. "A Red Team assassin would be the least of my problems."

Blade gripped his shoulder. "Rocco, Rocco, he's dead."

"No. I still feel him. He lives."

"You feel what an amputee feels—a phantom reality. The horror of his death is too terrible to accept."

The hard planes of Rocco's face turned rigid. He shoved free of Blade's hand. "No. I feel him." Rocco pounded his chest. "Here." His voice was raw, as if it came from his spirit not his throat. "He lives. He breathes. He cries for me."

Blade put his hand on Rocco's chest, his fingers spread wide. "That's because this is where he lives. It's where he will always be, where you will always know him."

Silence. Rocco choked on a harsh breath. His gaze darted around the room. Mandy saw the panic in his eyes, fear the likes of which she'd only seen in abused animals. He stormed out of the house, slamming through the front door. The dogs cowered and looked over at her.

Mandy didn't move. No one did. She covered her mouth, trying to bottle her emotions. She wouldn't cry. She looked over at her brother. He blinked the moisture from his eyes and glared at Blade.

Blade stood with his hands on his hips, his head

hanging low. Mandy started to follow Rocco. "Leave him," Blade ordered.

"I will not. I can't leave him like that. You saw how he was."

Blade's face was like stone, his gray eyes emotionless. "He needs time to process things. He has to think it through, has to accept his son is dead. When he does, I honestly believe the nightmares, all this crazy shit he's going through, will get better."

"Leave him to it, Mandy," Kit bit out.

Mandy picked up her oil and the towel Ty had used, then left the room. Her hands shook as she put the lotion away and the towel in the laundry. She heard Kit and Blade in quiet conversation as she took the two strays for their last potty break of the day.

She closed the back door and stood in the cool night air as the dogs saw to their needs. Folding her arms around her middle, she let her pain break free. She dropped down to the top step and wept for Rocco, for his son, his wife. He was like the wind. She could no more stop or redirect or soothe him than she could a tornado.

God, he had a son. Believing his boy was still alive, he must be going insane with worry. No wonder he was so broken. Had his boy been in the explosion with him? Had he been injured, too? Was he dead as Kit and Blade thought? She didn't doubt they'd scoured the countryside for his son. And she didn't doubt that Rocco still felt a connection to him. Her heart ached for all of them.

"Hey." Mandy heard Kit behind her. "Want some company?"

Mandy shrugged. He would stay no matter what she said. She moved to make room for him, drying her eyes on the sleeve of her wrist as she did so.

"I'm sorry about that. I guess you didn't know about his son."

She shook her head as she tightened her arms about her waist. "What other secrets does he have, Kit? What other things don't I know about him?"

"I don't know, and even if I did, it wouldn't be my place to tell you. I can tell you he's a good guy. He's someone who understands the arcane nuances that define a culture, a people. That makes him dangerous and effective as an undercover operative. Did you know he's a linguistic savant?"

Mandy looked at her brother. She sniffled and nodded. "You asked him to work for Owen's company, didn't you?"

"I did. He's very good at what we do. It takes a long time to train an operative. Even discounting Rocco's linguistic skill, he isn't easily replaceable."

"What are you guys? Why would you be sent to kill Rocco?"

From the look Kit gave her, she could tell he was considering his words. "We're an elite unit of soldiers. That's all I can tell you. We're allowed to quit or retire, but if any of our own were to go off-grid, one of us would be sent after him."

"He's broken, Kit. I don't think he can do what

you need him to do."

"You ever hear of getting back in the saddle, sis?"

"There's a time and place for that, Kit. This may not be it. He isn't whole yet. I've seen him crash." She shook her head and looked away. "I don't know what would happen if he were to break all the way."

* * *

A noise roused Mandy from sleep hours later. The room was dark. She felt like a kid again, waking when Grandpa rose early to run the plow. He'd give her a sip of sweet coffee from his Thermos, then send her back to bed. He'd grown crops on the lower plateaus—corn, wheat, alfalfa—to supplement their income, and spent many long days in the spring and summer working his two jobs.

She laid in bed now, remembering her Grandma in the kitchen, getting breakfast started on those early mornings. In her sleep-hazed mind, all was right in the world. As she woke, memory faded and reality settled around her like a thousand blankets—dark, heavy, and suffocating.

She reached out to the mattress beside her, searching for Rocco. He wasn't there. Had he come to bed at all? She remembered his revelation about his son and his intent to return to Afghanistan to search for him, a thought that filled Mandy with dread.

She went to the window and spread the curtains. Someone was in the far pasture, standing in the headlights of the tractor. Rocco. He was using the fence post jack to hoist the old metal posts out of the ground. The clock read 2:00 a.m. She drew a hoodie on over her long sleeping tee, leaving it unzipped, then shoved her feet into her work boots. She knew she looked ridiculous but didn't care.

She made a beeline for Rocco with the dogs close at her heels, crossing the first field to get to the far pasture.

"Rocco." He didn't respond, just kept working the jack to yank the post out of the hard ground. When the post came free, he tossed it down and set the jack over the next one a few feet away.

"Rocco!" He ignored her as he began jacking the post. "Rocco, listen to me!" she said, stepping into the tractor headlights, touching his shoulder. He shrugged her off.

"Leave me, Mandy."

"No. Rocco, don't do this. Stop."

The jack freed the post. He threw it aside and moved to the next post, shoving the jack handle hard for several pumps.

"Rocco—"

"Jesus, Em. What do you want me to do? I can't sleep—there's no fucking way I'm gonna lie down and let the nightmares eat at me. You'd think I'd lost my mind again if I took off jogging for a few hours. You don't want me to sit up, sit still, sit quietly, and let the night pass. I can't go to bed and just hold you because I can't be near you without wanting to fuck you. And that shit ain't happening because you're not ready for it and I'm not staying. I'm not staying, Em, and likely I won't make it back. So I'm not doing you any favors by letting you think we have chance. Because we don't. Not a single goddamned chance in hell."

The headlights illuminated the angry twist of his features, the fury and anguish in his eyes. He moved to the next post. She didn't know what to say. What was there to say? There was nothing he wanted to hear, nothing he would listen to. His hurt was so far beyond her reach, there was no aid she could render.

She felt empty inside. And very, very alone. She started back for the house, her heart ripping apart with each step. From the corner of her eye, she saw Rocco straighten. Metal clinked as he threw the latest post like a spear on top of other ones.

Rocco cursed. "What do you want from me, Mandy?" She didn't stop. She didn't know how to answer that question so she said nothing.

"He lives," Rocco shouted. "My son is not goddamned dead. He lives, Mandy." His broken cry stopped her. She looked at him standing with his shoulders slumped, his gloved hands empty, his heart laid bare in the bright headlights of her old tractor.

She started back for him, walking, then running. She leaped into his arms. He caught her up, held her in a vice grip as he buried his face in her neck and wept. She cried, too, as she stroked his hair. His sobs were ragged, broken, keening, so filled with pain she thought her own heart would rupture.

Eventually, he grew quiet. She pulled back and

looked at him. His eyes were searching her face, looking for answers she didn't have. She kissed his cheek, the corner of his mouth, pausing there, waiting for him to accept or reject what she was offering. He pressed her face into his, slowing his breathing to match hers. When a ragged breath broke free, he interrupted it by taking her mouth. She became his entire focus. He bent his head to fit his mouth against hers as his tongue swept inside to find hers.

Gradually, Rocco became aware of other things about them, the heat of her body against his, desire swelling, consuming him. He ran a hand down her back, over her bottom. He cupped her buttocks, lifted her against himself, moving them out of the headlights.

"Open for me. Wrap your legs around me." When Mandy locked her ankles around his hips, he groaned. She laughed against his mouth. Laughed. The sound did something to his insides. Tied him up, set him free. He didn't know, only that he wanted more of it, more of her and her joy. He lifted her higher and rocked himself against her, feeling the ridge of his erection move against her core, registering a oneness with himself, with the world, with this woman he'd never felt before. And still he wanted more, wanted all of her.

He drew his gloves off his hands with his teeth, switching the hands beneath her bottom as he removed the other one. "I want to be in you, Mandy."

"Yes," she answered, her mouth against his.

"Open my pants. Take me out. Let me in." She did as he ordered, flicking the button loose on his pants, unzipping his fly. The pressure of her hand on that part of his clothing was almost enough to unman him. He jerked hard against her touch. And then he felt her fingers in the waistband of his briefs, inside them, finding him, grasping him.

He tossed his head back and dragged a deep breath into his lungs. And then he was kissing her again, eating her mouth, hungering for more. More. He dragged the hem of her nightshirt free, baring her core. Now only her panties separated them. He didn't want to set her down long enough to have her remove them. With her legs still locked around his hips, he held her bottom with one hand and pushed the lacy covering aside, then slid his fingers into her sweet folds. She was wet, ready.

"Love me, Mandy."

"I do. I do, Rocco."

"Put me in you. Do it now." He watched as she moved slightly, positioning him. He lifted her, let her own their coupling. She slid him inside her, slowly, slowly, until he was fully seated. It felt so good. He gritted his teeth, aching for her, throbbing, needing to break free. He held her hips and began pumping himself into her, feeling every inch of his cock slide in and out of her warmth.

She kissed him, moaning into his mouth. Their tongues danced and pressed against each other, sliding and retreating as his cock worked her sheath. He gripped her with one hand again as he freed a hand to touch her curls, her clitoris. He gently pressed the swollen nub, feeling her tighten around his cock.

And then her legs tightened, and she was bucking against him, pressing, pleading for more, her small muscles gripping him, squeezing. He gave it to her, gave her all of himself. Holding her with both hands, he pumped all the way into her, out fast and in hard. Again. And again until he met his release.

He continued holding her until the last echoes of passion faded from them. "Rocco, take me to bed. If you can't sleep, I know we can find better ways to spend the time than having you out here working, or running for miles, or sitting awake in a chair." She cupped his face and smiled at him. "Yes?"

He smiled back at her, wondering at his incredible good fortune to have a woman like Mandy in his life. God, he hoped he made it back to her. "Yes," he answered. "Yes."

He set her on her feet, then righted himself. He climbed into the tractor seat and shut it down. They walked slowly back to the house, arms around each other. Mandy waited under the covers while Rocco showered. He drew his briefs on, then got into bed next to her. He lifted his arm and waited for her to scoot close to him.

"Why haven't you gone back to Afghanistan yet?"

He sighed. "I need to get my head on straight before heading back. And I have to remember what happened the day of the explosion. Afghanistan is a deadly place, full of mines and scorpions, snipers and assassins. I have to be fully engaged. The explosion was almost four months ago, now. When Kit had me extracted, it was by force. I was broken. I'd become more Afghan than American. I didn't want to be taken out. I wanted to stay and search for Zavi. I honestly cannot remember my first two weeks back stateside. They brought me back in restraints, heavily sedated. For the next ten weeks, they had me on a dozen different kinds of meds, trying to find the right ones that would numb my emotions, help me sleep, wake me up, enhance my appetite, calm my anxieties. I was fucked all the hell sideways.

"The only way I could get out of there was to settle down, eat whatever they gave me, pretend to sleep. I knew they watched me sleep. I would fake REM sleep cycles but stay awake. If they saw me having nightmares, I wouldn't have been released. I went to the therapy sessions. I listened when I was expected to, lied when I was expected to talk.

"Eventually, they thought I was recovered enough to be discharged. I went home, or at least, I went to the ranch where I grew up. My mom had died while I was in training, so there was no one there for me, no reason to stay. The rancher she worked for retired to Florida. The ranch had folded. No one was there. Just the wind and dust.

"And then Kit asked me to come here." He paused, looking at her. The moonlight caught a shimmer of tears in her eyes. "You're the best thing that ever happened to me, Mandy." He looked at her. "It's because of you that I can eat, can touch someone when I need to. I'm even sleeping better. I'm almost ready to go back. But I want to see you safe before I go. And I still need to remember what happened that day."

Mandy reached over to grip his hand, threading her fingers through his. She lifted them and brought them to her mouth. "You go when you have to go, Rocco. And you come back when you can. I will be waiting here for you. Do you understand me? This is your home. You belong here. When you find your son, you bring him home. I'll redo my old room in trucks and Transformers and Spiderman for him."

"His name is Zaviyar."

"I like that name." She grew pensive. "Do you think he could be happy here?"

"He'll love it. He'll love you." He pulled his hand free of hers so that he could cup the back of her head, letting his thumb stroke her cheek. "Thank you for believing that he's alive."

"I believe in you, Rocco. You'll find him, and you'll bring him home. Or you'll find his grave, and then we'll know."

Chapter 14

Rocco came to an abrupt stop when he entered the kitchen side door the next morning. None of the guys had been up when he left to feed Kitano, but they were gathered in the living room now. Seeing him, they grew silent.

A blast of tension sheered through him. He had no doubt this little gathering had something to do with what he'd revealed last night. He walked into the living room, confronting the group of sober-faced men. He looked from Kit to Blade, then Owen and the others.

Owen broke the silence. "Kit told me about your intentions to go back to Afghanistan to find your son."

Rocco shot a glance at Kit. "That's right."

"When you're ready, you pick one of the team to go with you. I'm not sending any of my men into a situation like that alone. If you don't want Kit or Blade to watch your six, you pick one of the others, but you don't go alone."

Rocco looked at Kit, who shrugged. "I don't want you to go—I know what you're going to find. But

Owen's right. If it's something you've got to do, then you don't do it alone."

Rocco looked at the other men. Every one of them gave him a solemn nod. Every one of them had his back. He gritted his teeth, more relieved than he should have been not to be alone in his quest. He nodded to Owen, then Kit. "Understood." He looked at the others again. "Thanks."

Kelan slapped him on the back. "We look after our own, Rocco. We always have."

When breakfast was finished, Kit gave out assignments. Greer was to set up surveillance cameras across the property. Max was to stay inside manning the command center and looking into Mandy's files. The others would go with Rocco for a tour of the grounds. Rocco would repeat the tour for the two who stayed behind.

"Afterward, I'm going to check out my place, talk to my foreman and his wife," Blade said. "I'll see if they've noticed anything unusual."

"Want company?" Kit offered.

"No. I go alone."

Mandy knew why Ty wanted to go alone—it was easier to face your ghosts without the distraction of witnesses or companions.

"I don't like it," Kit said.

"I know. I'll check in this afternoon. Mandy—don't plan on me for lunch," Blade told her.

"Don't plan on me either, Em," Kit added. "I'm going up to the diner to see Ivy."

"You want company?" Blade offered.

Kit smiled and shook his head. "No more than you do."

* * *

Kit stood across the street from the Wolf Creek Bend Diner at high noon, buffeted by an unfamiliar swirl of emotions. Part of him wanted to hold off meeting with Ivy. He hadn't seen her in thirteen years. They'd barely communicated over the years, yet he still knew everything about her.

And their daughter.

Casey was twelve now. She excelled in sports and mathematics, struggled with social studies and English. She was tall for her age, fiercely independent, and had a core of self-confidence that only a strong mother could have taught her. He was proud of her. Proud of them both.

And he ached to be a part of their lives.

For the first several years of his exile from town, he hadn't heard anything from his former girlfriend. He didn't know she'd decided to keep the baby. When he would ask Mandy if she'd heard from Ivy, her answer had always been no. Ivy and her family moved away after the scandal—she hadn't been allowed to communicate with her former friends, especially not the half sister of the boy accused of raping her.

Years later, she'd ended her silence, connecting first online with Mandy, then via email, and finally in long telephone conversations. It was then that Mandy had broken the news to him that he was Casey's father. When Ivy still had refused to contact Kit, he had called her.

He remembered that conversation, filled with more silence than words. Ivy didn't want him involved in Casey's life. He tried to tell her he wasn't the juvenile delinquent she'd known, that he'd made something of his life. Nothing he'd said had any impact until he'd offered to set up a fund for Casey, one that she could use for any of her needs—clothing, housing, tuition, healthcare, and education.

And so it was that he received copies of her report cards, photos from Ivy of important events in her life. When she'd turned ten, he'd asked Ivy to have her begin martial arts studies, which she'd loved. And when Ivy said she was coming back to Wolf Creek Bend, he'd covered the down payment on the diner and had funded the renovations.

It was the least he could for the woman whose life he'd destroyed.

He stepped off the curb and crossed the street, forcing each foot in front of the other. How would Ivy react to him? He intended to meet his daughter while he was in town. Neither Ivy nor his enemy could stop him, but he would have to keep it low key. He didn't want to tip off Amir that he had a vulnerability.

Kit stepped into the diner. He'd seen pictures of it, but a two-dimensional image did little to prepare him for the blast of colors or energy of the space. Originally used as a general store in the 1870s, it had been fitted out as a diner in the 1950s, and then abandoned in 2000. They'd bought the building for next to nothing, then spent a fortune refitting it with modern appliances and returning it to an old 1950's look.

Ribbed chrome, polished to a high sheen, edged the tables, booths, and barstools. The counter was finished in a teal blue Formica, the booths in yellow. The stools were red vinyl. The floor was a white and black checkerboard tile. 1950's era memorabilia covered the walls. It was ugly and exciting at the same time, and packed with patrons. Plenty of wait staff hurried about dressed in jeans, white tees, and yellow aprons.

Kit stood still for a moment, taking it all in. There was one free stool at the counter. He sat down and opened the menu, which was loaded with typical diner fare—hamburgers, meatloaf, pot roast, chicken fingers, breakfast selections, and milkshakes. He felt the weight of a gaze on him from behind the counter, but he did not look up. Ivy had sent pictures of herself standing with Casey over the years. She was still slim, still black-haired. He conjured up his favorite memory of her, naked beneath him, her hair loose on his pillow. Christ, she'd only been fifteen. What the hell had he been thinking? But then, he'd been seventeen—he hadn't been thinking.

She was the only woman he'd ever loved. And she wanted nothing to do with him ever again. If it weren't for Casey, they'd never have reconnected.

He didn't want to look up, didn't want to replace that sweet memory—a memory that had seen him

through many a dark day—with a new one. He felt
Ivy's approach. Was she seeing anyone? Was she in a
committed relationship? Had another man stepped in
to be a father to Casey? His hands fisted the laminated
menu at that thought.

"Kit?" Her voice was as soft as he remembered it,
overlaid now with the rich nuances of womanhood.

He lifted his gaze to the woman before him. She
was tiny. He didn't remember her being so small. She
wore the same uniform as her employees. Her black
hair was drawn back behind her. A ponytail or a braid?
he wondered. Bangs feathered her forehead. Her eyes
were still a gorgeous sky blue, but now they held stories
upon stories. Hardships. Triumphs. Joy and sorrow. He
wanted to hear them all.

He felt a tension ripple through several staff
members. Breaking free of her gaze, he looked around,
wondering how many of the people in this room knew
their history, knew he'd been run from town. The same
sheriff was still keeping order in town. People didn't
tend to leave small towns like this. They stayed in place
for generations.

He had not raped her. They'd made love, given
each other their virginity. Made a daughter, a child
whose life had been denied him.

He looked at Ivy again. "Hi." Christ, he could
hardly speak at all.

"Hi." She smiled at him, but the gesture didn't
warm her eyes. He looked at her ring finger, hungry to
know if she'd found someone. No ring marked her as

another's.

"Busy place," Kit said.

"We've been lucky."

"Ain't no luck about it, darlin'," the patron next to him joined their conversation. "You make a better meatloaf than half the wives in Wyoming."

Kit was about to make it clear theirs was a private conversation, but Ivy spoke up before he could. "Thanks, Sam. Kit, Would you like a tour?"

"You never offered me a tour," the man beside him complained.

"You're not an owner," she answered with a smile.

"Oh." He looked from Ivy to Kit. "Oh! You're Kit Bolanger, her angel investor. Glad to meet you." He held out a hand and shook with Kit. "You saved me from a life of fast food when I'm driving this route."

Ivy smiled at Kit. "C'mon. I'll show you around." She stepped through the counter, then led him toward a back hallway, pausing to look back at the dining area. "We can seat seventy-five at a time, between the booths and the counter. We're open for all three meals. Business has been good. We're grossing, on average, about three hundred meals served a day."

Kit looked across the room, noticing a small camera in the corner of the far wall. He looked at the counter and found one there as well. Interesting. He'd like to see how her patrons reacted to his team's arrival the day before.

Ivy led him through the kitchen to an office, then closed the door. "What's going on, Kit? Why are you here?"

"Can't a brother visit his sister every now and then?"

"This is your first visit in over a decade. Try again. Yesterday a whole platoon of commandos stopped in for dinner. Why are they here?"

"Just some buds. We're going fishing."

"Kit Bolanger." She put her hands on her hips. "Don't lie to me."

"I'm not lying."

"All right. Fishing for what?"

"That, I'm not going to tell you."

Ivy walked in a small circle—the room was clearly too small for her nerves and him. "What do you want, Kit?"

"I want to see my daughter."

Ivy's head jerked his way. "No."

Kit stepped toward her, into her space, backing her toward a cluttered bulletin board. He slapped a hand on either side of her head. "I will see her."

Ivy's big blue eyes filled with tears. Her gaze held him with same force he achieved with his entire body, pinning him in place. "Don't take her from me," she whispered.

"Never."

"She's my world."

As you are mine. And then he did what he'd dreamed of doing for thirteen years. He kissed her.

Chapter 15

Ty looked up at the towering log house. It was utterly unchanged in the long years he'd been gone. The windows were clean, the logs weathered to a nice patina. The grounds were neat. Daisies, poppies and other perennials made brilliant swathes of color in the flowerbeds. The air was lush with flowering lilacs.

He hadn't phoned the Jacksons to let them know he'd be stopping by. Truthfully, he didn't want to see them yet. He fished the key to the front door out of his pocket and let himself inside.

Shadows filled the foyer and living room. All the windows had their drapes drawn. Sheets covered three different suites of furniture. Though the house was clearly unused, there wasn't a speck of dust. The Jacksons were indeed good caretakers.

He paused at the side of the room where his father's bar stood, uncovered and stocked with his favorite whiskey. A chill skittered down his spine. It was as if the man had only gone on a protracted vacation, not that he was dead. The ache in Ty's leg became more pronounced as he battled memories he never wanted to revisit.

Leaning on his cane more heavily, he spun away from the bar. He forced himself to walk into his father's den, a place his father admitted him only when he wished to discipline him. He stared at the chair he'd occupied twenty years earlier in excruciating pain, his leg broken and untended because his father was on a bender and couldn't remember breaking it in one of his vicious fits of rage. One beating begat another, until the man finally sobered up.

Ty kicked the chair across the room, hating the memory, hating how weak he'd been. He turned and swiped everything off the surface of his father's desk with his cane, hearing a satisfying crash of lamp and containers and other clutter. Landing on top of the heap was his father's silver letter opener. Ty grabbed it and limped back to the desk. He knew his father watched him impotently from wherever his spirit had gone.

He stared at the smooth, highly polished, ancient, enormous, mahogany desk—his father's great pride—trying to decide what words to carve into the surface. "Fuck you" was too trite. "Go to hell" was foolish, because hopefully that's where the bastard already was.

"Mr. Bladen! You're home!" Dennis Jackson said from the doorway. Ty pivoted, expecting to see his father, but there was no one other than his foreman.

"Call me Ty," he barked the order. Dennis straightened, adjusted his black leather vest in the same way he'd done a thousand other times when Ty's father had rebuked him.

"Of course. There anything that I can do for you? Do you want a room prepared and the house opened?"

Ty swiped a hand over his face. "I'm sorry, Dennis. I didn't mean to be such a shit." He offered the older man a conciliatory smile. "I guess you startled me."

"It doesn't matter—Ty. You're injured?" he asked, nodding toward Ty's leg and cane.

"A lucky shot. It's healing well. And no, don't bother with opening the house. I'm not staying."

"I see." He glanced at the wall behind Ty. Was it his imagination, or was Dennis acting nervous? Ty leaned on his cane and took a few steps to the desk, using the motion to cover the look he sent around the room.

"Dennis, I noticed the paths between here and the Wolf Valley property are surprisingly well used. Do you know why? Have you had any trouble here? Odd visitors? Trespassers?"

"No. I haven't seen anyone on the property or in the house. I do a circuit of the grounds every few days."

Ty looked away. Dennis was lying. "I asked because Mandy is having some difficulties over at the construction site, and I wondered if you were experiencing the same."

"We'd heard about her troubles. Several folks in town were discussing it." His gaze flashed to Ty, adding a quick clarification, "I wasn't participating in the conversation. I just overheard their discussion."

Ty didn't react to how he'd gotten the news. His father had hated for their servants or any of their employees to participate in gossip. It had been a firing offense. Maybe Dennis was having a case of the nerves, unsure what to expect now that he reported to Ty.

"I'll be over at Mandy's for a while, helping her with the situation. Kit's home, too."

"Is it serious, then? Mandy's situation?"

"It is. I know you and Mrs. Jackson are due a vacation. I think it's a good time for you to take it now."

"If there's trouble, sir, I would prefer not to be away."

"You've served my family honorably my entire life. Would it be so terrible to take a month and visit your children? Your grandchildren? Spend some time on a beach? Make the arrangements and provide me with a bill. I'll cover the expense."

"Sir, will we have jobs when we return?"

Ty crossed the room and stood in front of the older man, one of the few who'd dared to make his childhood bearable. He set his hand on Dennis's shoulder. "This is your home, whether you work here or not. Take some time away. I will let you know when it is safe to return. And spend some money on Mrs. Jackson. I'll pay your wages while you're gone."

* * *

Kit pulled his chair closer to the monitors in the

command center. He'd asked Ivy to give him a copy of the footage from an hour before his team sat down to supper to an hour after they left, from both of the cameras in the dining area. He and Max were speeding through the gray-scale video, fast-forwarding to the moment the team entered the diner. Owen and Greer were sitting behind them, watching the monitors.

"What are we looking for, Kit?" Max asked.

"I don't know. We'll know it when we see it. *If* we see it," Kit told him. He phoned Mandy and asked her to join them. She came down the stairs a few minutes later, the dogs and Blade on her heels.

"What's doin'?" Blade asked.

"Ivy had video of the diner from last night. I thought it would be interesting to see who was there when the guys dropped in and what their reaction was. Mandy, you know these people. Tell me if something looks odd to you."

"Besides six mercenaries stopping at a diner in the middle of nowhere for a meal?"

"Right. Besides that."

They found the point where the team entered. There were some curious glances from other customers, but nothing worth noting. They moved forward, watching in slightly accelerated speed while the team sat, ordered, waited for their meal.

A man came in and sat down in a booth near the table the men occupied. Kit watched him, curious about his interested reaction to the guys. He kept looking at them surreptitiously. When the waitress came to take his order, he looked frustrated. He nodded toward the men and asked her something. She shrugged and shook her head. He must have said something that bothered the waitress, for she sent him an aggravated glance.

"Who is that, Mandy? Do you know him?"

"That's Alan Buchanan, the plumber."

The men received their food. They were laughing, had the waitress laughing. The plumber received his food. He barely touched it. He seemed to be avoiding looking at the men again, but he had his ears pinned to them. He picked up a French-fry and nibbled it.

"What were you guys talking about?" Kit asked.

"Sports. The surprise weekend celebration Greer's parents gave him when he came home from Afghanistan. Val's new boots. Nothing of any interest to anyone around us," Owen said.

"Look, he's texting someone."

"Or maybe he got a text."

"No, he didn't read then answer. He took out his phone and started typing."

Greer rolled away to a different computer. "I'm on it. I'll check his phone records."

"Maybe one of his employees was having problems and he sent a message to him," Mandy offered.

"If a worker's having a plumbing problem and needs to review it with the boss, he won't do it in a text message" Kit said. "That requires immediate contact via a phone call. A text could be ignored or not received."

"Got his records up. He did not send or receive a text yesterday at all."

"I want that phone." Kit looked at Owen. "I'll send Rocco and Kelan to his house to get it."

"You think Rocco's ready?" Owen asked, his pale blue eyes intense as he looked at Kit.

"It's the best thing for him."

* * *

Amir was already in the coffee shop when Alan arrived. Alan tried to keep all expression from his face, but he knew there'd be no good outcome from this meeting. He had not complied with the man's last directive.

"Hello, Mr. Buchanan. I have already ordered. Why don't you get what you would like and join me?" Amir asked in his deceptively gentle voice, his Middle Eastern accent making his words soft and lyrical.

Alan's only response was a brief nod as he accepted the short reprieve placing an order would give him. Minutes later, latte in hand, he sat at Amir's table. The man smiled at him, and it felt like a knife's unsheathing.

"You failed in your last task."

"I did not fail. The construction manager wound up in the hospital."

"He should have wound up in the morgue, no? It doesn't matter," Amir waved a hand dismissively. "I have another task. When it is complete, I will return your papers to you and release you from our agreement." He used his foot to push a bag over next to Alan.

Alan leaned over and looked inside. There were three large boxes wrapped in pretty bows.

"You will place these boxes, one each, in the pole barn, the stable, and the arena, next to the northwest corner of each. Understood?"

Alan nodded. "And when it is done, I will be released?"

Amir smiled. "Of course. You will call me from the phone in the bag. When it is done, I will overnight your papers to you." Amir studied Alan until he began to squirm. "You will not fail me in this task. There will be no second chances."

"They have men patrolling the site now. They'll see me. I may not be able to do it tonight." And his stepdaughter had returned from college. He'd have to work around her as well.

"We all have our challenges, Mr. Buchanan. I want it done in the morning, anyway—once the crew is onsite. They know you. No one will be suspicious to see you there. I am confident you will find a way to be successful. It is, after all, your future at stake."

Alan dropped his gaze to his cup. Tomorrow or the next day, this would all be over. He would be a free man. He'd go somewhere they could never find him. Mexico, maybe. He'd never be their puppet again. He raised his coffee cup to Amir.

"Here's to my freedom."

Amir nodded and lifted his cup. "To your freedom,

of course."

                        * * *

Rocco was the last to come in for supper that night. After a long afternoon working the fence line in the upper pastures, he'd needed a quick shower. By the time he had dressed and rejoined the group, they had all settled at the table, leaving only one empty seat between Mandy and Kit.

The smell of grilled meat hit him hard. The windows were open, drawing smoke from the grill back into the house. He took his seat, sending a look around the table. Maybe having so many men around Mandy made him feel off-kilter. She gave him a tentative smile as she poured him some tea. The ice cracked and clinked as the liquid filled his glass.

Kit brought in a tray of hamburgers and hotdogs. Another blast of grill smoke followed him inside. Rocco felt queasy. A clammy chill spread across his skin from the draft of the ceiling fan. He drew a deep, slow breath, trying to calm himself. The silence was coming—he could feel it stalking him. He didn't want it. He wanted to hear, to participate, to be a human among humans, not a ghost stuck between two worlds.

Mandy passed the platter of meat toward him. The hotdogs were blackened and blistered in places. He shook his head, staring at the platter. It's only hotdogs, he told himself. Grilled fucking hotdogs. He was breathing too fast. He knew it, but he couldn't stop. He was trying to get some air that didn't smell like singed flesh. And dust. He shut his eyes and saw the stuff of nightmares.

Everything was strangely silent. Women wailed, but he couldn't hear them. Men shouted and fired guns in anguished retribution, but the gunfire was silent. The village was a remote outpost. There was no one nearby to come to their assistance or witness the devastation. The world neither knew nor cared about the village's collapse. Ashes fell like snow to the ground. Fire burned the wood supports the explosion had exposed.

"Rocco? You okay?" The voice of an angel.

Mandy.

He opened his eyes. Her hand was on his arm. His fingers held the edge of the table in a claw-like grip. He yanked free of her hold, looking for the pieces of burned flesh on him. Nothing was there. He couldn't see it yet, but he could feel it. She'd said he could trust her eyes, but obviously she couldn't see the flesh when it was just forming, and by the time it covered his arms, it was too late. It would cover anyone who was touching him, like flames spreading from body to body.

Overhead the fan moved in a slow, nauseating circle, its blades cutting loudly through the air.

Wh-oo-oosh. Wh-oo-oosh. Wh-oo-oosh.

"Rocco, it's all good. You're cool. It's all cool," Kit told him, a hand resting heavily on his shoulder, another on his arm, as if to anchor him. Rocco looked down again, seeing the drying blood and burned flakes of flesh that covered his chest, his shoulders, his arms. He swiped it off, but for every bit he removed, more settled on him.

"No! No!" He didn't know if he spoke aloud, or even which language he used. Bile rose in his throat as his nose filled with the stench of rotting bodies. The black flesh was alive, it moved down his arms and onto Kit.

Rocco ripped his arm away from Kit's hold and jumped to his feet, his chair flying back across the wood floor. Every face at the table stared at him. He felt the weight of their eyes.

He wasn't crazy. He wasn't. He was just a man who lived in two realities, one of which they couldn't see. He spun away and stumbled across the room, escaping through the front door.

Silence magnified the echo the screen door made as it banged shut behind Rocco. Mandy looked at her plate, saw it waver in front of her eyes. Her mind replayed the fear she'd seen in his eyes. What the heck had just happened? She looked around the table, trying to see what Rocco might have seen, but nothing looked out of the ordinary.

"Shit," Kit growled. He shoved a hand through his hair. "How often does that happen, Em?"

"It's happened a few times since he got here. I don't know what set him off this time."

Kit picked up Rocco's chair and sat in it next to Mandy. Reaching an arm around her, he pulled her close. "Don't worry, sis. It's not something you did. His brain is haywire right now. He's been to hell and back, more than once. He needs time to heal."

"I told you that. He's not ready for this. I'll go talk

to him." Mandy swiped the tears from her face and set her napkin on the table.

"No. I will," Ty said. "Stay put. And eat up. Don't waste this food, but it would be best if it weren't here when he comes back. I'll get him something else to eat after he calms down."

"You think the food triggered this?" Mandy asked, frowning.

"Kit burned the hotdogs." Ty threaded his fingers together over his head. "You know what he looked like when we found him," he said to Kit. "Somebody had friggin' exploded all over him."

Mandy lurched to her feet and ran to her room.

"Well fucking done, my man," Kit complained as he stood up.

"He's not going for the phone tonight," Owen said.

"Oh, he's going. We need his head back in the game. The only way that'll happen is to give him work to focus on." Kit met Owen's implacable stare.

"There's too much at stake in this operation to use it as a therapy session. I don't want to endanger a valuable operative by using him when he isn't at full capacity."

"I know my boy, Owen. I know how to pull him through his hell. I've done it for seven years."

Owen leaned back in his chair and studied Kit through narrowed eyes. "You burned the dogs on purpose."

Kit sat down and filled a roll with a burned hotdog. He slathered it with mustard and ketchup, then took a bite. "Like I said, I know my boy."

Ty shook his head and went out after Rocco. He paused at the top step of Mandy's front porch, trying to get a read on which direction Rocco might have taken. He wasn't down in the construction area or outside the bunkhouse. Ty walked across the drive so that he could see the ridge behind the house—that's where he would have gone for some alone time. No one stood silhouetted there.

He checked inside the toolshed, then the bunkhouse. Nada. He walked out behind the collapsing barn, wondering if Rocco was making a tour of the back trails, and found him sitting in the dirt at Kitano's corral. He was leaning back against a support beam, his legs bent, arms propped on his knees. He held a long blade of grass that he was dismembering, inch by inch.

Ty eased himself down next to Rocco, his wounded thigh protesting the movement.

"You pull the short straw?" Rocco asked.

"I volunteered."

"Lucky you."

Ty made a dismissive gesture. "Whatever. I didn't come to talk about your little freak show. We need to talk about me. I went home today."

"I know."

"I goddamn hate that place. I think I'm going to burn it down."

Rocco looked over at him. "You're an idiot."

Ty shrugged. "I don't want it. I won't ever live there. And I'd love to send my father a message in hell that he can't fail to interpret correctly."

Rocco lowered his legs and leaned back. "So sell below market value. Hell, give it to Kit. If you believe that the spirits of the deceased watch us, seeing you give the house to the town's most hated kid will have your father spinning in his grave."

"I like that." Ty slowly smiled. "I like it a lot. Kit won't take it as a gift, but I could sell it to him for half the going price. Then he'd have a home here near his sister." He considered that a moment. "What about you? You want it?"

Rocco looked off to where the trails began. "Honestly, I don't know that I'm going to make it back. I prefer knowing Kit would settle near Mandy, eventually—if you do finally decide the house isn't for you." He looked at his friend. "When I go back, you'll go with me?"

Ty met Rocco's eyes. "Count on it." He extended his fist and Rocco bumped it with his. Silence settled between them, filled only by crickets and birds noisily chattering as they settled for the night. "What happened tonight?" Ty asked.

Rocco sighed. "I lost my fucking mind."

"Yeah, that part I got. But why? What kicked it off?"

"I don't know. The smoke. The burned dogs."

"I told Kit not to over-cook them," Blade interrupted.

"It was like a worm hole right back to the explosion."

"Did you see anything new while you were checked out?"

Rocco leaned his head back against the post behind him. He shut his eyes. Drawing a deep, slow breath to fight off the panic, he opened his mind to the memories triggered at supper.

"Kadisha was handing Zavi to me. She was going back in the compound for her mother. I grabbed her, tried to stop her. She said that I had done this, that I had killed them. She ran back inside, and the whole thing blew."

He looked at Blade. "Did I do it? Was there an order to level the compound? Did I have you or Kit call for an airstrike?"

"No. We got the kill order to take out her father, but without you, we didn't know where he'd holed up. And there were too many civilians living there for the whole village to be a target. It wasn't our side that blew the compound."

"Kadisha was pregnant with our second kid."

"Christ." Blade drew a long breath and slowly released it. "I'm sorry, bro. I didn't know."

"I would have loved that baby. I would have brought Kadisha and the kids here. And though we wouldn't have stayed married, I would have taken care of them, all of them."

"I know you would have, my friend. Wouldn't have expected anything less from you." He massaged his thigh. They sat in silence for a little while, listening to the sounds of birds settling in for the evening.

"So for the real reason I came down to talk to you—Kit brought back some interesting security footage from the diner. We noticed Mandy's plumber had an extreme reaction to the team when they stopped for supper. He texted someone, only it wasn't via his cell phone account—he used some other online account." He looked at Rocco. "Didn't you say he was in the diner the day you felt an enemy there?"

"He was there."

"Kit wants you and Kelan to go to his house tonight and retrieve his phone so that we can see who the hell he messaged and how."

Rocco looked at him and slowly grinned, feeling he was getting back in the game. "Sure, I'll go get it."

* * *

Alan made his routine circuit around the house, checking the lock in the front shop, locking the door between his apartment and the shop, then locking the back door. The whole action was preposterous, as if a locked door could keep him safe. It was an illusion of safety, nothing more.

And yet, house-by-house, his neighbors did the same safety checks he'd just completed, locking all the doors, shutting off the lights, slipping into their comfortable beds—ignorant of the fact that he had enough C-4 in his van to blow half the block.

He retrieved a bottle of whiskey and went into his room. Glasses littered his nightstand. One from the night before still had a little amber liquid in it. He tossed that back, then refilled it to wash down two prescription sleeping pills. He slumped down on his rumpled bed in the clothes he'd worn during the day, and waited for the pills to take effect.

When sleep didn't immediately quiet his mind, he splashed more whiskey into his glass to top it off and lit a cigarette. He caught sight of the amber vial of pills. His life hadn't turned out the way he'd expected it to when he was a kid. When he'd entered the plumbing business right after high school, he was proud of having selected a career in a field that would never be without customers—in good times or lean. But he'd been careless with his money and lost most of it gambling and drinking. He'd wanted more, always more. Nothing was ever enough.

One day, in his mid-forties, he realized he was broke, getting older and failing in every way that mattered. It had been easy to take the money he'd embezzled from the large plumbing franchise that employed him. So easy. And just as easy to lose it in gambling hells. He thought he'd win it back, but he only lost more. He'd sold his soul for that money. And then he had to run, hide, become less than he was. Become nothing.

It was at that low point that Amir had found him, offering sweet solace with that silky voice of his, assuring him his life would be better if Alan joined their cause. He could barely even remember what Amir had said their cause was. It didn't matter. They gave him a new identity. Found him a woman to marry, and cleared the way to this job. It was everything he'd ever wanted, and he took it. In exchange, he'd only been asked to make the drive down to Denver every few weeks in anticipation of an unknown assignment to be handed out sometime in the future.

He sipped his whiskey, remembering the vow he'd made when his wife had died; he'd decided to be different, to be what she had seen in him. She'd been a good woman, his Mary. Kind and honest. Married as strangers, he'd strived to be worthy of her. He'd stayed put in Wolf Creek Bend, and he'd honored his commitment to put her daughter through college—so far. But now that he'd made such a mess of things, Mary's girl would be better off without him. He looked at the pills again. He could check out. For good.

But if he did, he had no doubt that Amir's people would hunt Fee down. She was the only good thing left in his life. He'd tried to protect her from Amir by pretending indifference but doubted he'd fooled the bastard.

The only chance he had of getting them out of this situation was to blow Mandy's therapeutic riding center all to hell. Amir wanted it done while the construction crew was there. Alan couldn't stomach that. He'd blow the damn place at night when no one was there. He'd do it soon. As soon as he could bring himself to do it. Amir be damned. He'd do it when he was good and ready. Then he'd take Fee and hit the road. Again.

* * *

Kelan parked in front of the plumber's shop. Mandy had told them he lived in an apartment in the back of his store. It was approaching 1:00 a.m. The entire street was quiet and dark.

Kelan looked over at Rocco. "You okay to do this?"

"I'm fine."

"Then let's move. You take the shop, I'll take the apartment."

Only a double bolt lock protected the shop, which Kelan picked in a few seconds. There was no alarm system for them to disarm. Rocco began looking around the papers on the counter while Kelan slipped through the door between the shop and the residential area.

It was a seedy little space that would have looked shoddy even in its prime thirty years earlier. The current suite of worn and mismatched chairs and the odd collection of TV tray tables did little to improve things. The living room was open to the kitchen. Four doors led to other areas.

Kelan stood still for a moment, listening for a dog or a bird or anything that would give his presence away. Nothing stirred.

He walked through the open space, looking for Alan's cell phone. Not seeing it in the living room, he entered the first door to his left. A man was asleep in a bed. Clothes were scattered around the floor, over a radiator. Drawers were open in two different dressers. The room had the gamey smell of unwashed human.

The man's phone was on his nightstand, next to a full ashtray and several glasses. Kelan took it, plug and all, then returned to his exploration of the rest of the apartment.

One door opened to a bathroom, one a closet. The last was another bedroom, as threadbare as the rest of the apartment, but unlike the other areas, it was very tidy. There were no toys to indicate it was a child's room. The bed was rumpled, as if someone had been sleeping in it. Kelan had a bad feeling as he looked around the room. An unmade bed in a room this neat meant someone had just left it. He looked under the bed and around the other side of it, but didn't find anyone. A suitcase sat on the floor in front of a dresser. He knelt down beside it and lifted the top flap, curious about who was visiting the plumber. Inside were neatly folded jeans, a stack of tiny T-shirts, and a cluster of stringy panties and bras.

Kelan jack-knifed to his feet. This was a woman's room. The closet was the only other space someone could hide. He stood to the side as he opened one panel. He spanned the space with his flashlight, but found it empty of anything other than clothes and boxes. He pushed the other panel open and flashed the light in that half, catching a pair of big eyes and an enormous Colt revolver. The girl cocked the gun as she lurched forward out of the closet. Kelan backed a step away, his hands held in front of him.

"Easy now, kid. I didn't mean to scare you."

"What are you doing in my home?"

"I didn't know you lived here."

"That's not the answer I was looking for." She pushed him back through room, the gun pointing straight at his heart. Her grip was incredibly steady. She wore only a skimpy pair of knit shorts and one of those tiny, strappy tees he'd seen in her suitcase. Her hair was a mop of little curls—it was hard to tell the color in the dim light, but it appeared to be blond. And she was half his size. He had at least a foot in height on her, which would have made her about five foot three.

"Now, hold on there. We're the good guys."

"Show me some ID."

"I don't have any."

Her gaze darted to the dresser. Kelan saw her cell phone sitting there. He grabbed it and shoved it in his pocket.

"Give that to me," she ordered.

"No can do. How about you put that gun down?"

"How about you get the hell out of my house?"

"Okay. I'm leaving." He took a huge gamble and turned his back on her at the threshold to the living room. Rocco stood there.

"What's taking so long?" he asked Kelan.

"Ah, we got a situation."

"What kind of situation?"

Kelan moved a half step from the door and looked back, keeping the girl blocked from entering the living room but letting Rocco see what the issue was.

"Shit. How did she see you? You're supposed to move like a shadow."

"I never said that," Kelan argued.

"Who is she?"

"We haven't exactly exchanged pleasantries."

"Hells bells. You're going to have to bring her with us."

"Right." Kelan spun around, gripping the girl's wrist and elbow to stabilize the gun. She fought him in the no-holds-barred way of a desperate woman, stomping her heel down on his booted foot, clawing at his hand, trying to bang her head into his nose. With very little effort, he pinned her against the wall so that he could remove the pistol from her hand.

She turned her head and drew air to belt out a loud scream, but Kelan quickly slapped his hand over her mouth, holding her in a way that kept her from being able to bite him. He was wondering how the hell they were going to get her out of the place without waking the plumber and the entire neighborhood when Rocco returned with a roll of duct tape.

They taped her wrists, ankles and knees, then Kelan placed a piece across her mouth. He straightened and slung her over his shoulder.

"I've got Buchanan's phone," he told Rocco. "You find anything interesting?"

"I got his appointment book. I hate having to take her."

The girl was still struggling over Kelan's shoulder, hitting his kidney with her fists. "It's a real party for me, too." He took the appointment book from Rocco. "Go get her stuff. Her suitcase is in her room. No idea how old she is—see if you can find her purse. I'm going to get her settled in the Expedition. Don't dawdle. I saw sleeping meds in the plumber's bedroom, but I'm not sure how much noise Buchanan can sleep through."

Kelan made his way through the living room and into the shop. She got in another good strike at his left kidney. He swatted her backside. "Knock it off. How about you don't hit me and I won't hit you?" Kelan growled at her bottom.

She settled for a minute, but as soon as he stepped outside, she pushed up against his back, whimpering. He shoved her farther over his shoulder, closing his mind to her muted pleas. If she was involved in the plumber's treason, she'd receive no mercy. He doubted she was, however. He thought she looked to be about twelve—until he remembered the lacy lingerie he'd seen in her suitcase and reevaluated that assessment. Little girls didn't wear stuff like that, did they?

Hell, if she was under age, they'd have to turn her over to social services. And good riddance, he told himself as he settled her in the backseat of the Expedition. He fastened her seat belt, then sat beside her. Rocco was right behind them. He put her stuff on the passenger side of the front seat, then took the wheel. Neither man spoke on the return trip.

When Rocco opened the front door for Kelan and his package, he couldn't help giving his old friend a grin. "This is not going to go well."

Kelan moved into the living room, ignoring the

humor in Rocco's voice. He unsheathed his knife and sliced through the tape at the girl's ankles and knees while she still hung over his shoulder. He set her on her feet in Mandy's living room, then cut the tape on her wrists, leaving the one across her mouth for her to remove.

"What's going on? Why did you take me?" She punched his shoulder. Her little fist barely made an impact against his lean strength.

Kelan's face darkened. "What did I tell you about hitting?"

Several pairs of boots thundered up the stairs ending any chance of a reprieve he might have had before having to face the team.

"This better be good," Blade said as the men stopped in a half-circle around Kelan and the girl.

"What the hell have you done?" Kit asked, shouldering his way through the ring of men. The girl stepped back against Kelan, her arms folded over herself. The top of her head barely reached his chin. The look Kit was giving her would make a seasoned warrior nervous. Wanting to deflect Kit's focus from the girl, Kelan wrapped an arm across her arms, pulling her close.

Val gave the girl a warm look-over. "Kelan! How many times do I have to tell you, 'female good, jailbait bad?'"

Kelan's normally effervescent mood was rapidly diminishing. "We found her at the plumber's. She'd already seen us. We couldn't leave her there."

"Who is she?" Kit snapped.

"Fiona Addison," Rocco said, holding up her driver's license and school ID. "Age 20. A student at Colorado State University."

"Well, Ms. Addison, mind telling us what you were doing at Alan Buchanan's apartment?" Kit asked.

"I live there."

"Mandy didn't say anything about anyone else living there," Rocco said.

"Mandy? Is she here?" the girl asked, looking around.

"She's here. She's sleeping," Rocco told her.

Kelan felt the girl relax a little upon hearing that Mandy was here—until another thought hit her. "Is she also a prisoner?"

"She's not a prisoner. Nor are you. Mandy's my sister. I'm Kit Bolanger."

She straightened and faced Kelan. "If I'm not a prisoner, then I'll thank you to take me back home."

"No."

"What's your connection to Alan Buchanan?" Kit continued with the questions.

"How about you show me some ID first?" she demanded.

"We're private investigators," Owen explained.

"I didn't know private investigators traveled in packs." She answered with more bravado than Kelan would have expected from someone so young and so small. "What are you investigating? What has Alan done?"

"We're not at liberty to explain. Answer the question," Owen told her.

"He's my stepfather. He asked me to come back and work the office for the summer. His counter help keeps quitting."

"There was no sign of your mother at the apartment," Kelan said, wishing she were still leaning against him, wishing the guys would back off a bit and give her some room.

The girl shoved her dark blond curls off her face and glared at him. "She died a year ago. She was murdered when I was a freshman at CSU."

"How long have you known Buchanan?" Owen asked.

The girl shrugged. "My mother married him two and a half years ago, just before they moved up here. I don't know him very well. I've spent most of that time at school." She looked at the stockade of men standing shoulder to shoulder around her.

Kit and Owen exchanged a look. Kelan clenched his jaw. He could see they intended to press the girl for every bit of info she had on Buchanan. It was going to be a long friggin' night. And he did not intend to let them question her without him.

Chapter 16

Mandy woke to loud voices coming from the living room. She'd tried to stay awake until Rocco returned from his mission, but she'd been too tired. She pulled her robe on over her pajamas and hurried out to see what had the men so excited.

As soon as she stepped into the hallway, she saw the guys standing in a tight circle and heard a familiar voice. The plumber's daughter.

"Fee?" she asked, pushing her way into the ring of men.

"Mandy?"

Mandy reached out to hug her friend, who was ice cold. She glared up at Kelan. "You couldn't have let her get dressed?"

"It wasn't a social call, Mandy."

She drew Fee to the sofa and wrapped her in the quilt before pulling her down to sit next her. "What's going on? I didn't know you were out of school already. Why are you here?"

Fee folded her legs in front of her on the cushion

and glared at Kelan and Rocco. "They broke into Alan's home and kidnapped me."

Mandy gasped. She looked at Kelan's shuttered face, then at Rocco for confirmation. He shrugged. "She was an unforeseen complication."

Kit looked at the men gathered in the room. "I think you have some work to do downstairs," Kit ordered. "Owen and I will chat with the girl."

"I'm staying." Kelan crossed his arms and planted his feet. "She's my complication. I'm responsible for her."

"True, that. And we'll discuss it shortly. In the meantime, I need you to do as I asked and give me an update ASAP."

Kelan didn't move. "Rocco will get your update. I'm staying."

"Why are these men in your house, Mandy? And don't tell me they've come out for a vacation—I won't for a minute believe it," Fee asked.

"They're friends of Kit's. They've come to help me with the center. I've been having all sorts of problems." Mandy said with a sigh, unsure how much she could or should tell Fee. "They have some questions for you. Please answer them as completely as you are able."

Fee frowned. "I don't know anything about what's happening here. I just got back from school."

Mandy nodded. "This isn't only about the center."

Fee looked at Kit and Owen. "My stepfather's in trouble, isn't he?"

"What makes you think he's in trouble?" Owen

asked.

"He was always a little off." Fee got up and started pacing. "I've always wondered about him." She looked at the men. "I never understood why my mother married him. She wasn't in love with him, I don't think. They didn't even know each other. I was a senior in high school. She came home one day and said she'd found a way for me to go to college. They got married, and we moved up here. They seemed happy enough. And he did pay for my college. It was just odd, that's all."

Mandy watched as Fee moved around the room, gesturing with the blanket as she spoke. "And when my mother died, I really became suspicious. They said she ran off the road in a drunken stupor, that her blood alcohol level was higher than .14."

"That's good and drunk," Kelan commented.

Fee glared at him. "She was a teetotaler. She never drank. Ever."

"Was her death investigated?"

"No. I had a fight with Alan over it. He didn't want me to raise any questions, or make any noise. I did anyway, but the sheriff couldn't see beyond the coroner's irrefutable conclusion that she'd been drinking. They had only been here a year by then. No one knew my mother very well. No one could vouch for the fact that it was exceptionally odd behavior from her."

"Does your stepfather ever have unusual visitors? Is he a member of any associations or groups that you know of?" Kit asked.

"I don't know about his professional organizations. I don't think he belongs to any social groups. That's another weird thing about him. He doesn't have friends. He's been in half of the houses in Wolf Creek Bend. Everyone knows him, yet he eats by himself at the diner most nights. He doesn't socialize with anyone. Every now and then, he'll go down to Denver unexpectedly. I usually work in his office in the summers. Several times I'd have to rearrange his schedule so that he could take a day off and drive down there."

"Do you know where he went?" Owen asked.

"No. He never talked about it."

"How would you describe his demeanor those days?"

"I don't know. Edgy. When he got back, he'd take out his whiskey and finish off whatever he had left in the bottle."

"Kit," Mandy looked at her brother, "I don't think she can go back. I think she should stay here."

"Agreed," Kit said. "Give her my room," he offered.

Owen gave Mandy a dark look, clearly not pleased to have to deal with this complication. "Get her settled. Fiona—hold off calling Alan until we talk in the morning."

She glared at Kelan. "I can't call anyone. He's got my cell phone."

Owen nodded to Kelan. "Good. We'll give it back

to you in the morning."

* * *

Rocco tossed Buchanan's phone to Max, who immediately started digging into the plumber's online accounts.

"Any problems—besides the obvious one upstairs?" Blade asked Rocco.

"None."

"You look around while you were there?"

Rocco handed him the appointment book. "Seems at least once a month he clears out an entire day, as if he decides to take off without any forethought or planning. The bounced appointments all get rescheduled. No idea what that might mean, but it's a pattern worth checking into."

"Can you tell what he texted the night we came in, to whom, and how?" Blade asked Max.

"He's got an email account, but there are no in-coming or out-going emails stored. He has no saved drafts, either. The only social networking app on here is Twitter. Last night, he sent a direct message to @A__akbar. No text, just a picture of our guys."

"Who's A Akbar? That short for 'Allah Akbar'?" Rocco asked, remembering the crazed battle cry of Afghan insurgents.

"There's no profile data for that account. I don't know."

"What was Akbar's response?"

"No response. @A__akbar has never interacted

with our plumber. He isn't even following him. The
next thing @A__akbar posted, barely an hour later, is,
'Lovely evening to drink coffee in Denver. I've ordered
a single espresso.'"

Blade and Rocco looked at each other. "Does he
say something like that a lot?"

Max shook his head. "Can't tell from this phone. A
search shows nothing. He might have deleted his
Tweets. Let me get into Twitter's database to see what's
passed through his account."

"I'll a make copy of his appointment book," Rocco
said. "I want to return it and the phone before
Buchanan wakes up."

Kelan came downstairs after Fiona was settled. He
handed her phone to Greer. "This is the girl's phone.
Best check it out before we give it back to her."

* * *

The house was silent as Rocco made his way to
Mandy's bedroom later that night. He felt an
unexpected rush of joy at the prospect of spending a
few hours with his woman—sleeping and anything else
that might happen while they were together. He
stripped, then sent the dogs to their pillows. Slipping
beneath the covers, he pulled Mandy to his side. This
was the closest he'd been to heaven his entire life.

He eased her long T-shirt up, hoping not to rouse
her too much. He liked her this way, warm and sleepy
and soft, wanted to feel her skin against his. She
shrugged out of the tee when he had it up about her

arms and head, then snuggled back into his side. Rocco tossed it off the bed. He pulled her over his chest, then drew the covers around them. Slipping his hands under the blankets, he rubbed her back, her hips, her buttocks. She sighed and nuzzled her cheek against his chest.

He lifted his knees between her legs, nudging them apart as he rocked himself against her core. He captured her nipples, rubbed them, pinching just slightly. She sucked in a sharp draw of air as she responded viscerally to his touch.

"Shh. Don't wake up. Don't move," he whispered. "I want you like this." He pulled back and positioned himself at her opening, then slowly entered her, letting his cock stroke her feminine channel as his hands stroked her back. In and out. Up and down. Slowly.

"Rocco—"

He held her to him, keeping her from rising. He didn't hurry this coupling. He wished it could last forever, leisurely and sweet. "We'll go slowly."

"Rocco—"

He could feel her body tightening, urging his to a faster pace. He took hold of her upper thighs, just below her bottom, keeping her still. "Not yet. Go back to sleep. I'm gonna fuck you for hours, so relax. Dream. Of me. Of this."

He moved in her, his cock like hot iron. The restraint he imposed on himself strained his entire body. He could feel her passion heating up, rippling through her body. She cried out, her body tightening like a fist over him, pumping, grinding into him. She arched up and rode him hard. Rocco could feel his balls tightening, seizing. He gripped her hips, lifting and driving into her, over and over as he reached his own climax.

They both settled against the bed, still joined. It felt wonderful to have her warm, sated body on top of his. He tried to close his mind to the shadow stalking his euphoria, but it wouldn't be silenced. One day soon, he would have to leave her. His arms tightened around her shoulders. He kissed her forehead. Leaving her was going to tear a piece out of his soul.

* * *

Mandy was hard at work in the kitchen the next morning when Fee came in. "What are you doing up so early?" she asked.

Fee shrugged. "I wait tables during the school year. I figured you could use an extra hand."

"Well, I certainly could. There are only nine men, but I swear they eat like a whole battalion. Why don't you get a cup of coffee, then I'll have you make the biscuits."

Fee paused beside the coffee pot. "Thanks for letting me stay here." She looked over at Mandy. "After hearing that Alan is being investigated, I didn't feel safe going back there."

"I'm happy to help, Fee."

Fee looked around them, checking the two kitchen entrances to be sure they were alone. "What do they think he did?"

"I don't know exactly. I'm not sure they know, but I have no doubt they'll figure it out."

"So how long has your brother been with these guys?"

"Not long." Mandy was gun-shy about answering questions. "He joined this private firm when he left the service."

Fee looked down at her coffee, then back at Mandy. "This is really happening, isn't it?"

Mandy squeezed her arm. "I'm afraid so."

"Who hired them?"

"I don't know. I'm just grateful that they are here." She filled Fee in on the crazy things that had been happening with her construction site.

"Do they think Alan is behind that? I don't know him that well, but it doesn't seem like something he would do."

"They are trying to follow the threads. That's all."

The next half-hour passed in a blur of preparations. Fee made the biscuits and cut up the fruit. She gathered a stack of plates and silverware. When she turned to take them out to the table, the big guy who'd kidnapped her stood there. Kelan, they'd called him last night. He looked to be of Native American descent and had to be at least a foot taller than her, about twice as wide, and whipcord lean. He'd carried her as if her hundred and ten pounds were nothing.

She felt the warmth of a blush creep up her face. "Morning," she said, in as clipped a voice as she could muster.

He gave her a curt nod, then looked her over, his gaze clinical. "You slept well?"

"I did, thank you." She stepped around him and carried her dishes out to the table.

Mandy saw Kelan turn and watch her. "She's cute, isn't she?"

"She's an infant." He poured himself a cup of coffee.

"She's older than you think. She's in college."

He sipped his coffee, squinting from the heat as he watched Fee. His gaze shifted to Mandy. "That's what I said." He went to the dining room. "Want help with that?" he asked Fiona.

"Nope. I've got it covered."

"Fiona, I'm sorry about last night. You must have been terrified."

"I wasn't scared. I had the Colt—which I want back, please. That was my grandfather's gun."

"You may not realize this, but guns are usually more effective loaded. You should have shot first and asked questions later. If we'd been the bad guys, you wouldn't have stood a chance."

Fee glared at Kelan. "That gun hasn't been fired in a hundred years. I doubt it still works. And I didn't realize what trouble Alan was in—I thought you were common burglars that I could bluff into getting out of the apartment. What about my phone?"

"Max has it. He'll give it to you after breakfast." He moved away, but Fee stopped him.

"Kelan?" He looked at her over his shoulder. "Thanks."

He gave her a lopsided grin of brilliant, white teeth. His eyes crinkled, easing his stoic mask. He nodded. "I'm glad you're here instead of with Buchanan."

The other guys started to congregate as she and Mandy set food out. One of them introduced himself to her. He was even taller than Kelan. He had reddish-brown-blond hair, almost the color of a malt whiskey. It was longer on top and lay in waves of rich color. His eyes were the azure blue of a Caribbean shoreline. He had dimples when he smiled, which he did as he held out his hand to her.

"I'm Valentino Parker. Mandy says you'll be staying with us awhile."

She took his hand and felt it swallow hers. "Valentino? Seriously?"

"I know, right? I begged my mom to rename me Sue or Jodeen. Hell, I could even have pulled off a Rachel. But no, she had to be a romantic."

"Well, you certainly fit your name."

His smiled widened. It was electrifying. She realized she was still holding his hand. Their palms were becoming warm—all of her was warming up.

"Don't talk to him," Kelan said, interrupting her embarrassing stare.

Reluctantly, she pulled her hand away. "Why?"

"Because he's bad news. He has about twelve concurrent relationships in flight at the moment, some of them even monogamous. You don't want to be the thirteenth. And you won't like his definition of monogamy."

Fee looked over her shoulder at Valentino. He didn't seem inclined to refute what Kelan said.

"He's jealous," Val explained with a shrug. "He can't grasp that his frown is not his friend when it comes to women."

"She's not a woman. She's a girl. Don't talk to her."

"Leave poor Fee alone, you two. She has enough stress in her life as it is." Mandy interrupted them. "Kelan, why don't you introduce the guys before we all sit down?"

A muscle bunched in his jaw. He looked like he was going to refuse, but took one glance at Owen and relented. He called out their names in quick succession. Val pulled out Fee's chair for her, grinning at Kelan as he stood behind it.

The guys filled the dining room with noisy chatter while they loaded their plates. No one spoke about their plans for the day other than innocuous things like exercise rotations, which they planned to do in groups of two or three at various times during the day.

"Fiona, we'll make the call to Buchanan after breakfast. We'll do it downstairs. I want to record it," Owen told her.

Fee pushed the fruit around on her plate, too nervous to eat after hearing that news. She was dreading that call. She didn't know what Alan had gotten himself into, but it couldn't be good if a team like this had come in to investigate him.

She looked up and noticed that Kelan was watching her poke at her food. She stabbed a strawberry and shoved it in her mouth, then followed it with a piece of biscuit. He continued to glare at her until her plate was empty.

After breakfast, the men ushered her to the stairs, half in front of her, half behind her. She felt like an enemy of the state being escorted to an interrogation. When she descended the last step, she moved into a different world. Two sofas had been pushed into the middle of the room and now sat back to back to make space for tables that, loaded with computers and equipment, surrounded most of the outer perimeter.

This was no simple investigative team. They had a war room here in Mandy's basement. It was looking more and more as if these guys were a pseudo-military operation.

The man the others called Max hooked her phone up to the one of the computers, then gave it back to her and told her to dial Alan. "Keep it casual. You're here to work for Mandy—simple change of plans, that's all," he coached her.

Fee looked around the room, nervous at having an audience. Her gaze stopped at Kelan, who stood the furthest away in the stance of a warrior, with legs braced and arms folded across his chest as he had done last night when Mandy's brother and the one named Owen had questioned her. He met and held her gaze. For some reason, she took courage from his strength.

She dialed Alan.

"Fee? Where are you?" he answered the phone.

"Hi, Alan. I'm at Mandy's."

"What the hell are you doing there?" he asked.

She looked at Max. He was broadcasting their call to the room. He nodded at her and mouthed the word "Focus." She pressed a finger to her other ear so that the echo wouldn't distract her.

"I ran into her yesterday. She's desperate for help up here. I hate to disappoint you, but I've decided to work for her this summer instead of at the shop. If you like, I can arrange for a temp to come in."

"What I'd like is for you to get the hell out of there."

"Why?"

There was a brief pause before he answered. "I want you to come home, goddamn it. Why do I have to explain myself?"

"I don't understand. That's all."

"You know what? I made a promise to your mom and I've kept that promise."

"You did, and I'm grateful for that."

"Now you come home. Before it's too late."

"Why would it be too late, Alan? What's happening?"

He sighed. "Just do what you're told, or I wash my hands of you."

"I'm going to stay here for a little while."

"Then we're through. We're done. We are not family. You're on your own." Alan hung up.

Fee's hand was shaking as she set the phone back

on the table. She held no great fondness for Alan, but he'd kept his word to put her through college—a promise he'd honored even after her mother's death. He was her very last connection to her mom. The room was deathly silent. She looked up at the men who watched her so solemnly. She would not cry, she told herself. Not in front of them, not in front of anyone.

Her glance moved to Kelan. He uncrossed his arms. More than anything, she wished she could go to him, have him hold her, hear him tell her everything would be okay.

But it wouldn't. Not ever again. Alan was right. She was on her own. She walked across the room, her head up, her gaze on the stairs. She needed air, and lots of it.

Kelan broke the silence once the sound of Fee's footsteps faded upstairs. "He's up to something. Want me to go keep an eye on him?"

"Yes," Owen said. "And, Max, I want to know about any out-going phone calls, emails, Tweets, or any other communication the bastard makes. Angel, there's a connection between our plumber and Mr. Akbar. Find it. Get me some dirt on what they're up to."

* * *

A few hours after supper, the guys were fighting over a Nerf football and driving Max crazy. They'd been trolling their Internet sources, examining data, playing with different scenarios for the last fifteen hours.

When the football hit Max in the back of the head

for the third time, he spun his chair around and winged it at Val. "Get out of here. All of you. Leave me in peace. You're like a herd of buffalo down here."

Val grinned at him. "Okay. You sure you don't need us?"

"I need you to get outta my hair," Max growled.

"I'll keep him company," Owen told the group. "If we discover anything interesting, I'll phone you."

The guys took the steps two at a time. "I'll be D.D.," Blade offered when they reached the living room. "Rocco, you comin'?" he asked.

"Not me." Rocco grinned at Kit, who still hadn't warmed to the fact that he and Mandy had a relationship. "I've got other plans for the evening."

Kit glared at him but accepted Blade's invite. "I'm in."

"Where are you going?" Fee asked.

"Out," Kelan said.

"Hey, can she go?" Val asked the group.

"Don't think she's legal," Angel wondered aloud. "Unless they lowered the drinking age to, like, twelve?"

Fee made a face. "I'm twenty." She was blushing.

Val watched the color rise on her skin. "Damn, she's cute in pink. You sure she can't come? Take a minute to make a fake I.D."

Kelan stepped in front of her. "She's not going. Guys night out," he said to Val. When the last of the team had filed out the door, he faced Fee and bent close to her ear. "He's right," he whispered. "You are pretty in pink."

Rocco led Mandy through the dining room and into the living. "We're calling it a night, Fee. Max and Owen are downstairs if you need anything. Don't leave the house. It isn't safe yet."

Fee glared at him. "I'm going to bed to read." She started down the hall, mumbling as she went, "I've gone from a terrorist step-father to nine surrogate fathers."

"Brothers," Rocco corrected. "We're not old enough to be your fathers."

Mandy laughed. "We'll be just down the hall, too, if you need something."

"Right. But don't need anything for a while, 'kay?"

"Rocco! You embarrassed Fee," Mandy scolded as he closed the bedroom door behind them.

"I'm not talking about Fee. I'm not thinking about anyone or anything that doesn't involve you in my arms, right here, right now." He took her hand and led her to the bathroom. Her favorite candles glowed by the sink and in the far corners of the tub, washing the room in a muted, flickering light.

Mandy looked at Rocco, her eyes tearing up. "When did you do this?"

He started to help her out of her clothes, unfastening her jeans so that she could step out of them. She was already barefoot. "While you were getting the dogs settled for the night." He pulled her tank top over her head. She stood before him in only her bra and panties. Desire filled him with heat. He forced himself to keep his hunger under control as he popped her bra open. While she stepped out of her panties, he flipped on the water in the stall, letting it warm up. He shucked his clothes, then drew her into the shower stall.

The water was on the hot side of warm. He held her hand and pulled her into the shower. She dropped her head back and let the water stream through her hair. Blocking it from her face with her hands, she arched her back in a slow, delicious stretch that brought his gaze to all the sleek curves of her body. He stepped into the water in front of her. She looked at him through the sheeting water.

He took her hands and lowered them to her sides, twining his fingers with hers. She was so beautiful. He smiled at her, committing every second to memory. He leaned forward, looking at her through the water, letting it splash from her face to his as he kissed her. Her mouth opened to his. Water rushed in, and then his tongue. Softly stroking. He kissed her nose, between her brows.

He poured shampoo into his palm. She covered his palm with hers, rubbing it back and forth until he cupped lather. She took some and rubbed it into his hair. He did the same, drawing her long, copper mane up into the lather. It felt like he was creating her even as she made him, from suds and dreams. But she was real. Flesh and blood. And he was so goddamned blessed he could barely breathe.

They rinsed the shampoo from their hair, then he took up a bar of soap and started to wash her. She stopped him. She handed him a pink scrubby and poured a body wash on it. He lifted it to his nose. Jasmine. God, he would never in his life forget that scent. He rubbed her with the pink mesh ball, lathering every inch of her body.

He knelt to wash her feet. He leaned forward to kiss her belly, low, between her navel and her mound. He went lower still, pressing his face into her coppery curls. "Open for me, Em." She rested a foot on his thigh. He licked her soft folds, rubbing his tongue over her clit. She gasped and grabbed his hair, holding him to her.

His fingers stroked where his tongue had just passed. When he slipped inside her, she cried out, frowning down at him with stormy, green eyes. He smiled up at her.

"Rocco, I'll fall. I can't do this."

"Lean against the wall. I've got you." He kissed her thigh, sucking on her skin as he worked his way back up to her core. He ran a hand up her thigh, over her hip and belly, to cup a breast. Mandy gripped his hand with hers. His tongue circled the swollen nub at the top of her core, then slipped along her folds as he entered her with a finger, two fingers. And then her body was writhing against his face, her channel tightening around his fingers. Fire shot along his cock as he imagined being joined with her for her orgasm.

When she grew still, he kissed her hip, her belly. He dipped his tongue into her navel, then licked along her ribs as he rose to her breasts. He kissed her collarbone, ran his tongue over the center of her throat, captured her chin between his teeth, and grinned at her.

Mandy laughed. He looked pleased with himself. His black eyes, so often sad or tormented, looked happy. She switched places with him.

"Your turn." She pressed his hands against the tile wall, flattening his arms. "Don't move." She drew her hands down the muscles roping his arms. The dark hair of his chest and underarms streamed with water down his torso and abdomen. His penis stood upright from its nest of black hair, like turgid iron. His muscular thighs were spaced apart, bracing him against the wall.

"Kiss me," he ordered, his eyes becoming hooded and intense. Mandy smiled. She leaned forward and kissed his pec, then his shoulder, then his other pec. "That's not what I meant." He breathed heavily through flared nostrils, his gaze held hers, his hands sticking to the wall as if shackled.

She stepped up on her tippy toes and kissed his neck, his jaw, slowly, working her way up to his mouth. He groaned as she pressed her lips to his. Mandy tilted her head, fitting her mouth against his. Her tongue did not penetrate his lips. She licked the circumference of his mouth. He growled, a low, rumbling sound when she reversed her direction and started kissing a long line down to his navel.

Water rained on her back as she knelt before him. She looked up to see the way desire tightened the features of his face. Without touching him, she flicked her tongue against the head of his penis. He spread his legs wider. She licked the sensitive underside of him.

"Do it," he rasped. "Take me in your mouth. Now." She turned slightly, mouthing only a portion of him, flicking her tongue back and forth over the engorged vein at the base of his cock.

"Jesus, Mandy. You're going to fucking kill me. Take me now."

She smiled and moved her mouth leisurely upward until she wrapped her lips around the crown. He groaned and thrust forward, pushing himself as deeply as she could take him. "Yeah, like that." Every time he pulled out, her tongue caressed the hard length of him. He'd wanted this to go on forever. She sucked and stroked and pleasured him. She gripped his balls and gently massaged, even as she squeezed the base of his cock. He pushed into her mouth, feeling as if he was fucking her throat. His balls tightened, his only warning before semen shot like fire into her mouth.

He knelt before her as she lifted her face to the shower, rinsing her mouth with the streams of water that were growing cooler. He kissed her throat, her chin.

His eyes looked sad again. She touched his cheek. "What is it?"

"You're looking at a man without a heart. It belongs to you now. Keep it or throw it away—do what you will with it. I can never take it back."

She shook her head. "How is it that I feel as if I've known you my whole life, not just these past few weeks?" She wrapped her arms around his shoulders, buried her face in his neck. "I've been alone for so long. Most of my life."

"But you're not alone, now. You have my heart." His arms tightened around her. "You give me a reason to live, to want to come back."

She took hold of his face. "I'm counting on it."

* * *

It was just before 11:00 p.m. when Ty parked in the side lot at Winchester's. The place was packed. The band's bass throbbed across the parking lot. Inside, the noise was almost deafening. It was odd, Ty thought, how disproportionate the number of men to women there were. The men were large and poorly groomed. Many had shaved heads. Some sported beards and moustaches. Most of them wore leather vests over wife-beaters, maximizing their display of ink. Not what he would have expected for a Western bar's clientele.

Three women sat alone at one long table—two of them looked like Jersey Shore transplants complete with big hair, heavy make-up, and form-fitting clothes. The other few females in the place were on the dance floor or in crowded booths. Every table and booth was occupied, leaving nowhere for the group to sit together.

Val looked the situation over, spotted the table with the three women, then grinned at Ty. "Get me a Fat Tire. I'll get us a table."

Ty and Kit got their drinks first, then paused at a half-wall separating the bar from the booths, waiting for the others. Val was now sitting at the table with one of the women on his lap. Across from them was the other Jersey Shore princess. A third woman sat at the far end of the table, her nose buried in her phone. Wearing a T-shirt, jeans and hiking boots, she seemed an odd companion for the others. While Ty watched, she made short work of a guy who approached her. No one spoke to the other two women, which, given their come-fuck-me attire, surprised him.

Val waved them over.

"The guy's a man-whore, but he got us a table," Greer grumbled.

"You don't hear me complaining," Kelan commented, following him. They pushed their way through the crowd. Ty handed Val his beer, then sat between him and the hiker chick. Kit sat at the end near Ty, and the other guys filled in around the table. The brown-haired girl looked up at him. Her lips were compressed in a tight line. She offered no welcome but simply went back to her phone.

Ty leaned toward her. "If you don't want to be here, why are you?" he asked, honestly curious about her answer. Again, she looked up at him. She wasn't wearing any make-up. She didn't need any. She looked like she'd come here right from a lengthy hike outside. What color would her smoky topaz eyes be in the sunlight? Her hair was wavy and looked unbearably soft. She was like a draft of fresh air someone had let into the thick, crowded room.

"I had no choice. They needed a D.D."

Ty set his cane against the table and leaned back,

absently rubbing his thigh. "Same here. I'm unstable enough as it is with this. Figured I didn't need to be stumbling around in a drunken stupor."

The girl's smoky eyes studied his. "What happened?"

"War injury."

She frowned at his thigh, lost to her thoughts. "I'm sorry," she whispered.

"Why?"

"That you're hurt."

"Wasn't your fault. You didn't do this to me." Ty wondered, as he said it, if he wouldn't have voluntarily taken a bullet just so that he could sit here with this girl and have this conversation. He stuck out his hand. "Name's Ty Bladen."

Her eyes widened then narrowed. "Bladen?" She shook her head. "We got no further need to chat. No offense intended, Bladen." She returned her focus to her phone.

Ty frowned. What was that about? He'd been gone for more than a decade. He'd done nothing to earn her frosty attitude. He could only think of one reason why she'd had that reaction. "Did you know my father?"

"No," she said without looking up.

"Eddie! Get your nose out of your phone. We have visitors, honey," the Jersey Shore girl cuddling with Greer leaned forward to call down the table. "Be nice to the man."

Eddie flashed the woman a look, but stayed silent. "S'all good," Ty spoke up, deflecting the woman's attention. "The two D.D.s'll just sit here and keep tabs on you guys."

Ty sat silently for all of a minute before leaning over to Eddie and asking, "So—what're you reading?"

The girl looked up at him with the hardest, ball-busting glare she could summon. "Listen, Bladen. This is how it's going to go. You're going sit in your chair and talk to your boys and leave me alone. Otherwise, someone's going to get hurt."

Ty couldn't help but grin. God, she was hot. "Right. No talking." He crossed his arms and slumped farther in his chair, his legs spread wide to ease the tension in his groin that his interest in the girl had caused. He tried to think of something other than the spitfire sitting next to him, but all he came up with were more questions about her. Why had she shut him down when she discovered his name? What had his bastard of a father done to her to cause such a reaction?

Val smiled as a waitress set a margarita in front of him. He paid her with a hundred dollar bill and asked her to keep drinks coming for him and his friends. The woman on his lap snuggled tighter while he spoke to the waitress. Val felt his body heating up. She was all curves—big breasts, narrow waist, plump ass. He didn't care that her assets were medically enhanced. The very fact that she wanted to look sexy *was* sexy. He grinned up at her as she rubbed those assets against his chest.

God, he loved women. They were delectably different from men, soft and cuddly and sweet smelling. It didn't matter if they were thin or heavy, small- or big-breasted, young or older. All of them equally fascinated him. They were truly a gift to mankind, and he intended to spend his life showing his appreciation.

She wiggled on his lap. His dick responded in kind. She giggled. "You know you have a girl's name." He drew her down for a kiss, putting her mouth to a different use than talking. He savored the sweet, chemical flavor of her lipstick, imagining the sticky, pink imprints she'd leave on his body as she kissed her way down to his cock.

"Do I kiss like a girl?" he asked, his voice rough.

"I don't know. I've never kissed a girl," she said, wrapping both arms about his neck.

"You're lying." More wiggling. Christ, he was going to lose it. Right here.

"Well, there was one time..."

"Did you like it?"

"Wouldn't you like to know?"

He gripped her hair, positioning her face where he wanted it. "Yes, I would." He tilted his head and took her mouth with a force and authority that was all male. While she was distracted with the kiss, he lowered his hand to her thigh, bared for his consumption by the short skirt she wore. He stroked her skin from her knee up until his fingers brushed the hem of her skirt.

She didn't protest. She drew back from the kiss and watched his hand on her leg. He lifted the margarita glass and held it to her lips, then turned the glass and sipped where she'd sipped.

"How is it that such a beautiful woman is here alone?" he asked, resuming his slow stroking.

She made a lovely pout. "We weren't alone when we came here, but they took off a while ago. I'm so glad you showed up."

He pulled her ass a little closer. "Just left you, did they?" He made another pass up her leg, his hand now fully beneath her skirt. Would she let him get her off here? Now? Would she quietly peak, her pleasure a secret between the two of them? Or would she go all wild on him with a screaming orgasm? He couldn't decide which he'd prefer. Both, maybe.

Her phone beeped with an incoming text message. She huffed, but got off his lap to answer it. A quick look at the text had her sending a dark glare toward the woman at the end of the table. "Not funny, Eddie."

She sat back down on Val's lap, this time facing the other way—effectively blocking his advances since he was right-handed. He leaned in to kiss her neck and caught sight of the tattoo she wore below her left ear. A crescent moon and star.

I had them branded so we'd know them when we saw them, Rocco had said during the briefing two days ago. Val pressed his lips to the mark of his enemy and sent a surreptitious look around the room, searching for men with the same mark.

Ty looked between Eddie and the floozy warming Val's lap, wondering what she'd texted. Probably a warning about the audience they were attracting. Man, he couldn't even live vicariously. He decided to get up and move around. "I'm going to get another Coke. Want one?" he asked the girl next to him. Their waitress was being plenty attentive, thanks to Val, but his leg was stiffening up—he wanted to stretch it out.

Eddie kept her eyes on her phone. "No."

"Hungry?" he asked, wishing he could get her to look at him one more time.

She did—and caught the sight of his grin. Her eyes narrowed. "No, thank you."

Ty grabbed his cane and walked through the crush to the bar. He shouldered his way in and leaned an elbow on the counter. The man currently waiting for his drink was one of the many gangbangers clustered about the place. Ty's gaze wandered over his tats, curious to see if he knew any of the images the guy sported. He followed an unimaginative hate message up the guy's neck, where it terminated with a crescent moon and star.

A cold feeling started at Ty's neck and worked its way down his spine. He sent a look around the crowded bar area, seeing the same mark on several men. The man at the bar must have felt his curiosity, for he turned and glared at Ty.

"Nice ink," Ty tapped his neck. "What does it mean?"

The man's brows lowered. "Why the fuck are you talking to me?"

Ty laughed. "Just makin' nice conversation. Got some social anxiety there, big guy?" The gangbanger grunted for an answer and reached for Ty's throat with his free hand—the other still held his money and was resting on the bar. Ty grabbed two of his fingers and bent them backward as he pushed the hand away. The man should have caved instantly to avoid the pain, but he kept up his forward momentum. He either didn't feel the pain or didn't need those two fingers.

Before the situation escalated, the barkeep slammed a baseball bat down on the counter. He looked at the skinhead. "You know the rules. No fighting." The immediate area around the two of them got quiet, but Ty doubted anyone beyond a few feet from them heard the bang. He eased his hold on the guy's hand, ready for anything. The man took his drink and paid, glaring a warning at Ty before he stepped away.

Ty looked at the frustrated bartender. "They part of your regular clientele?"

"No. Once a month or so, they come into town and take the place over. I made an agreement with their leader, Pete Conlin, to keep the place open longer when they're here in exchange for no property destruction. Still, it's a battle every time." He eyed Ty. "You're with the Feds who came into town earlier this week." Ty didn't bother correcting him. The less he knew about Owen's team, the better. The bartender shook his head, grinning as he rubbed the counter down. "You picked a helluva night to come here."

"Why's that?"

"They aren't normal biker dudes. They're WKBers and they hate government employees."

Ty took his drink and returned to the table. He tapped Kit on the shoulder. "We've got a problem. And not a three girls and six guys kind of problem."

"What is it?" Kit asked as he stood up next to Ty.

"It's a six guys and fifty WKBers kind of problem."

Kit mouthed a curse as he glanced around at the clientele, his gaze snagging on man after man bearing the mark of Ghalib Halim. Val caught his look, and Ty could tell he'd figured out the problem as well. Kelan noticed the loaded glances. He hit Greer and Angel on the shoulders. They stood up.

"I'm sorry to cut our time short, sweetheart, but it looks as if we're heading out." Val stood up, his arm still around the woman he'd been fondling.

She arched against him like a cat stretching, her hands kneading the contours of his chest. "Why do you have to go? Stay and keep me company."

As Val leaned in for a good-bye kiss, the woman was yanked out of his arms. A fist connected hard with his jaw instead. Stunned by the abrupt change in his circumstances, Val barely had time to focus on the bearded, bald man in front of him before Kelan intercepted the next blow. His friend grabbed the skinhead's throat in a hold so tight, the man could neither breathe nor pull away. It stopped the others who'd come forward in a close circle.

"Take it down a notch." Kelan glared at the guy. "I'm going to let you go so we can have some nice convo about what's got you freaked out." The guy held his hands up. Kelan eased his hold.

"The bastard was touching my woman. I'll be doing my talking with this—" He pulled a switchblade out of his pocket and popped the blade. He swiped at Kelan. It was the only strike he managed to make. Kelan hit his throat with the edge of his hand, then kicked out his knees.

When he turned to the next man, Kelan realized all his bros were likewise engaged. The space was too tight for them to take on more than a couple of men each. It was hard to tell how many they were going to have to fight, but the odds were definitely not in their favor.

Ty and Kit were fighting back-to-back, dodging chairs. For every man they put down, another took his place. Ty looked over where Eddie had been sitting. She was gone. At first, he was relieved, thinking she'd slipped away with the other women who'd been at the table. But then he caught a movement under the table and realized she was trapped inside the ring of fighting men.

He moved toward her, putting himself between her hiding spot and the circle of angry gangbangers kicking and thrashing their way into the line the team was holding around the table. As soon as he saw an opening in the crush, he drew her from under the table.

"Go. Get out of here. Find the other women you were with and go home."

She looked at him for what seemed several heartbeats. He wondered if he'd ever see her again. He touched his hand to her cheek, unable to live out the night without knowing the feel of her skin. "Stay safe,

Eddie."

"It's Eden. My name's Eden."

Ty smiled. *Eden.* He'd no sooner indulged himself in repeating her name than another fist plowed into him. He pushed into the bastard to give Eden enough space to slip away. When he looked back, she was gone.

The fight seemed to last for hours but probably was only minutes. Ty's knuckles were torn and bleeding. He had a split lip and one rib felt as if it might be broken. His thigh was protesting its extended strain. He noticed a ring of downed WKBers was clogging up the fight zone just as a shotgun went off.

"It's over. Get out," Hal shouted, his shotgun poised for another blast into the ceiling. "And if you ever want to come back, you'll pay for tonight's damages."

"We didn't start it," Pete said.

"Of course. I have no doubt who threw the first punch. But don't worry—you'll be splitting the bill—half to the Feds, half to you. Now get out."

Ty and the others watched as the WKBers helped their friends up. They had to carry a few of them. He looked around the room for Eden but didn't see her. Val clapped Kelan on the back. Being slightly behind him, he didn't see the wince that tightened the man's face.

"Thanks for the quick save earlier. Was expecting a pair of soft lips, not a hard fist," Val said.

"Happy to help. And thank you for getting us all fucked tonight," Kelan groused. "Next time keep your hands to yourself."

Val sighed. "Yeah, sorry about that, too. She was just so damned sweet."

"We didn't all strike out." Greer held up a torn napkin. "I got Trudy's phone number." He leaned over and spoke to Ty in a lower voice. "Might come in handy if we want an in with the WKBers. She lives in their compound."

"Great. Maybe you and Val can double date," Ty growled. He had a reason to get in to the compound too, but he doubted he'd get a warm welcome.

Kit handed Hal, Winchester's owner, a business card. "Send our bill to Mandy's house. Sorry things got out of hand."

"Next time, don't come here on WKB night, got it?"

"Loud and clear."

* * *

The next morning, Mandy thought the guys were unusually quiet but she was too busy cooking breakfast to notice why until she sat at the table. She sat next to Rocco. As he poured coffee for her, she looked around the table.

"Good heavens! What happened?" Every man, except the three who had stayed home last night, looked as if he'd been run over by a herd of horses. They had swollen, split lips, red, bruised cheeks, swollen noses, black eyes. Kit sported a butterfly bandage on his eyebrow. "Were we attacked? How could I sleep through such an event?"

"No attack," Kit told her. He filled his plate as if nothing extraordinary had happened. "We went to Winchester's last night."

"I go there all the time. I never come home looking like you do now. I've never even seen a bar fight there. Really, Kit, you should have outgrown that long ago."

"I'm guessing you don't go there on WKB night."

"Oh. Oh, no!" Mandy's eyes widened as she processed what must have happened.

"And lucky for us," Kelan explained, "Val hit on the lead guy's hoochie mama."

"She voluntarily sat on my lap. How was I supposed to know she was spoken for?" Val said in his own defense.

"Tell me the other guys look worse," Mandy commented.

"We have owies, Mandy. We need massages." Val gave her a soulful look.

"No massages," Rocco growled. "Mandy is not here for your amusement."

"And don't even look at Fee. She's under our protection," Kelan warned.

Val grunted. "So that's how this team's gonna roll, is it?"

"I'd be happy to put you out of your misery," Rocco offered.

Mandy laughed and set her hand on Rocco's forearm to calm him. "I have a friend I can introduce you to, Val. I'm sure she'd be quite taken with your injuries."

Kit glared at her. "Not Ivy."

Mandy frowned. "I do have more than one friend, Kit."

"Wow. No one's sharing. What happened to the team that fights together has fun together?" Val shook his head and glared at Owen. "If I'd known women were so scarce here in Wyoming, I would never have taken this assignment."

* * *

As evening cast long shadows across the ranch, Rocco stood with Blade at the high fence of Kitano's corral watching Mandy work the Paint. He loved how she handled the gelding, eased his fears, respected him, asserted herself. It seemed to Rocco that the Paint looked forward to his twice-daily workouts with her. Soon she'd be able to ride him.

Blade's phone rang. He had a short conversation with the person on the other end, then hung up. Rocco looked at him. "Problems?"

"No. I asked my foreman to take an extended leave for a while until we get the situation here cleared up. He said he was ready to go, but had a few things to discuss with me. I'm going to head over there. I'll be glad when they're safe."

"Want company?" Rocco offered.

"No need. I shouldn't be long."

Ty walked into the foyer of his house a few minutes later, calling for Dennis.

"In here, sir."

"Glad you could make arrangements so quickly," Ty said as he walked into his father's office. A sound caught his attention over by the private bathroom off the study. He caught a quick glimpse of Kathy, Dennis's wife, gagged and bound. Hearing someone behind him, he spun around as a tranquilizer nailed his shoulder.

His world began to wobble, his vision narrowing, closing. He looked at his caretaker, who rushed forward to catch him. "I'm sorry. I'm so sorry. I had no choice—"

The rest of his words were lost to Ty.

Dennis looked up as Amir led his whimpering wife out of the bathroom. "It's done. I shot him, now let her go."

"Take him out to your car and put him in the trunk."

Dennis looked at his wife, then at Amir. "He's too heavy for me to move by myself."

Amir cocked his gun and pointed it at Kathy. "I suggest you figure it out, Mr. Jackson, or you'll have two bodies to move."

Dennis lifted Ty under his arms, but before he could pull him out of the office, Amir told him to stop. "Give me his cell phone." Dennis handed it over. Amir dropped it on the floor and crushed its case beneath his heel. "Get moving," he ordered.

Dennis dragged Ty across the foyer, out the front door, and down the steps to the waiting SUV. He opened the back hatch and lifted Ty into the empty cargo area. Amir led his wife out and shoved her into the backseat. "Get in and drive," he ordered Dennis.

"Where?"

"Head up toward Hwy 130 West. I will tell you when to turn off."

Dennis drove as fast he dared. Police patrols were scarce out this way. He didn't know if he should comply or if he should try to get someone's attention. In the end, the gun pointed at his wife's head made his decision for him. Once they'd gone a little ways into the Medicine Bow National Forest, Amir directed him to pull off the highway onto a windy dirt road that hugged a few cliffs and crossed a couple of creeks.

"Stop. We're here." Amir ordered Dennis and his wife out of the car. The night air was cold in the mountains. Dennis took his coat off and wrapped it around her shoulders.

"Where are we going?" he asked Amir, who'd taken a flashlight out of the trunk. Dennis looked at Ty to see if he was rousing yet. He didn't move. God, he hoped he hadn't killed the boy. Though if he had, it might be better than whatever Amir had planned for them.

"Follow the path. I'll show you where to drop his body."

The ground was rocky, the path barely discernible in the dark. Amir jerked the flashlight around, using it more for his footing than theirs. Dennis almost fell into a deep fissure before realizing the path had ended right where he stood. He reached out and grabbed his wife.

Amir stepped up and poured light down the narrow hole, a hole too deep to see the bottom in the darkness. "That's where you'll dump the body." He pulled out a long knife and turned to Kathy.

Immediately, she started crying, pleading. "Silence," he complained, backhanding her. He grabbed her wrists, slashing through the rope that bound them. "Help your husband move the body."

They trudged back to the SUV. Dennis's mind was churning quickly, spinning through different options. Amir stayed in the Explorer as they pulled Ty out. He tried to hold most of Ty's weight to spare his wife as much of the burden as he could.

"Is he dead, Dennis? Have you killed Ty?"

Dennis looked around. He could still see Amir with the flashlight in the driver's seat. "No," he whispered. "Let's be careful how we get him into the hole. I saw a ledge not far below where we were standing. Maybe he can get out when he comes to. Hurry now. I don't want him to awaken while we are here."

Kathy was sobbing quietly, broken by fear. She stumbled and hurt her knee. "There is no one to help us, is there?"

"We'll see. We'll see, Kathy."

At the edge of the crevice, Dennis positioned Ty so that he could slide down the one side, hopefully without getting any broken bones, though what good that would be if he couldn't get out and no one knew where he was, Dennis didn't know. When it was done,

Kathy leaned over and tossed Dennis's coat after him.

"Why did you do that?" Amir asked, his voice almost a scream. Gone was his knife, in its place was his sleek Glock. Dennis hadn't heard him come up behind them. He drew Kathy a step away from the ledge. "It slipped is all. It fell off of her when we tossed him."

"He is still alive isn't he? Isn't he?" Amir shouted this last when they didn't answer quickly enough. "Go back to the car and wait for me," he ordered.

Dennis grabbed Kathy's hand and hurried to do Amir's bidding. Amir shot a couple of rounds into the fissure where Ty was. Dennis had never felt such terror in his life. An idea took form as they rushed down the jagged hillside. At the SUV, he opened the back passenger door and ordered Kathy inside. He jumped in the driver's seat, then put the SUV in gear, expecting a blaze of gunfire at any moment.

He could see the bouncing light of Amir's flashlight as he ran back toward the SUV down the rough trail. Dennis cranked the steering wheel and spun the vehicle around. They drove fast down the dirt road. The trail seemed to take forever. Kathy kept a watch behind them. The narrow road made a sharp turn to the left, hugging a ridge. Dennis reminded himself to go slowly. His heart was pounding so that it drowned out Kathy's whimpers in the backseat.

He hated leaving Ty with Amir. God, it probably didn't matter. Amir had fired shots down into the ravine—the boy was probably already gone. They made a sharp turn onto another side road. The incline was steep, and the tires did not seem to grip the road through the dirt and gravel. He tapped the brakes.

Surely, there were cops ahead in the town of Centennial, or if not, at least there were people. He could get help there. He tapped the brakes again, realizing he was going too fast for the sheer, winding back road. Nothing. He tapped again.

The brakes were gone.

He tried easing up on the handbrake. He was so focused on the brake that he didn't steer the SUV around another sharp bend. He looked in the rear view mirror, caught Kathy's panicked gaze as the SUV launched itself over the mountainside.

Chapter 17

"Owen! We got it! We broke @A__akbar's code!"
Max shouted gleefully. Night had fallen. The team had
been at this the entire day. "Every time he mentions
coffee in Denver, the plumber goes to Denver. The
number of espresso shots correlates to the number of
days between the Tweet and the meeting. They met
two days ago."

"Where did they meet? Get me some video
footage."

"We're getting Buchanan's bank records now. If he
used a credit card, we'll know shortly."

Three hours later, Rocco stood up and stretched.
He hated paper trail work. They'd discovered the name
of the coffee shop, and had found receipts in
Buchanan's bank records going back two years, ever
since he first arrived in Wolf Creek Bend. From the
schedule recorded in his appointment book, it looked
as if he'd been having regular meetings each month at
the same location. They were still awaiting video
footage to confirm, but it was an interesting lead.

Rocco found Mandy curled up on the sofa upstairs, sound asleep, a book open and forgotten on her lap. He knelt beside her and tried to wake her by gently brushing a bit of hair from her face.

"Hey," he whispered. "You didn't have to wait up."

She opened her eyes, giving him a soft smile that filled him with warmth. She touched his face, palming the rough hair of his beard that was growing thicker every day. "I missed you."

"I'll put the boys out, then come to bed. You go on and get settled." He drew her to her feet and turned her toward her room. He whistled for the dogs and held the door open for them. They moved as sleepily as Mandy. They hadn't been with her for long, but already they'd become accustomed to the routine she kept.

Something caught their interest down at the construction site. They began barking. Rocco walked out, his eyes searching into the darkness. It had to be after midnight. Had Blade had come back yet? The dogs were now barking in earnest. He caught their collars before they could charge down the hill.

Someone was down there. A phone rang. Rocco could feel the hackles on his neck stand up. He was taking the dogs back to the house when the first explosion lit up the sky. The dogs broke free from him and ran into the darkness, away from the fire. The second blast blew him off his feet. He never heard the third one.

* * *

Max sat in front of his monitors, searching for what had tripped the motion detector down at the construction site. A man was standing in the skeletal framework of the stable.

"Kit! Get out here!" he called out. He, Kit and Greer were sleeping in shifts so that one of them manned the monitors around the clock.

Kit sat down next to him, rubbing the sleep from his eyes. "Whatcha got?" He wore his jeans and black T-shirt, but was barefooted.

"Not sure. Someone's down at the construction site. Can't make out who it is. Can you?"

Kit studied the video feed. "Is that Buchanan? Who's he calling?"

A second later, light flashed on the cameras as they heard the explosion outside. Kit jumped to his feet and ran to his room to gear up, shouting orders to Max as he went.

"Stay at the monitors. Watch for anyone else stalking around." Greer was rolling out of bed seconds after the explosion, awake and battle ready. "Greer, call down to Owen at the bunkhouse. Tell him to get the rest of the guys up here. We need to secure the house and check the perimeter for more bombs."

"Shit! Rocco's out there!" Max pointed to a monitor. They watched Mandy run from the house and fall at Rocco's side, Fee right behind her. Kit strapped on his Beretta. He buckled his Kevlar vest, grabbed his rifle, then took the stairs three at a time.

Owen, Angel, Val, and Kelan were running from

the bunkhouse, armed and ready. Kit hurried to where Rocco lay still in the dirt. Mandy was crying, trying to get him to respond to her. Kit pressed his fingers to Rocco's neck, checking for a pulse.

"He's alive, Mandy." Kit set his hand on Mandy's shoulder. "Look at me. Em, look at me. You've got to keep it together."

"What the hell just happened?" Owen asked as they reached the main house.

"Buchanan blew the riding center. Help me turn Rocco onto his back."

Angel held his head, keeping his neck immobilized as Kit and Owen slowly rolled him to his back. Rocco appeared to have no major injuries, though he was nicked and scraped from the explosion. Sirens began to wail in the distance. Kit checked Rocco's pulse again, made sure he was breathing.

"Angel, Val, do a sweep of the buildings, make sure there are no other nasty surprises waiting," Owen ordered. "Kelan, guard the porch. No one goes in or out unless it's one of us. And take Fee with you."

"Was Buchanan alone?" Owen asked when Kit stepped away from Rocco.

"He's the only one we saw. The other cameras were not triggered." Kit looked at Owen. "Max and Greer are manning the monitors. Where's Blade?"

"Don't know. Wasn't he at the house with you?"

"Haven't seen him since this evening."

"He wasn't down below, with Buchanan, was he?" Owen asked.

"We didn't see him on the monitors. Go get some blankets, Em," Kit told Mandy. "I don't want Rocco going into shock."

Kelan wrapped a hand around Fee's waist and led her back to the house. At the porch, Fee pulled against him. "Rocco's hurt. Mandy needs me. I can't go in yet."

"He's hurt, but he's got all the help he needs. You'll just be underfoot," Kelan told her. The sirens were sounding louder. "It's not safe out here. I want you to go back inside."

Fee turned in his arms and buried her face in his chest, surprising the hell out of him. He wished he weren't wearing his Kevlar vest, wished he could feel her against his side. He wrapped an arm about her shoulders and pulled her even tighter against himself. He could feel her trembling. She looked up at him, her big, blue eyes swimming in tears.

"What happened, Kelan? I heard the explosion. I thought I dreamt it, but then Mandy went running out of the house."

"We don't know yet."

"Do you think Rocco was hurt badly?"

Kelan shook his head. "I wish I had more info for you."

She straightened and smoothed her hands over her eyes. "What can I do?"

Kelan didn't want her to do anything. He wanted her to go back inside and stay safe, but he suspected her panic would only deepen if he didn't give her a task. "First, get dressed. Then put on some coffee and see if you can wrangle up some food. I think it's going to be a long night."

She nodded, still hesitating to move inside. He caught her chin, forcing her to meet his gaze. "I will keep you safe, Fee."

Fresh tears spilled down her cheeks. Damn, that wasn't the reaction he was after. She pulled away and hurried back inside Mandy's house.

Rocco stood in the middle of the mayhem surrounding the compound where he and Kadisha lived. She handed Zavi to him and tried to push him away. He grabbed her arm, not letting her go back into the building. She fought with him. They both stumbled to the ground. Her coat parted, revealing a wide band of C-4 belted around her waist, secured across the slight swell of their child.

"Kadisha! What are you doing?"

"You did this!" She gestured to the explosives. "You killed us!"

Rocco stared at his wife as she got to her feet. "Don't go! I will defuse it."

"It is too late. There are other bombs in the house. I have to get my mother out of there."

Rocco jumped to his feet, and reached for her, but she slipped away. He looked at Zavi, who was crying. He reached for him, and then everything went black.

When he came to, the dust and ash was so thick, the sun had darkened to night. Rocco crawled on his belly, dragging himself over shards of brick and twisted bits of metal to a small, bleeding body a few feet away. Zavi. Oh, God, Zavi. Only the torso remained of his boy, his skin singed beyond recognition. Rocco reached him and dragged him to his lap, weeping and rocking. His own face and body were nicked with dozens of small and large cuts, though he felt none of his injuries as he held what remained of his son's body.

He'd done this, Kadisha had said. He'd done this. He couldn't have—he hadn't wanted his boy or his wife killed.

Women were running around in the debris, crying, screaming, looking for lost loved ones. He couldn't hear them. His ears were ringing too loudly. Time moved in a strange, distorted way, going too fast sometimes and too slow others.

Men tried to get him to put Zavi down, to stop the prayers he wailed over his son's body. He threatened them with his knife. He would not surrender the body. Not yet. Not ever. He would never let his son go.

Gradually, the orange sun dipped below the horizon, shutting itself away from the horror and devastation the day left behind. Still, Rocco rocked his son, singing prayers, begging Allah to accept his innocent child into heaven.

Again, men tried to take Zavi from him, wanting to prepare him for his burial, and again Rocco would not let them come close. By the time the sun rose the next morning, Rocco's throat was raw and his soul was empty.

The stench from Zavi's body was unbearable. Some of the burned skin had torn off his son's body and was stuck to Rocco. When the men came this time, there were too many to fight off. They pulled Zavi from him and went to prepare him.

Rocco sat alone on the hill, looking at the place where Kadisha's house had been. Zavi's blackened flesh and dried blood were all over him, his arms, his neck, his face. Still he rocked.

Still he tried to sing the prayers for the dead.

When the men came to him next, they came with guns. These were not the village elders but his father-in-law's warriors. They beat him with their rifle butts. He did not fight them off. Perhaps it was Allah's vengeance for his prayers—prayers from a man who had killed his son.

They stopped their assault, sooner than he'd thought they would. His flesh hurt now, but it still didn't equal the anguish in his soul. The men dragged him to a rickety van and threw him the back. He didn't know where they were taking him. It didn't matter. He was dead already.

Zavi was dead. And Kadisha was dead. And their next little baby was dead. The whole, goddamned village was dead.

They drove for a while over rough roads. They didn't offer him any food or water. But of course, you cannot feed a corpse. Eventually, they stopped somewhere. Another village.

They dragged him out of the van. He tried to walk, but he couldn't keep up with them. They moved some crates and then some boards, revealing a dark hole in the ground. His grave. They'd brought him to his grave.

"Rocco? Rocco, can you hear me? Are you hurt?"

Rocco floated toward that voice. An angel's voice. His angel. Perhaps God had heard his prayers after all. She was touching him. She shouldn't do that—he would soil her, would get Zavi's death on her. He eased away from her, warning her. She frowned at him as if she didn't understand.

The irony of that made him laugh. With all of the languages he knew, he still couldn't speak Angel.

A man shook him. He shoved at the man. The man grabbed him again. Rocco punched him. The man tried to wrestle him down. Rocco didn't want anyone touching him, but the man wouldn't quit. They rolled on the gravel, hot metal shrapnel cutting and searing them.

"Goddamn it, Rocco! It's me. Kit. Open your fucking eyes and look at me!"

Kit? Rocco did as ordered. He relaxed the hand he held braced against Kit's chin. "Kit?" he asked, touching him with one hand, then two, anchoring himself to this reality. "Kit?"

"Yeah, bro. It's me. You hurt?"

"No."

Kit studied him. "You remembered, didn't you?"

Rocco dropped his hands and shut his eyes. He nodded.

"You okay?" Kit asked.

Rocco looked at him. "I'm alive."

"Yeah. Yeah, you are."

Rocco lifted his head to look around, seeing the warm glow of the destroyed equestrian center, Owen, and Mandy. He shoved free of Kit's hold and tried to stand. His legs didn't hold him. He fell down. The world was spinning. Time warped again. He felt nauseous and dizzy. He tried to stand, managed to take a few steps before again hitting his knees. His head was ringing like a fucking bell tower. He bent over and covered his ears with his forearms. Christ, his head hurt.

Mandy knelt in front of him. She reached out tentatively and covered one of his hands with hers. "Rocco? Where does it hurt?"

"Mandy—" He barely recognized his raspy voice. He couched in front of her, afraid to move too much while the world was spinning so crazily. "I feel it. I feel the flesh," he whispered, lifting his head to look at her. He caught her gaze and refused to relinquish it. If he looked at himself and saw the blackened skin and blood, he would be lost. "It's sticking, burning, pulling. Do you see it? Is it real? I can smell it. I can feel it. Help me, Mandy."

"Oh, Rocco." Her voice broke. She brushed his hair from his face, her touch infinitely gentle. Her eyes filled with tears. She took hold of his face, her thumbs brushing his cheeks. She shook her head. He sat up a bit farther so that she could look him over. She ran her hands down his neck, over his shoulders, down his arms, to his hands. Lifting her gaze, she met his look and shook her head. "It is not there. But you are cut-up pretty badly. Can I take you inside?"

"No," Kit answered. "The ambulance is almost here."

The sirens were close now. Fire engines were rushing up the hill toward the center.

"Where are the dogs?" Rocco asked, looking around. "They were with me right before the explosion."

"I'll go look for them," Mandy said as she stood up.

"No!" Rocco and Kit both stopped her.

"You're not going anywhere until we secure the site," Kit ordered. "Where's Blade?" he asked Rocco.

Blade. Rocco knew something about him. He tried to reach that memory. It danced at the edge of his consciousness. They'd stood at the corral and watched Mandy earlier that evening.

"He said he was going to meet with his foreman, that Dennis had some things to cover with him before he and his wife headed out of town for a while," Rocco looked at Kit and Owen. "But that was hours ago. He's not back yet?"

Something else claimed Rocco's attention. "Oh hell, Kit." He remembered what he'd seen immediately before the explosion. "There was someone down there, in the arena. I saw him before it all blew. The dogs were barking at him. A phone rang, and then the bombs went off. They were triggered by the cell phone."

"That was Buchanan. Max and I saw him on the monitors," Kit said.

Val and Angel came back with the word that the grounds were clear. Owen sent them to move the cars so that the fire trucks would have room to maneuver if they needed to come up to the higher level. Soon the lower terrace was filled with fire engines and cop cars. An ambulance pulled into the upper terrace. There were no fire hydrants to connect to, but the Wolf Creek Bend Fire Department was often called upon to tackle wild fires in the nearby mountains and so came well equipped to deal with a remote fire like the one at Mandy's ranch. Two water tankers pulled up by what was left of the construction site.

A couple of paramedics rolled a stretcher over to Rocco. He felt a cold sweat break out over his skin at the thought of being strapped down while they worked on him. He stood up, using all his concentration not to wobble on his legs.

"No," he told the paramedics when they reached for him.

"Rocco, you have to go with them," Kit ordered. "I want them to check you out. You might have a concussion and God knows what other injuries."

Rocco tore his gaze from Kit and nodded toward the gurney. "I'm not going on that. I'll walk."

Mandy came to his side and wrapped an arm about his waist, providing her shoulder to lean on. "Let's go." She didn't give him time to argue but started walking him toward the back of the ambulance.

The paramedics cut his shredded T-shirt off. One of them wrapped a blood pressure cuff on his arm while the other checked his pupils. Then they began examining the many cuts and scrapes he'd suffered when the explosion threw him to the ground. He had to fight a rising panic at being crowded, touched.

He could feel the burned skin and blood tightening on him. He shut his eyes. It wasn't real, that phantom flesh. Mandy had said so. It was a memory, all that had remained of his son after Kadisha's house blew up. It wasn't on him now. He looked over the shoulders of the men tending to him. She was there, watching the proceedings, her face taut with anxiety.

He took a deep breath to calm himself before motioning her over to hold his hand. The paramedics looked from her to Rocco. In a small town like Wolf Creek Bend, everybody knew everybody and who their significant others were. He bet there'd been speculation in town about the two of them, especially after his freakout at the diner. And now this explosion. He brought her hand to his mouth and kissed her cold knuckles, making sure there was no doubt to any observers that she belonged to him.

"Sir, several of these cuts are going to need stitches. And you may have a concussion. We're going to take you down to the hospital in Cheyenne."

"No. You'll put butterflies on them, and we'll call it good." He felt a growing pressure to get to Blade's. He had to have seen the explosion, even from his place. If he were able, he'd be here. Something had happened to him. Rocco couldn't screw around with little cuts when Blade was in trouble.

The two paramedics looked at each other and shook their heads. "If you won't go to the hospital, we've got Doc Reynolds on call. At least let us take you into town to have him take care of these cuts, check you out more thoroughly."

Before he could refuse any attention, Mandy tightened her hold on him. "Rocco Silas, you go see the doctor and let him fix you up."

"Fine. But you're staying here. I'll get Kelan to take

me. I don't need to be driven in an ambulance."

"I'm going with you."

"You're going to stay here, Em. I don't know what's going on, but shit's hit the fan. I need you to stay here with Kit. It's the only way I'll go the clinic."

"You're hurt. I should be with you."

He looked at the paramedics, who were observing their conversation with rapt attention. "Please," he told her. "Stay with Kit." He nodded to the paramedics as he grabbed his shredded T-shirt and stood up. He took hold of Mandy's arm and led her back to her brother.

Kit and Owen were talking to a couple of men—one was the police chief. Rocco assumed the other was the fire chief. "Sheriff," he nodded to Tate. "I told you there was more going on here than common pranks."

"And I asked you for more information," the sheriff grumbled. "If you thought this was a matter for Homeland Security, you should have said something."

"I had nothing more to go on than a gut feeling. I guess we all are on the same page now."

"Rocco warned you?" Kit growled as he glared at the sheriff. "You should have listened to my man."

"There was nothing I could do. I had no facts to work with. Besides, your man here was having psychotic episodes. Didn't exactly help his credibility."

"Yeah, well, now you got a dead man and a whole hive of terrorists," Owen told him. "I want this kept quiet. If anyone asks, it was a prank gone wrong and it's under investigation. I don't want OSHA up here asking questions. And I don't want to alert the townspeople."

Rocco pulled Kit aside. "Kelan's taking me to see the doc in town to get a few stitches. Then he and I are going to Blade's. Something's wrong. He should have been back by now. Keep Mandy with you. The bastards are playing a game—she may be their next target."

Chapter 18

Kelan shut off the SUV's lights well before he and Rocco reached the turnoff to Blade's ranch. They drove slowly up the long dirt road, their path marked only by the moonlight. Kelan cut the engine at the last hill before the house. They closed their doors quietly, knowing how sound traveled in the night's cool, thin air. They made a circuit of the main house, keeping to whatever slim cover they could find—fence lines, shadows of outbuildings, and a few scraggly bushes.

The house was completely dark. Blade's car was parked by the front steps. Rocco swallowed an oath, wishing he'd gotten over here sooner. What if someone had gotten to Blade?

He and Kelan made a fast dash toward the back door. It was unlocked. Kelan wore night vision goggles, so he went in first. Room by room, they cleared the main floor. Blade's place was a huge, sprawling log home. Rocco had never been there before—he was a little surprised at how Blade hated the property. It was magnificent. They split up, Kelan taking the basement, Rocco the upstairs. The house was empty.

So where was Blade? Had he gone somewhere with the Jacksons? Rocco went back to the den, which was the only room where anything was out of place. He flipped on the overhead light and studied the room. A big mahogany desk had been swiped clear, everything plowed to the floor. A broken lamp lay in shattered pieces on the floor.

Rocco stared at the debris, trying to make sense of it. The papers were displaced but not torn or wrinkled. There hadn't been a fight.

"Anything?" Kelan asked as he entered the room, his M16 shouldered, and his night vision goggles sitting on his forehead.

"Nothing. Just the mess in here. What happened, do you suppose?"

"It's hard to say. You tried his cell?"

"Several times." Rocco began walking around the room, trying to see what else might have been disturbed, looking for a clue, something that could lead him to Blade.

Kelan cursed and held up a crushed cell phone. Rocco shoved the door open farther, his movement fast and angry. The panel hit something on the floor, rolling it toward the shadows against the wall. Rocco bent down and picked up a small syringe. He showed it to Kelan. "They've got Blade."

"Looks like they wanted him alive," Kelan observed. But neither of them voiced the unthinkable—how long would he be allowed to live?

"Found the mutts," Val said as two excited dogs swarmed Mandy. She knelt and hugged them both, then ran her hands over them, checking for wounds. They were uninjured but still nervously trembling.

Kit's phone rang. "Mandy, take them up to the house. Val, stay with her." He looked at his screen and saw that it was Rocco. "Go," he opened the conversation.

"Blade's been taken," Rocco's said on the other end of the line. "His car is here but no sign of him or his caretakers. They tranq'd him, Kit."

Kit cursed even as another call broke into their conversation. "Get back over here. Owen's called a meeting." He ended the call with Rocco and accepted the new one from an unknown caller. "Bolanger here."

"Hello, my friend."

Kit snapped his fingers to get Val's attention as he was climbing the porch steps. Kit pointed to his phone. Val pulled Mandy into the house, in a hurry to get Max to trace the call. "Why would you think we were friends, Amir?" Kit asked as he started walking toward the house.

"You may not like me, Mr. Bolanger, but I am indeed your only friend at this point. How do you like the game we are playing? Rather exciting, don't you think?"

"You owe me a new equestrian center. But don't get in a dither about coming up with the money to pay restitution. I'll be taking it out of your hide. Personally."

"Tsk-tsk. You really shouldn't be making threats you can't see to completion. You cannot fight me. I am terror. I am all around you. You'll never know what I'll do next. One by one, each of your friends and family members will die, in most horrible ways. I will crush their dreams first, then fill them with terror as you filled my people with fear, then kill them."

"What do you want with Ty?"

"I just told you. Are you not listening to me, Mr. Bolanger? Your friend, Mr. Bladen, will see his death coming but will be able to do nothing about it. Do you remember the pit your friend Mr. Silas was in? We have a similar one for Mr. Bladen. Unfortunately, there aren't any scorpions in Wyoming, but I found rattlesnakes were a fair trade. There are so many of them. He will die slowly, painfully, as his body shuts down, knowing all the while that you will never find him. Such is the will of Allah."

Kit made it to the basement where Val gave him a thumbs-up sign. "Don't make this about religion, Amir," Kit scoffed. "Nor is it about an eye-for-an-eye retribution. If it were, you would be building roads for us and schools and hospitals, finding jobs for our unemployed citizens, as we did for your people in Afghanistan."

"You did not improve my country. You made every man stand between two lines of guns—yours and the Taliban's."

"This is not a debate I'm gonna have with you, Amir. We both know your complaint with my men and me is that we crippled al Jahni's main drug and arms trade route. For that, I will not apologize. I took you down there, and I'll take you down here. And when I'm done with you, I'm going for al Jahni." Kit dropped the call.

"The call originated in Jalalabad, Afghanistan," Max told him.

"Impossible," Kit growled. "We know Amir was in Denver two days ago. He's bridging his call somehow."

Owen replayed the recording of the phone call. Twice. Kit struggled to find meaning in the words Amir spoke. Sounded like Blade was in a pit. With rattlesnakes. In Wyoming. Was it man-made, as Rocco's had been, or was it naturally occurring? He started pacing. What if Amir had mentioned it knowing they would go off chasing that lead? What if it took them in the opposite direction of where they needed to be looking?

"Pull up a topographical map of the area within a hundred mile radius of Blade's home," he ordered Max. "I want to know about all rock formations that might house crevices or holes or pits wide enough to dump a man deep enough that he can't get out."

"Hold up," Owen called out. He shut off his phone and looked at Kit. "A vehicle registered to Dennis Jackson was just reported to have been in a roll-over accident near off Highway 130 not too far from here."

"Were there any survivors? Any bodies?"

"No word on either yet."

Kit sighed and swiped a hand over his eyes. He

looked at the guys. "Greer, get over there. If they are alive, stick with them. Give me an update when you can. Max, concentrate on the area within a fifty mile circumference from the accident location."

* * *

When Rocco and Kelan came back to the ranch, they both went their separate ways. Rocco knew Owen was waiting for a meeting, but he had to get rid of the dirt, ash and blood still clinging to him from the explosion. And, he needed a few minutes to process everything that had happened that night. Whatever the team wanted could wait until he cleaned up—or they could catch him up when he joined them.

The coffee pot was gurgling, filling the house with the rich scent of freshly brewed coffee. The dogs had returned and were happily chowing down their breakfast. Though dawn was only a faint hint on the eastern horizon, Mandy was already starting breakfast prep. He stood there, watching the woman he loved.

A strange sense of being beside himself, observing his life instead of living it, came over him. His present and his past had collided a few hours ago, and he wasn't sure what remained of himself. Believing his son still lived was the only thing that kept him alive in the months following the explosion in Kadisha's village. And now that he knew the truth, he realized he'd lived beyond that terrible event long enough to begin again, to heal, to start a new life.

A life he had no right to live.

He headed down the hallway before Mandy caught him watching her. He wasn't ready to talk to her or anyone yet. Christ. He'd remembered what happened. All of it. And the freshness of it was like losing his family all over again.

In the shower, he bowed his head in the streams of the hot water. Revisiting the memories the night had unlocked, he forced himself to walk through the minutes before the explosion had destroyed Kadisha's village. He saw again the panic that had women and town elders fleeing about, gathering their loved ones. Kadisha was helping them to hurry, bombs still strapped to her waist.

He thought of how much C-4 she wore, realizing it wouldn't have been enough to wreak the destruction the explosion had caused. She'd said there were more bombs placed about the village. Whoever had set them wanted it to look as if an airstrike had hit the remote mountain town.

Rocco scrubbed his face, his hair, every inch of his body. The salt of his tears stung the cuts on his face as he thought about his son. Beautiful. Precocious. A child full of laughter and light. As a grandson of the region's most powerful warlord, he'd been the darling of the village. He'd made a vow to himself that the taint of war would never darken his son's spirit. His boy was born to stand in two worlds. Rocco had intended he would know and love not only his mother's people, but his father's as well.

Instead, he'd let the war snuff his boy's life out.

Rocco shut off the water. He grabbed a towel and mopped his face, trying to compose himself. Now wasn't the time to break down. His son was gone—he couldn't undo the past. Terrorists were loose, Blade was missing, and Mandy and the team were still in danger. He had to stay present and on task. He could compartmentalize it, as he had all his feelings and desires and dreams for ten long fucking years. It was what he'd done when he'd let himself forget the truth of that day. But no matter what he told himself, that wound was raw and gaping, exposed as it was to the air and the light of day.

Stepping to the sink, Rocco made the mistake of catching his reflection in the mirror. He swiped at the steam and looked at the visage of a man he didn't know. Tall, lean, gaunt, eyes filled with shadows, chin covered with a few weeks' growth of beard—a beard he no longer needed now that he knew his son was dead.

That realization was heartbreaking. Paralyzing. He didn't move. Didn't blink. What was there left to him?

Nothing. Not a goddamned thing.

He reached into a cabinet and retrieved his shaving kit. His movements were angry and jerky as he slapped shaving cream on his face, sending white foam everywhere. He reached into his kit for his razor, but it caught in a bit of netting and wouldn't come free. He yanked at the razor's thin handle, knowing logically that wasn't the way to free it but unable to stop himself. He yanked and yanked, flapping the kit around, emptying its contents in a noisy clatter across the counter, but still not freeing his razor.

Rage built within him, a fire in his bones, his being, his empty, empty soul. He wanted to pound the walls, rip the medicine cabinet off its mounting.

Catching himself before his fury spooled out of control, he felt the ugly wash of emotion slam back into him. His legs crumpled beneath his weight, and he slumped on the floor by the cabinet, wracked by soundless sobs.

His son was dead. His wife was dead. Their second child, still in the safety of his mother's womb, was dead. Two beautiful, innocent children given to a pair of monsters. Gone.

He rested his arms on his knees and bowed his head, sucking in air as he tried to calm himself. He should have died with them. He was their father. Kadisha's husband. Though he hadn't loved his wife, he had loved his children. He should not have lived when they didn't.

In every way that meant anything about being a man, he had failed his children, his wife. Himself.

Rocco didn't know how long he sat there. Gradually, noise of the men gathering in the living room drifted to the back of the house where he sat. He got to his feet and faced his reflection. The shaving cream had thinned and dried on his face. He rinsed it off, then wiped the counter down, and tried again.

And when he looked at his eyes next, he saw banked anguish and determination that was raw and unbounded.

Amir, who was one of Abdul Baseer al Jahni's lieutenants, as Kadisha's father had been, was here. In America. Threatening Mandy and men he'd come to think of as brothers. The bastard would die a hard and bloody death if Rocco had anything to do with it.

He straightened the bathroom, then dressed. When he opened the door to the hallway, he stood unmoving as he looked at his future. He was hollow inside, a shell of a man. He had a choice to make. Live or die. Fight or quit. Be or stop.

He heard Mandy laugh in the kitchen. In the middle of the hell that had become her life, she could still laugh. The guys were gathering in the living room, hungry for breakfast. They'd been up all night. Like him, they were anxious to find Blade.

It seemed, whether he was done with life or not, it wasn't done with him. It beckoned at the end of the hall. He knew if he accepted what it offered, he would be starting over. He would have to put the past behind him. Become a man reborn, a man who looked forward rather than backward.

He stepped across the threshold and made the long walk down the hallway and into the kitchen. Mandy took one look at him and hurried to his side. "Rocco, what is it?"

He ached to hold her. She didn't resist as he pulled her against himself. She leaned into him, wrapping her arms around him, holding him as tightly as he held her. His arms moved across her back, one folding around her tiny waist, the other circling up to wrap around her head, pinning her to him.

"I love you, Mandy," he whispered against her hair. He stroked her hair. "It's important for you to know that."

She pulled back and looked up at him, searching his face, his eyes. Her hands lifted to his cheeks. "I love you, Rocco." A frown wrinkled her brow. "Are you okay?"

He shook his head. He felt the cool track of tears on his cheeks. Zavi. His boy was dead. "No. I'm not." He sighed. "But I think I will be." Blade had been right—what he felt was the ghost connection of a father and his son. "I remembered, Emmy. I remembered everything."

Mandy studied his eyes. "I'm so sorry." She touched the smooth skin of his jaw. "Your beard—"

He shrugged. "I don't need it anymore. I'm not going back after all." He pulled her close again, then kissed her temple. "Blade's been kidnapped."

She tensed in his arms. "I heard. What happened?"

"Someone took him from his house. We have to go after him fast. I want you to be careful. This Abdul Baseer al Jahni is a bad guy—he's rich, connected, and determined to make examples of Kit, Blade and me. If you must go outside, I will go with you. If I'm not here, take a couple of the men. You are not to be alone outside of this house, ever. They used a tranquilizer on Blade, so even if you don't see anyone nearby, you still may not be safe. I don't know how long it'll take us.

For Blade's sake, I hope not long."

He pulled back and looked at her. "I need to know you'll do as I ask. I hate how indefensible this property is." He frowned down at her as he considered other options. "Maybe I should take you down to Warren or Fort Carson."

"I'm not leaving here. I'll do as you ask, but I won't be going to any safe house on a base somewhere. I don't want to be away from you during this."

He leaned down and touched his lips to hers in a gentle kiss, breathing her scent, feeling the soft curves of her body. She was everything he was not: kind, gentle, strong, soft, warm. The ugliness of his life had invaded her existence, and he regretted that. She deserved be sheltered, protected, not warned and guarded, afraid to even to walk the grounds of her property.

He straightened, then wiped his cheeks against his shoulders. "Can I help you with breakfast? I don't know how you keep up, cooking for all of us. I need to hire some help for you."

"No. I'm fine. Fee's a big help." She frowned at him, her gaze catching on the various scrapes on his face. "How are you feeling? What did the doctor do?"

"I feel like I tangled with a sewing machine and lost. I think he put a hundred stitches in me, here and there. And he gave me some prescriptions."

"Leave them on my desk. I'll get them filled for you this morning."

"No you won't. The doc said the pharmacy

delivers. Get them to bring it up here. I'll leave cash for you. And you don't answer the door—one of the guys does it if I'm not here. Understood?"

She smiled. "Yes. Don't worry about me."

After breakfast, Rocco joined Owen, Kit and the whole team in the dining room. A topographical map of taped sheets of paper covered one end of the table, various rifles, pistols, knives, and ammo covered the other end. They were all dressed in tan, green, or black T-shirts with black jeans or tan cargo pants, Earth colors of civilian camo. All of them were strapping on holsters and knife sheaths. Owen and Max were carrying Sig Sauer 9mm pistols. Kit and the others all had Berettas. Rocco found it odd that they were handling battle maps and lethal weapons in the homey dining room of Mandy's grandparents' house, like revolutionaries instead of trusted associates of the U.S. government. He had only his shotgun and a hunting knife in his personal armament, but it didn't matter. He knew plenty of ways to kill a man.

He crossed his arms and looked beyond the men to Mandy. She was leaning against the doorjamb to the kitchen, watching them. He caught her gaze and held it, hoping to reassure her with a look that said this madness was temporary.

He wished to fucking hell it was.

Kit called him and the others over to the map. He pointed to an area about fifty miles northwest of where they currently were. Color-coded squares layered several blocks in one portion of the map.

"This is where the Jackson's SUV was found. These are rock formations thought to have deep crevices where a man could be stashed." Kit looked up at the men around him. "This is the White Kingdom Brotherhood's compound," he said, using his finger to outline an irregular shape that surrounded the rock formations in question.

Owen assigned teams. "Rocco, I want you and Max to stay here. Kelan, I want you to take Fee and go back to Buchanan's house. Look for anything that would give us more information about who he was working with, others around town he might have bought, or where they stashed Blade. Val and Angel check out this sector," he pointed to an area on the map. "Owen and I will take this area. Max has sent the coordinates to your phones. We've connected with state police and the U.S. Forest Service. They'll be helping us cover the maximum area we can."

The men picked up their comm equipment. Rocco thought that was the end of the briefing. There was still a set of gear and a full complement of weapons, including an M16, a Beretta, the associated ammo, and a KA-BAR ankle knife on the table. He looked around, trying to see who hadn't geared up.

Kit nodded toward the rifle, then handed Rocco the pistol. "You said you're still in. You might need these."

Rocco grinned. "Hell, yeah." He strapped on the ankle holster, feeling like himself for the first time in months.

When the house had settled after the men left for their assignments, Mandy headed out to the porch with two fresh cups of coffee. Rocco was standing at the edge of the steps, his hands in his pockets. He took the mug she offered.

"Rocco, what does all of this mean for the center? Should I move it to a different town? Stop construction entirely? I expect George to come by this morning and don't know what to tell him."

He touched her face, letting the velvet softness of her skin warm his palm. "I won't let you give up your dream, but it's too early to know what's best to do. Tell George you can't give him an answer yet. If you've become one of Amir's targets, they will find you wherever you go. So relocating wouldn't help. Either way, the construction can't resume until we put an end to Amir and Abdul Baseer al Jahni."

Mandy bent her head and rested it against his chest. "I wish you were getting out, Rocco. I don't want you to fight. I don't want to lose you. I don't care about the war or stupid skinheads or druglords. I don't care about saving the world. I want you safe."

He stroked her face with his thumb and gave her a sad smile. "I do care about saving the world, from this threat at least. I'm good at what I do. So are Kit and Blade, as are the rest of Owen's team. I hope you'll understand we have no choice but to end this. Now."

Chapter 19

Rocco filled the water and feed buckets and set them in the wagon to take down to Kitano. Worried about exposing Mandy to any threats lurking on the property, he'd refused to let her out of the house to tend to the horse. He didn't know how long he'd be able to keep her inside and safe—hopefully long enough for the team to capture Amir.

When he got halfway to Kitano's corral, a white delivery van pulled up the driveway and parked in front of the house. There was a sign on the side of the van with the local pharmacy's name. He watched as a man wearing a white lab coat got out of the van. Seeing him, the man lifted a hand with a white bag. Rocco waved back and continued to Kitano's corral. He knew what was in that bag—the antibiotics and pain meds. He'd take the antibiotics, but wouldn't touch the Vicodin. He'd worked too hard to get his head clear to mess with that stuff.

When he returned the wagon to the toolshed after feeding Kitano, the van was gone. He walked up to the house. The dogs were outside. He looked at the porch to see if Mandy was standing in the doorway. The door was open, but no one stood there. A frisson zipped along his spine, spurring him forward. Just inside the door, Max lay on the ground, his Sig still in his hand.

Rocco felt for a pulse even as he looked around the room. Max was alive. He didn't see any injury. Had he been tranq'd like Blade? What the hell had happened? No furniture was disturbed. He called for Mandy, but got no answer. He ran down the hall to her room—it was empty. He checked her bathroom. Empty. He dialed her cell, then heard it ring in the kitchen.

He cursed and looked around the room, trying to determine what might have happened. He saw the white pharmacy bag on the floor, along with the money he'd given Mandy to pay for it. She wouldn't have just dropped everything and left with the delivery guy.

She'd been taken.

Max sat up and shook his head. Awake again, his mind cleared in a flash. He roared and leapt to his feet, ready for intruders. The man moved with the fluid grace of a martial arts master.

"What the hell happened to you?" Rocco asked.

"Chloroform. Where's Mandy?"

Rocco cursed. That's why it didn't look like there'd been a struggle—there hadn't been. "Gone. They took her," he told Max. "I'm going after her. They can't be more than a few minutes ahead of me. I'll radio Kit on my way. Call Sheriff Tate and tell him the delivery guy took Mandy. Get him to put an APB out on the van.

Then look around and see if there's anything missing, any surprises left for us. You should sweep for bugs, too."

Max grabbed his arm, stopping him. "Don't go alone. Let me call one of the others back."

"I'm not waiting for a ride-along."

Rocco fired up his truck and started down the long drive, which passed between two steep hills before it met the road. He exited slowly—it was hard to see what might be waiting ahead. He didn't expect to see the delivery van parked off to the right.

He parked, then walked around the van. He looked in the front windows. It appeared empty, but a divider wall kept him from seeing into the back. When he opened the rear doors, he found a man lying inside, out cold. No sign of Mandy.

He radioed Max. "Found the delivery van parked on the road in front of the drive. He switched cars. No idea what we're looking for now. Get the paramedics up here. There's a guy in the van, breathing but unconscious."

On the opposite side of the driveway, there were fresh car tracks. Looked as if someone had taken off in a hurry. Rocco circled the area, trying to see if they made a u-turn and headed back toward the town. As far as he could tell, they hadn't.

He got in his truck and started down the road, heading away from town, then radioed Kit. "The pharmacy delivery van was hijacked. They took Mandy and switched vehicles. Don't know what they might be driving, but they appear to be headed west. Can't be more than a couple minutes ahead of me. They have to be taking her to the compound. Where else would they go with her?"

Kit hissed a curse. "No idea. I expect I'll be hearing from Amir shortly—he never lets any good deed go unnoticed. Will let you know if I find out more." There was a pause ripe with unspoken words. "Rocco, you okay?"

"No. I'm fucking pissed."

"We'll find her. Owen and I are starting back now. We'll meet-up midway. You got to keep it together, bro."

"I will, at least until I can start pounding faces." He signed off and hit the accelerator. The highway headed northwest, deep into the Medicine Bow Mountains. He took the sharp turns as fast as he dared, frustrated that the steep, twisty route kept him from seeing very far down the road. A half hour later, he'd seen no cars driving in either direction, none of the dirt roads that led off the highway onto private property were dusty or looked recently disturbed.

Up ahead was a rustic rest area with a car parked in the lot. He wouldn't have thought to stop except the car was backed into its parking space, and the man behind the wheel dipped lower in his seat as he spotted Rocco's truck approach.

Rocco pulled in and stopped his truck right in front of the car. A short, slim man with dark coloring got out and started running. Rocco couldn't tell if he was

Middle Eastern or of some other ethnicity, but it didn't matter. He ran like a guilty man. Rocco chased him past the facilities and up a steep path that led into the woods. Warning signals were firing in his head. He was either getting Rocco to waste precious time or running him headlong into a trap. He tackled the man before the path took them out of sight of the parking lot.

"Where is she?" Rocco asked. The man beneath him shook his head. Rocco pounded his face into the hard dirt. "Where is Mandy Fielding?" Again no answer.

Rocco wrapped an arm about the man's throat and pulled tight. "I'm asking one more time, you son of a bitch." He jerked his hold tighter.

"I don't know!" the man rasped, his words carried the heavy accent of a native Pashto speaker.

"Then you will die." Rocco tightened his grip. The man began gasping out a question in Pashto. Rocco eased his hold slightly.

"Are you the Gray Ghost? Are you the one?"

"I am," Rocco answered in the same language. "You cannot escape me. In this life or the next, I will follow you and get my answer. Where is the woman?"

"I don't know. I was only supposed to get her to this place. They came and took her."

"Who?" Rocco asked. "Where did they take her? What are they driving?"

"A green van. They are driving a green van. It is all that I know. I swear!"

Rocco tightened his hold until the man passed out,

then he carried him back down to the car. A black SUV pulled into the lot, stopping behind Rocco's truck. He waited behind the decoy's car, cautious about the new arrival until Angel jumped out of the passenger seat.

Rocco holstered his Beretta and started for his truck. "Get his ID and the car's registration," Rocco ordered Angel. "Call it in to Max. He said they took Mandy in a green van. Get that info to the cops and to Kit. I'm going after the van."

"And I'm going with you," Val said. "Toss your keys to Angel and get in. Val had it in gear even before Rocco had shut the door. They drove another few miles down the road, looking off to each side, trying to find a spot where a car might have driven off the road. A car drove by, heading in the opposite direction, a woman at the wheel. A truck passed. It was as if nothing unusual had transpired here at all. No one knew that the woman Rocco loved had been kidnapped, disappearing like smoke in the wind.

He radioed Max in the control room at Mandy's house. "Give me some good news."

"The State Police have several road blocks set up between Centennial and Ryan Park. They're looking for a green van or any vehicle that looks suspicious."

"If they've got the road covered, get me info on any properties that might be abandoned up here. Properties that are far enough off road as to have some privacy. Anything that sold recently and could accommodate several fighters. Something. Anything. I don't think they are still on the road."

"On it."

Max radioed back a few minutes later. "There's a property on your left less than two miles from your current 20. It was a cabin rental site that has been without an owner for the last three years. I'm sending the map to your phone."

"Thanks. Get someone to pick up Angel. He's holding a package for us at a rest stop. Be sure to check out that car before moving it. And keep looking for other sites in case this one doesn't pan out."

"Roger that. Kelan is already en route. Keep us posted."

Rocco's phone pinged when the message came through. He studied the map a moment, then pointed to an upcoming drive. "There's another private drive a little farther down the road. Turn there."

Val pulled off the road. Rocco handed him the map he had open on his phone. "Looks like the cabins are about a mile up the road," Rocco said. "Let's go see what we're dealing with." They put their phones on vibrate, then jogged as far up the drive as they could go. They moved silently into the woods, creeping up a small rise that overlooked the lodges.

Parked in front of one of the cabins, among several other cars, was a green van. They eased into position. Val settled on his stomach and arranged his rifle. Rocco snapped a picture on his cell phone and sent it to Kit. The vehicles definitely looked parked, not abandoned. As he watched, a man stepped out of one of the cabins, slung an AK-47 over his shoulder, then lit a cigarette.

When he walked around the other side of the cabin, Rocco radioed Kit.

"Found the green van. Got a nest of camel spiders up here armed with AKs. Permission to use lethal force."

"Negative. We're not giving those bastards any virgins today. We need to question them—there's a bigger op at play than this one. Any sign of Mandy yet?"

"Negative."

"The FBI's coming up from Denver. Got a bomb unit from Carson in the air. Owen and I are on our way. Hold your position until we're in place."

"What's your ETA?"

"Ten minutes."

"Roger that." Rocco nodded to Val. They watched the site a few minutes, waiting to catch the rhythm the guard used in his patrol.

"Looks like there's only the one guard. He makes a simple loop," Val commented.

"I'm going in closer," Rocco said. "I want to see where Mandy is."

He held his position until the patrol strolled by. There were eight cabins in an L-shaped formation. All had a front and back window and door. It was hard to tell from the way the vehicles were parked which cabins might be occupied. Looking in the rear window of the first cabin, Rocco could see the space was configured in an open floor plan. The front door stood open, but no one was inside. He motioned to Val that it was empty.

He walked casually across the alley between it and the next cabin. Looking in the window, he could see the space was empty. The third cabin held five men sitting on the floor. No Mandy. He signaled the count to Val, then moved on to the fourth. The window was broken in the back. It was empty. He kept on until he moved to the next to last cabin around the bend. Three men were inside, but no Mandy.

Where the hell was she? Had the green van not been the one that had taken her? Could she still be in the van? Had they stashed her somewhere?

Rocco checked the last cabin, which was empty. He stepped back into the woods, keeping absolutely still while the guard walked between his position and the cabins. When he'd circled around in front again, Rocco went up the hill and crossed to Val.

"Any sign of her?" Val asked.

"No. I didn't check the van, though. Maybe there were two vans. Maybe the bastard lied. They could be holding her in one of the bathrooms. The third cabin has five guys. The next to the last in that row has three. The others are all empty. I'm going to wait for Kit near the SUV."

"When you come back, bring my bag. I've got plenty of zip ties in there."

Rocco waited in the cover of a scrub pine. He wanted to rage, to storm the cabins, to kill the bastards working on al Jahni's terror campaign. Instead, his training and his years of covert ops work kicked in like a core instinct, keeping him calm and focused.

At last, a black Expedition pulled into the drive and parked in front of Val's SUV. Kit and Owen got out.

"What's the situation?" Kit asked.

"A quarter of a mile up the road is a ridge that overlooks the campground and cabins." Rocco knelt down and took up a stick to draw the layout they were working with. "Val's there. A hundred and fifty meters below him is a line of eight cabins. This one has five tangos, that one has three. One guard patrols the circumference. The green van is here," he marked an "x" in front of one of the cabins. "Three other vehicles are here, here, and here. No sign of Mandy, so go carefully."

"Right. Kit will take the patrol," Owen directed. "Then he and I will take the cabin with the three men in it. You and Val take this one. Let's go." They caught up to where Val was lying in wait.

"Any change?" Kit asked.

"Negative," Val answered without looking away from his scope.

"When the guard is down, radio us," Owen told Kit. They waited for the patrol to move around the corner before getting into position, four men moving silently as shadows down the steep slope of the ridge. The trees around them were mostly lodge pole pines, with a few aspen mixed in. Soft pine needles covered the ground, damp from the recent snowmelt. If the enemy looked at the right time, they might catch their movement, but they couldn't be heard.

Rocco's heart was pounding. With the man he'd

caught earlier and the nine here, they'd take ten terrorists out of circulation today. One of them had to know where Mandy was.

As soon as Kit radioed he'd handled the patrol, Rocco and Val stormed their appointed cabin, Rocco coming in from the front, Val from the back. They filled the room with noise and shouts, throwing it into chaos.

"On the floor! On the floor! On the floor! Hands on your head!" Val shouted. Rocco repeated the order in Pashto and then Arabic. Two men complied, crashing to the floor with their hands over their heads. One tried to run past Val, and two turned on Rocco. Rocco slammed the butt of his rifle into the shoulder of one of the men who lunged at him, then jammed his elbow into the other man's jaw.

"Give me a reason. One goddamned reason," Rocco shouted at both of them. They didn't try for him again. "Get down on the floor, hands on your heads." In short order, they had all five men subdued. Once Val had secured them with zip ties, Rocco collected their weapons.

"Where is the woman, Mandy Fielding?" Rocco asked, watching their expressions. He switched to Pashto, then Arabic, repeating the question, all to blank, impassive faces.

"Was she your woman?" one of the captives asked, his expression smug.

"She *is* my woman."

"Perhaps, but not for long. Allah's will is just. She

will pay the price for whoring herself to an infidel."

"What do you know of her? Where is she?"

"Beyond your reach, I would expect."

The room fell quiet under that open threat until the metallic sound of Rocco unsheathing his knife broke the silence.

"What are you doing?" Val asked Rocco.

"I'm going to get him to tell me what he knows about Mandy. If he won't talk to me, I'll cut out his tongue so that he can't talk to anyone ever again." He looked at the row of men sitting against the wall. "And if he loses his tongue, I will start on the next, and the next. One of them knows something."

"Huh." Val walked to door and looked out toward the cottage where Kit and Owen were. "Better be quick about it. I doubt Kit would approve."

Rocco pulled the man away from the line of the others. He forced him to the floor, pinning him with a hand on his throat. "Where is the woman?" The other four captives watched with pale faces and wide eyes.

"Go to hell," the man spat.

"You first." Rocco put a knee on the man's abdomen and gripped his jaw in his left hand. The man clamped his teeth shut and struggled against Rocco's attempts to get his mouth open.

"Come hold him," he ordered Val.

Val shouldered his rifle and knelt down, pinning the man's head between his knees. "Go for it. Just don't cut me."

"Stop!" one of the other men shouted. "She is not

here. They took her up the hill to another building."

Rocco sent Val a quick look. "Go," Val told him. "I got this."

As he reached the door, a man he'd not seen before stepped inside. He took one look at Rocco and Val, then glanced around the room. Seeing what was happening, he took off. Rocco ran after him. He got almost to the foot of the hill where a drive led up and out of sight before Rocco tackled him. He was shouting a warning—to whom, Rocco had no idea. A quick right hook silenced him.

Rocco heard someone running fast behind him. Kit was closing in on him. He left Kit to deal with the terrorist and continued up the hill, scoping out the area, watching for threats. Straight ahead was another building. An old sign hanging askew over the front door read, "Office & Mercantile."

Rocco ran up to the entrance, then flanked the front door, straining to hear any sound inside. All was silent. He cleared the main room, then each of the smaller rooms. The building was empty of humans. Its sole occupant was a chair set in the middle of the room. Freshly severed ropes lay discarded on the floor.

Rocco kicked the chair across the room as he bellowed a curse. He took another turn through the building, trying to see if there was a basement, a closet, another space where they might have stashed Mandy, another clue as to what they might have done with her, all to no avail. The place was clean.

When he came back into the main room, Kit was

finishing a call. His face was pale, his eyes bleak as he met Rocco's gaze.

Chapter 20

"Highway Patrol reported a woman matching Mandy's description walking east on Highway 130, not far from here," Kit told him.

"Alone?" Rocco asked.

Kit nodded. Rocco ran down the drive to the main road. He turned right and kept jogging. Flashing lights at the crest of a distant hill told him the cops had shut down the road. He rounded a bend in the road and saw Mandy walking up ahead.

"Mandy!" he called, relieved to find her. She didn't acknowledge him. What had happened to her? Why wasn't she responding to him? She kept moving forward in a slow, determined stride, like a sleepwalker. She wore a shirt that was too large for her—one he didn't recognize.

"Mandy!" He came even with her. When she didn't acknowledge him, he caught her arm and pulled her around, revealing the thick belt of C-4 tied to her waist. He recognized that particular configuration of explosives. Kadisha had worn one just like it when she'd handed Zavi to him.

A paralyzing bolt of fear shot through Rocco. His nightmare was about to repeat. His body felt brittle as he hit his knees.

When she saw his reaction, Mandy drew a ragged breath. "I can't stop." She shook her head. "He said I had two hours to get back to my house." She kept moving, but backward.

Rocco looked up at her as the distance between them slowly increased. "Who said?"

"One of the men. I don't know his name. Asan, Asand, I don't remember."

"How many men were there?"

"Two."

"Hold still."

"I can't. He said he's watching the progress the belt is making. If it stops, he will detonate it. And if anyone tries to disarm it, he will detonate it."

Rocco pushed to his feet as he glanced around them, shoving his hands into his hair. Highway 130 looked like a war zone. Cops were everywhere. Several black SUVs had parked in haphazard places across the road. The woods were crawling with soldiers and search dogs. He could hear various radio conversations. A helicopter was parked on the upward rise of one of the hills. He couldn't tell if the bomb disposal team had arrived, but he wasn't waiting another minute to get Mandy safe.

"Ehsan Asir is what his name is." He walked toward Mandy. "I can disarm it."

"No!" She turned around. "No. Don't come near me."

Rocco jogged to get in front of her, walking backward as she continued her relentless stride forward. He opened the edges of the man's shirt that she wore.

She shoved him away. "Please, Rocco. Please, go. You don't have to die, too."

"No one's going to die."

A sob caught on one of Mandy's exhalations. A tear splashed on his hand. He looked up at her.

"I love you," she whispered, lifting her hands to cup his face. "I want you to live. I want you to find the joy that's been denied you so far."

Rocco clamped his mouth shut as he tried to stem the tidal wave of hatred that filled him for Ehsan Asir—the man Kadisha had been expected to marry before Rocco came into her life—the man he now knew had killed Kadisha and turned Rocco's life into a living hell. He'd had Rocco in his sights ever since Halim had favored Rocco. The bastard needed to die a bad death.

"Look at me, Mandy." She did, then dropped her gaze again to the belt of explosives. "Don't look down. Look at me. Only me." She did as he ordered. Tears were pooling in her eyes, drowning her gaze. He clamped his jaw shut, calming the rage that simmered so close to the surface.

He pulled the detonation wires from the blocks of C-4 and twisted them away from anything they might touch, then he pulled the cell phone free and pocketed it. Finally, he unbuckled the belt and set it on the wayside.

Mandy wavered on her feet. Her face had gone pale. Rocco pulled her into a tight hold as he radioed Kit. "I got her. She's safe. They'd strapped a bomb to her. It's Ehsan Asir. I'm going to kill the motherfucker and it will be self-defense. The belt is here on the wayside. Have someone come get it."

He wrapped both arms around Mandy. His woman. She *loved* him. She loved *him*. She'd told him this morning, but he'd still been in a daze then. Her declaration sunk in now. He could feel her trembling in his arms. He tore the shirt Ehsan had made her wear off her, leaving her in just her tank top. He didn't want another man's clothing on her—especially not that bastard's. She pressed her face against his chest. He knew he probably stunk—he'd been running in full on panic mode for hours—but he didn't care and she didn't seem to mind.

"I can't believe how easy that was for you to disarm. I could have done it." She pulled back and glared at him. "I'm an idiot. I don't know anything! Leaving it on as I did, I could have gotten us killed." She looked up at him. "I thought I was dying, Rocco."

He felt her anger grow, swallowing her love, filling her with hate. He'd done this to her. Brought darkness to her world. He had to get her out of there, had to get her back home where things could appear normal again before she lost herself to the realities of his life.

A black SUV pulled up. He opened the door and shoved her inside, then climbed in after her. Shock had made her movements sluggish. He leaned over her and fastened her seat belt, then slapped the driver's seat. "Let's get out of here."

The driver turned and faced him. "As you wish," he said in a heavily accented Middle Eastern voice. Mandy gasped.

"Yes, do take us out of here," another man said from the third row of seats. Ehsan Asir. "But do go slowly. There is no need to call attention to ourselves."

"What do you want, Asir?"

The terrorist smiled. "I want what you took from me. Kadisha was the light of my life. We'd planned for years to be married. Did you know that? Did she never mention me?"

"That why you killed her? Blew her whole fucking village to hell. You call that love?"

Ehsan's face tightened, his eyes darkened as he sifted through memories. "Ghalib Halim set me aside when he saw that you had your sights on her. He wanted you. The Gray Ghost. He used Kadisha as bait to draw you in. It worked. Just like he'd said it would. He knew who you were, the whole time. You thought you were so brilliant, fooling all of us."

"What he knew was that you were playing him, spying on him, and selling information. Of course he wasn't going to let you marry his daughter."

He thrust his chin at Rocco. "No it was I who fooled you. I discovered who your contacts were from my friendly askars. They told me about Mr. Bolanger and Mr. Bladen. I knew if we got to them, we'd get to you here in America. We found men here to assist us, used their greed to buy them. Our rage was righteous and our cause was just. Praise Allah."

Rocco looked around them. They were slowly weaving among the vehicles parked all over the road. As soon as they cleared the police barricade, they'd escalate in speed. He had to act fast if he wanted to get Mandy out of the SUV.

Asir lifted his hand, his thumb depressing a trigger. He smiled calmly as if the SUV weren't rigged with enough C-4 to blow a huge crater in the state highway. Up ahead, there were only a few hundred feet between the last of the team's vehicles and the long line of waiting civilian traffic stopped by the roadblock. This was the only opportunity Rocco was going to get, and he knew it.

He released Mandy's buckle, then lunged toward Asir, grabbing his hand to control the trigger as he punched the man's face, over and over with lethal blows. Dragging his limp body forward, he kicked the driver in the head. Once. Twice. The SUV began to drift off toward the ditch on the right side of the road.

"Get out. Roll with the fall, run back away from this SUV. Go! Now! Tell the others there's a bomb in here."

Mandy shoved the door open and dropped out of sight. The driver's forehead landed on the horn, but the noise barely registered against the blood pounding in

Rocco's head. He saw Mandy get up and run screaming toward the team. She was waving her arms. Her hair was streaming behind her. It was déjà vu, all over again, thanks to the bastard whose limp hand Rocco still held.

The SUV dipped into the wayside and stopped. Asir wasn't wearing a suicide belt—the wires led under the seat. Rocco cursed. It was impossible to determine quickly how much C-4 was packed throughout the vehicle. He pulled his comm unit from his ear. There was no way these two bastards were going to survive this day. He noticed a backpack on the floor next to Asir and tore into it with his free hand, searching for something, anything that would let him rig up a way to detonate the bomb from a safe distance. He found what he was looking for—a roll of the black electrical tape that was used to build the bomb that had been strapped to Mandy.

Mandy ran toward Kit, her throat raw from shouting the bomb warning. The response from the emergency crews was immediate. Men were calling out orders, moving vehicles farther away from the SUV, getting the civilian cars to turn around and leave the way they came, clearing the area.

She looked to see if Rocco had left the SUV after her, but she was alone. Perhaps Asir's bomb was more complex than the one he'd strapped to her, and it was taking Rocco longer to disarm it. A minute passed. Then another. Her stomach was in her throat. Owen and his team congregated around her and Kit.

As she watched, the whole SUV blew, lifting the vehicle high into the air with the force of the explosion. She screamed and lurched forward, but someone caught her around the waist, dragging her against an immovable wall of muscle, pulling her back to the line of men and vehicles in case there was a secondary explosion. She fought against his hold, but could not break free.

"Mandy, it's me. Kit. I've got you."

She dragged in a breath, slowly letting reality sift into her mind. She stopped clawing at his arm and looked up at him. Kit. She was safe. But Rocco wasn't. "Rocco was in that SUV. He's gone, Kit. He's gone."

She looked at the SUV sitting like a big fireball on the side of the road. And then men blocked her view. Not just any men—Owen's team. Val, Angel, Kelan, and Owen stood like a shield in front of her, protecting her from the sight of the burning SUV.

She buried her face in Kit's chest, giving in to sobs that ripped from her heart. A lifetime passed in the next handful of minutes.

"Hey, Kit," Kelan called over his shoulder. "Looks like your boy is fireproof."

"And bomb-proof," Angel added.

"Some guys are hard to kill," Owen said, grinning at Mandy.

Kit laughed. "I'll be goddamned."

Frowning, she pulled back and looked up at her brother. He nodded to something behind her. Rocco! He was walking around pockets of burning debris. His shirt was ripped. He had more cuts on his face and arm. He was searching the crowd that had gathered, his black eyes intense, focused on only one purpose: finding her.

Mandy gasped and pulled free from Kit. The movement caught Rocco's attention. The men parted, giving him access to her. He grinned, his teeth white in his soot-stained face. She ran toward him, throwing herself into his arms. He grabbed her in a solid hold. She touched his face, his shoulders, reassuring herself he was real and essentially unharmed.

"Hold me," she ordered him.

"I am."

"Tighter."

"I got you, sweetheart. And I'm not ever letting you go." He bent and pressed his mouth to hers as his hand cupped the back of her head. His jaw pressed against hers, forcing her mouth to open. She gave herself to him without any hesitation, surrendering to the sweep of his tongue.

"Mandy," he breathed against her lips. "I need you. Now. I want to be in you."

She nodded, her forehead brushing his. Rocco looked around for another vehicle and was in luck to find the guys were standing next to one. He pulled Mandy along behind him as he made a beeline for that SUV. "This vehicle clear?" he asked Kit.

"It is. Why?"

"Because I need some privacy to talk to Mandy, make sure she's not injured. I don't want anyone bothering us. Make it happen, Kit."

Rocco opened the back passenger door without waiting for Kit's response. He checked the whole vehicle before helping Mandy inside. He locked the doors, then drew her toward the long back bench, pulling her shirt off as they went.

"Rocco! Someone will see!"

"No one will see. The windows are tinted and we're too far back for anyone to see from the front." He sat on the backseat and drew her onto his lap. He ran his hands over her ribs, her chest, her arms, then pulled her down for a kiss. He was breathing heavily, sucking the scent of her into his lungs, filling his body with her essence. She was here. And he was here. They were together.

His dick was as hard as a marble pillar, aching to be inside her. He reached up and opened the front clasp to her bra, letting it slip from her shoulders. He cupped her breasts, checking for bruises or other wounds. He knew what Asir was capable of. In Afghanistan, Rocco had seen what happened to several of the women who'd had the bad fortune to cross the bastard's path.

"Are you hurt? Did they touch you?" he asked her.

She gave him a look that caused his heart to stop beating, then lurch forward. "I'm not hurt. But they did touch me—not in that way, but they were free with their hands. I couldn't understand much of what they said, though I knew from the tone they used it didn't bode well."

Rocco pulled off his shirt and drew her close,

feeling her skin against his, using his body to push away the bad memory of Asir touching her. He would replace it, here and now, with another, healthier one. One of love. He reached down to remove her boots. He wanted her naked, bare to his touch, his eyes. He wanted to see all of her, love all of her. She was barefoot. They hadn't even let her get her shoes when they'd taken her. She winced when he touched her feet.

"I'm sorry," he whispered, trying to keep the anger he felt for Asir out of his voice, away from her.

She shrugged. "It's fine. I'm fine. It's over."

"Yes. Take your pants off. I want you naked. Now. Hurry."

She leaned up on her knees, bringing her belly close to his face and unfastened her jeans. He yearned to look down, watch her undress, but her breasts were so close, so warm, he let his mouth latch on to one instead. She gasped and arched into him, clasping his head. He sucked her nipple, feeling it tighten and bud against his tongue. It took every ounce of willpower he owned to take hold of her waist and lift her off his lap so that she could remove her jeans.

He kicked off his boots, pulled off his socks, and shucked his pants. His cock nearly lifted off his belly as he watched her mount his lap. His balls were so swollen—any and every movement hurt. He guided himself into her sweet sheath, then shut his eyes. He was home. She was safe. He drew a deep breath, the first full breath he'd been able to take since he'd discovered she'd been abducted.

She started to move over him, but he held her hips still. This was not a moment he wanted to rush. He never wanted to be apart from her body. He ran his hands up her thighs, over her hips to her soft narrow belly, then dragged his eyes up to hers.

"Mandy, I love you." She didn't answer him, other than to brush the hair from his face, and smooth her thumb over the corner of his eye. "Did you mean it when you said you loved me? Or was it just the fear talking?" he asked.

"I meant it. I love you." She smiled.

Rocco released the breath he'd been holding, and his hunger for her broke free. He began moving inside of her, letting his hands wander over her body, holding her, touching her until her hips moved in a sensual arch, drawing him out of her, pulling him back in, taking over the rhythm.

"Rocco! Rocco, I can't stop. I don't want to stop. I need you. I need you to come." She ground herself against him, pounding down on his cock, grinding against his aching balls. He spread his legs wider beneath her, wanting to hold out as long as he could. He touched his thumb to her clit, rubbing the swollen nub until he felt her body squeeze him, grabbing and milking him.

He cupped her head, pulling her mouth against his, capturing both of their cries as he erupted inside of her. Just when he thought he'd finished, he experienced something extraordinary. "God, Mandy, I'm coming again. Do it. Ride me. Fuck, yeah. Ah, sweet Christ."

He felt his balls squeeze a second burst of semen up his cock and into her. The pulses of aftershock pleasure rocked them both. Long minutes later, when they'd settled somewhat, she collapsed against him.

He tightened his arms around her, thanking God and Allah and every other deity for the miracle he held in his hands. He turned slightly, lying back against the seat, keeping their bodies connected. When Mandy finally lifted up enough to look at him, he smiled and brushed her beautiful copper hair back behind her ears.

"Rocco," she broke the silence that held them enthralled. Her face was serious. He braced himself for what she would say. "If I'm going to live in your world, there are things I must learn. I need to know how to protect myself, how to protect you. I need to know how to spot danger, as you did in the diner that day. I need to know how to keep us safe."

He blinked. He didn't want this to be her life experience. He wanted so much more for her. "I wish that the world was different. I wish that I could build a haven for you where I know you'd be safe and happy. But I also know that evil moves where it will, finding the path that leads to its destination. I don't want you to be its target again. I will teach you all of those things and many more besides."

She studied him, considering the depth of his resolve to keep his word. She nodded, then leaned forward and pressed a soft kiss to his lips. "We'd best get moving. People will be worried about us."

"Forget them." His arms tightened around her

waist, then his hands strayed to her soft buttocks, grinding her hips against his cock, still nestled warmly inside of her. "I want to stay here and fuck you again."

She smiled, wiggling on top of him. "Then take me home. Eventually someone is going to want this SUV. And judging from the way Kit is pacing outside, it'll be sooner rather than later."

Rocco groaned. "I love you, Mandy." He cupped her face, his eyes locked with hers.

"I love you."

They both dressed, bumping into each other in the small space. Mandy giggled when Rocco tried to help her straighten her hair, making it more of a snarled mess than before. He opened the door on the side of the SUV that faced the woods.

"How do I look?" she asked him, smoothing her hands over her hair, her hips.

God, she was hot. He wanted her again, with the same fierce hunger he'd felt only moments before. "Like you've just been well and thoroughly banged." He grinned at her horrified face and kissed her. Her mouth was warm and pliant beneath his. He groaned against her lips and pressed her back into the open door. "Let's go again."

"No!" she laughed and pushed him away. "You are insatiable!"

"I am." He took her hand and led her around to the other side of the SUV, where Kit and Kelan stood impatiently awaiting them.

Kit looked at Mandy then at Rocco. "I assume my

sister is unharmed based on your thorough inspection?"

"Hell, no, she's not unharmed. She was grabbed from her home by men she didn't know, stashed in a forgotten building in the middle of nowhere, threatened and frightened and alone, and then sent on her way with a bomb strapped to her. It's been a bad fucking day and I'm taking her home."

"Good. Val's bringing your truck over. I'll be following you shortly."

Rocco frowned, studying Kit. "What's going on?"

"Nothing. We're done here. The FBI is taking over custody of Asir's men and handling the crime scene. I expect they will be opening the road again shortly. So go home. There's nothing more to be done here."

Val pulled up in Rocco's truck. He got out and held the driver's door open for Mandy. Once she was inside, he gave Rocco a wide I-know-what-you-were-doing grin. "You were rocking that Expedition, man."

"Not the time or the place," Rocco warned.

"I know, right? I tried to tell you that, but Kit wasn't letting anyone near the SUV. Didn't look too happy to be standing guard. Bet you wish you could have seen his expression."

Rocco grinned, then shook his head. Val clapped a hand on his shoulder. "You okay?"

"I'm good. Mandy's safe."

"And we got twelve bad guys off the street. It's a start. We'll get Amir and his puppet master."

Rocco nodded. It was a mission the entire team had

taken to heart. "What are you doing after this?"

"When Kit cuts us loose, Angel and I are going for Blade."

"Call if you need me."

"Like hell I will." Val nodded toward the truck. "You got something important to do—take care of your woman."

Rocco got into the truck. Val closed the door, then thumped it with his hand. "See you back at the ranch." He straightened, frowning. "Those are six words I never thought I'd hear myself say," he mumbled as he walked away.

Rocco looked at Mandy. Seeing the shadows under her eyes and the pale color of her skin, he wished they didn't have the long ride home. He lifted his arm, urging her to his side. "Come closer to me." She didn't hesitate to scoot over. He kissed her temple, then wove his way through the cars and people and police cruisers onto the open road. "I promise you a hot bath and a cup of tea as soon as we get home."

"I have to feed Kitano and the dogs."

"I'll feed them. And I'll deal with supper. You get a night off. You were brave today. Beautiful. Fierce."

"I meant what I said. I need to learn to live in your world."

He sighed. "I regret that I've tainted your life. But I will teach you everything you want to know and all that I feel you need to know beyond that."

"You haven't tainted anything, Rocco. You've made it beautiful."

They drove the remainder of the trip in silence. Rocco was glad she stayed next to him. He could feel her tension ease out of her as they neared her house. He pulled into the driveway and had just crested the top of the drive when he spotted a green SUV parked in the circular drive in front of the main house.

He cursed and parked the truck where it was. "Stay here. And get down." He palmed his Beretta, then got out and started forward, moving away from the truck, hoping to make Mandy less of a target if whoever was waiting for them was in a shooting mood.

Chapter 21

A woman got out of the backseat wearing army fatigues. Rocco pointed his gun at her. "That's enough moving. State your business."

"Mr. Silas?"

"Who's asking?"

"I'm Lieutenant Kelly Froman. I have a surprise for you."

"It's a bad fucking day for surprises, Lieutenant." He lowered his gun but didn't ease his stance, not trusting that anyone was who they said they were anymore.

The woman held her hands up, but still moved closer to the back door. "Sir, I need you to stand down. I have your son."

Zavi? She had Zavi?

Another soldier got out of the front seat as the lieutenant reached inside for something. When she turned around, Rocco saw two little legs, then a boy's small torso, then a little face appeared as he squatted down and peeked under the door.

"Papa!"

Rocco's lungs quit pulling air. It was Zaviyar. Alive and well. Then he remembered his pistol and quickly holstered it as his son charged toward him. He grabbed him up into his arms. He'd gotten so big in the months since Rocco had last seen him. After a moment, Rocco knelt down, setting him on his feet so that he could get a good look at him. He smoothed his hands on either side of his head, down his neck to his little shoulders.

"Zavi, do you remember the accident?" His son nodded. "Were you hurt?"

"No. But you were, Papa. Rafiullah told me I had to go with him so that you could go to the clinic. And then I didn't get to see you again. Where did you go?"

A memory slammed into Rocco at the mention of Rafiullah's name—the final piece of the puzzle. He shut his eyes as he absorbed what it revealed. When he'd been unable to stop Kadisha from running back into the compound, he'd given Zavi to Rafiullah Kahn, an area shepherd who had hurried by in the melee. He'd only taken a few steps toward the compound when it blew. Christ. That was why he'd been so certain that Zavi lived. It all made sense now.

He hugged his son. "I've been with the doctors. I've been waiting for you. I'm sorry it took so long for us to be together."

"Kelly said this is America. A different country."

"It is. Do you like it?"

"I do so far. But don't they have any children here?"

"There are lots and lots of children."

"Is this our home?"

"For now. Zavi, who taught you to speak English?"

"Kelly. She said I needed to know English for when I saw you again. She said I couldn't speak Pashto anymore."

"You can speak any language you like, son. If you don't know it, I will teach it to you. If I don't know it, I will learn it with you."

"I can speak Pig English?"

"You mean Pig Latin?"

Zavi thought about that, his little face frowning with concentration. "No. It isn't Latin, is it, Papa? I've heard that before, and it doesn't sound like that. So it can't be Pig Latin."

Rocco laughed and pulled his son in close for another hug. "Where did you hear Latin?"

"Kelly and a man took me to a church where the man was speaking it. That was the day they taught me Pig English."

Rocco's hackles went up at the realization that the Army had apparently been casually testing his son's ability and now knew about his linguistic capabilities.

The sound of gravel crunching alerted him to Mandy's approach. He drew a breath, forcing himself to remain calm as he reached up for her hand.

"He's home, Em. He's really here." Rocco drew her down to kneel beside them. "Zavi, this very special lady is Mandy Fielding."

Zavi straightened and pushed away from Rocco.

He made a polite bow, as regal as any village elder. "How do you do? I'm Zaviyar. I'm pleased to meet you."

"What a polite young man you are. It's lovely to meet you as well."

Just then, the dogs came charging out of the house. Max stopped at the porch, watching from a distance. The dogs greeted the trio enthusiastically with wagging tails and wet tongues.

"You have dogs!"

"Yes. This is Yeller and this is Blue," Mandy said, pointing out the Golden and then the Heeler.

"I never had a dog before. Other boys did, but I wasn't allowed." He sent a dark look over his shoulder at Rocco.

"Oh, that is a shame. Every boy should have a dog," Mandy laughed.

"She has a horse, too," Rocco told him.

Zavi looked from Mandy to his father. "She is a special lady." He patted Yeller, who was leaning against his side. "My family had donkeys. And sometimes my uncle would bring camels to our village. We loved riding them."

"You rode a camel?" Mandy asked, her eyes widening at the thought of so tiny a person on so large an animal.

"Papa took me. Sometimes we raced them."

"Then I think you'll like riding horses. I'll have a few here soon that you'll be able to ride."

A black SUV pulled up into the turnout area. The

windows were rolled down, letting them see that it was Kit and Kelan. Kelan jumped out to park Rocco's truck. Kit nodded to the soldiers waiting by the SUV, then joined their group. Seeing him, Zavi moved closer to his father, wrapping his arms around Rocco's neck.

Kit gave Rocco a sad smile, as if realizing all he'd been insisting Rocco walk away from. He knelt next to Rocco and Zavi, who seeing him, turned his face away, burying it in Rocco's neck. "I should have trusted your instincts. I told Mandy once they were never wrong."

Rocco smiled at him. He offered Kit his hand. "It's done, man. We're cool. How long have you known?"

"Got the call while you were inspecting Mandy. That's why I sent you home."

Rocco laughed. "Zavi, this is Uncle Kit. Can you please greet him politely?"

Zavi saw Kit's flattop haircut, his height, his weapons, and shook his head. "He is a dushman, Papa," he whispered into Rocco's ear. "Be careful."

Rocco sighed. Everything his son had been taught was backward now. The people he now needed to be wary of were some of his countrymen and fighters from the region of his homeland—not the coalition troops the warriors from his village had fought. It could be a difficult transition for a child. He hoped he could help Zavi learn without deepening his hatred for one people or another.

"He's not an enemy, son. He's my friend. He's a good man. I would like you to meet him."

Zavi turned in Rocco's arms, still leaning back

against him. "Hello, Uncle Kit."

Kit grinned at him. "Hello, Zavi. Your father's missed you something terrible. I'm so glad you came here to find him. Was the trip very hard?"

Zavi straightened and glared at Kit. "I was not afraid."

Kit laughed and looked at Rocco. "He growls like his daddy."

"Zavi, would you like to go meet my horse, Kitano? I can see him watching us. He's either very curious about what's happening or he's just hungry. You can help me feed him."

Zavi nodded and reached for Mandy's hand. "Do you speak Pig English?" he asked as they walked away.

Rocco heard Mandy answer, "Pig English? You mean Pig Latin?"

"No. I mean Pig English. It isn't Latin. You take an English word and change it around. It's a word game."

Rocco and Kit stood and watched the two walk away. "He has my faculty with languages," Rocco commented.

"Looks like it. He's quite gifted."

"I want him protected, Kit." He nodded at the soldiers who brought Zavi. "The Army already knows what he is capable of. They will exploit him. Why else would they challenge him to speak Pig Latin?"

"It isn't a skill that can be easily hidden."

"I'm not raising him to be a warrior."

Kit sighed. "Rocco, what you can do linguistically, what Zavi can do, is rare. It's something extremely valuable to our country."

Rocco looked at Kit but could not pursue their conversation because the lieutenant was approaching. She handed him an envelope. "Here are your son's papers—his birth certificate, passport, vaccination records, and such. I'm sorry it took us so long to get him to you. We had to do a paternity test to be sure he was yours. I put his carseat and suitcase on your porch."

"How did you find him? What happened to him after the explosion?" Rocco remembered the small body he'd held so tightly thinking it was his son. Whose lost child had he held then?

"A shepherd who was a friend of yours turned him in. He said he tried to get you to come with him after the explosion, but you resisted. He had his wife guard Zavi and went back for you, but by then your shock was so bad, he could not make you understand. When Halim's men came for you, he began to fear for Zavi's life, and then for his and his wife's lives as well. He wasn't sure if the things they said about you were true, but your son put his entire family at risk. He fled with the boy and his wife to hide at a cousin's home several villages away.

"When some of our guys came to that village for a *shura* that was being held with the elders, he met with one of the officers and explained that he had Zavi. Fortunately, that captain knew about the search your team was conducting for your son. He gave the man a substantial reward and took the boy.

"Zavi was hidden and moved from fort to fort until he could be flown out of the country. And then in Germany, we had to wait for the results of the paternity test. I regret it took us so long to bring him home to you, but we couldn't do anything until we were certain. Everyone who spent any time with Zavi fell in love with him. He's a special kid, sir."

Rocco shook hands with the lieutenant. "Thank you." As the SUV pulled away, he and Kit crossed over to the house. Rocco sent Max to stay with Mandy and Zavi while he and Kit went inside.

"What did you find out about Blade?" Rocco asked as he set the packet on Mandy's desk.

"Owen and I covered several miles of rock formations. We even sneaked onto the WKB's property to examine the ones there. We did find several fissures, but all were empty. The Forest Rangers know the area intimately. Val and Angel are working with them closely. Kelan and I are going to keep a watch on Blade's house, see if the bad guys come back."

Kit put a hand on Rocco's shoulder. "We'll find him soon—if the information Amir gave us was valid. I'm not convinced it wasn't a distraction to let them get to Mandy. Had we not run off this morning, she wouldn't have been taken. It's interesting that we haven't heard from Amir again. I think he's playing us, and I don't like being such an easy target. We may have to wait for Blade to check in." Kit looked at Rocco. "He will. He's too ornery to stay down for long. Go spend the afternoon with your son and my sister. Put this day out of your mind."

* * *

Ty held himself perfectly still as he listened to the small sounds the rattler made in its slow approach toward him. The viper's head was wide and its body long. He knew he'd have one chance to capture it, but every second he waited thickened the air in the dark pit. A rock with jagged edges pressed against his back. He didn't know how much longer he could hold his pose without his body beginning to resist, but he didn't dare move until he had control over the snake's deadly mouth.

The rattlesnake appeared to consider the dark opening of his jeans by one of his ankles, no doubt sensing the warmth of his skin. Christ, he hoped it would see the opening was too short and narrow to be of use.

He was not so lucky. The viper inched closer to his leg, then stopped, testing the air with its tongue. Ty wondered how much it relied on its sight versus its other senses as it eased over his ankle to lie against the warmth of his skin. He had to resist all instinct to hop up and dance away from the cold feel of the snake against his skin.

The beast moved slowly up his shin, almost to his knee, where the pant leg was too tight to go farther. It drew as much of itself inside as it could, leaving a good two feet of its body outside, its rattle up but not sounding. Ty watched the fabric move as the snake settled inside his pant leg. It grew still, resting where it was, comfortably absorbing the heat of his leg.

His back cramped painfully as he watched the shadows shift across the pit, marking the day's progression. When the sun was directly overhead, the air began to warm up, and the snake slowly reversed its position.

Ty leaned forward, hoping the snake's movement would camouflage his slight change in position. When the spear-shaped head popped out of his pants, he grabbed the snake. Its mouth opened with fangs drawn. It looked big enough to swallow an adult prairie dog.

Ty had been in this pit for a night and a day without food or water. The viper in his hand looked like his salvation, right about now. He pulled his knife from its sheath and cut the snake's head off. His stomach growled in anticipation of the coming meal.

Chapter 22

Mandy was sitting on the sofa, having a quiet conversation with Fee later that night. Rocco had spoiled her the whole afternoon, first with a hot bath and tea, then getting Fee and Zavi into the kitchen to help him make dinner. Mandy joined them, but was only allowed to sit at the table and call out instructions. The house was quiet now. Zavi was asleep in Ty's room. Owen and Max were downstairs. Greer was at the hospital. Kit and Kelan were staking-out Ty's house, while Val and Angel were still searching for their lost teammate.

Mandy reached up to hold Rocco's hand as he stood beside her. "What an awful, wonderful day this has been."

"That about sums it up," he said with smile.

"Has there been any word on Ty?"

"Nothing so far." He picked up the quilt that lay across the back of the sofa. "Let's go outside, Em," he said as he drew her to her feet. On the porch, he led her to the swing that hung from one end of the rafters.

He wrapped the quilt about them both, keeping her close as they sat down. She leaned her head against his shoulder and folded her legs against his thighs, melting into him.

So much had happened today, he didn't know where to begin with what he wanted to say. "How are you holding up?"

"I'll be fine. It's wonderful having Zavi here. I've been thinking that, like it or not, you'll need to raise him in a way that prepares him to be your son. He has the same rare ability with languages that you have."

"I know. And that scares the hell out of me. I don't want him to be a warrior. I want him to be a thinker, a scientist, a writer. Something that adds to the world rather than taking from it."

She leaned back to look up at him. "That's not a fair assessment of yourself and what you do. You are a kind, honorable, and brilliant man. Warriors like you and Kit and Blade, and all others like you, keep me and Fee and those of us who aren't warriors safe. When I told you I wanted you to stop fighting, it wasn't because I think what you do is bad. It's because I'm selfish. I don't want to risk losing you, and I want to keep you to myself. If your son wants to be a warrior like his dad, the world would be a better place for it."

Rocco savored her words, humbled by her opinion. "I realized this afternoon why I had been so certain that he was alive." Mandy looked at him, waiting for what he would say. "Kadisha had second thoughts about blowing up the compound."

"Your wife blew it up?"

He nodded. "With help from Ehsan. She was clearing everyone out. She brought Zavi out and handed him to me, then went running back in for her other relatives. Ehsan had filled the village with enough bombs to make it look like an American airstrike had hit the town." He looked at Mandy. "He also strapped a suicide bomb around Kadisha, exactly like the one he made you wear. I handed Zavi off to a local shepherd, then went after her."

Mandy straightened. "But the blood and the burned flesh?"

"After the explosion, I didn't remember I'd handed Zavi over for safekeeping. There was a child's burned body next to me when I woke. I assumed it was Zavi. But it was someone else's child. I said prayers for him, and the villagers buried him. He was mourned. It was his phantom flesh I kept seeing on me."

"Oh, Rocco." She touched his cheek. "I'm so sorry that you and Zavi and the village had to go through that hell. How could Kadisha do something like that?"

He sighed. "She was a product of her culture, her people, her time. She wasn't allowed to think for herself. And perhaps, she was a woman scorned. I think she knew I wasn't in love with her." Rocco rubbed his thumb across the back of Mandy's hand. He thought about telling Mandy that Kadisha had been pregnant with their second child when she died, but that was a wound he didn't need to share. Mandy's world was dark enough now. Kadisha was gone. His time in Afghanistan was done. They both needed to look to the future.

"Em, do you want Zavi and me to find other quarters?" She started to object, but he interrupted her. "You and I have happened so suddenly. What we have is special. I don't want to rush it, rush you. I don't want my burdens to fall on you. Having Zavi here changes things."

"Zavi is not a burden. He's a gift." She threaded her fingers with his. "If you need room and space to reconnect with your son, then go and do what you must. I'd prefer we stay together. I'm afraid without you, and I'd like to work through this with you. But I understand if you need time to get situated. After what you've both been through, you deserve to do what you must to feel settled and safe."

Rocco blinked, relieved. "I'd prefer to be here with you as well. I can hire a nanny to watch him when I have to go out. She could help with chores."

Mandy smiled. "How about this? When I need help, I'll ask for it. Right now, with this house being the nerve center of your operation, I think it would best not to have someone from town come in—I don't want to expose another person to the danger we're all in. Zavi and I will get along just fine if you need to pop out. I'm sure Fee will help, and the other guys, too. There's plenty here on the ranch to keep him occupied."

She leaned against his shoulder again. "He does need some toys. And I need to do some studying about early childhood development. I suspect that boy will be three steps ahead of us all the time."

"He will. I'll have to teach him Spanish." He looked at her and grinned. "Then Pig Spanish, just to challenge him. He already knows Pashto, English and Pig English. Probably a little Latin as well."

Mandy smiled at him as she squeezed his hand. "Are you happy, Rocco?"

"Immeasurably." He rubbed his cheek against her hair. "Everything I dreamed about, and everything I didn't dare hope for, has come true in you and Zavi. You are my world, Mandy. I would do anything for you. I will spend my life making your life what you wish it to be."

Mandy sighed. "I like that." She touched his cheek and looked into his eyes. "I'll do the same for you. How about we start by going to bed? You need to get some rest before you join the hunt for Ty tomorrow."

He lifted her and started across the porch. "I was thinking about getting you to bed, too—but not to rest."

Elaine Levine lives on the plains of Colorado with her husband, a middle-aged parrot, and a rescued Bull Mastiff. In addition to writing the Red Team Contemporary Western series, she is the author of several books in the Historical Western series, Men of Defiance. Visit her online at www.ElaineLevine.com for more information about her upcoming books. She loves hearing from readers! Contact her at elevine@elainelevine.com.

If you enjoyed this book, please consider leaving a short review at your favorite online retailer or at Goodreads.com to help others discover this story.

Made in the USA
Lexington, KY
16 March 2013